THE RISEN HORSE

Sequel to *Horse of Seven Moons*

THE
RISEN
HORSE

Karen Taschek

University of New Mexico Press
Albuquerque

Library of Congress Cataloging-in-Publication Data

Taschek, Karen, 1956–
The risen horse / Karen Taschek.
p. cm.
Sequel to: Horse of seven moons.
Summary: In 1905, Bin-daa-dee-nin sends his fifteen-year-old
daughter, Isabel Chavez, to Carlisle Indian School in Pennsylvania,
where she has trouble reconciling her father's traditional views with
the Anglo community's expectations. Includes a timeline of the
Indian Industrial School.
ISBN 978-0-8263-4837-1 (pbk. : alk. paper)
[1. Boarding schools—Fiction. 2. Schools—Fiction. 3. Race
relations—Fiction. 4. Mescalero Indians—Fiction. 5. Apache
Indians—Fiction. 6. Indians of North America—New Mexico—
Fiction. 7. Horses—Fiction. 8. Pennsylvania—History—20th
century—Fiction. 9. New Mexico—History—1848——Fiction.] I.
Title.
PZ7.T211132Ris 2010
[Fic]—dc22

2010005180

To Lillian once again, an inspiration to us all

PART I

THE MESCALERO INDIAN RESERVATION,
MESCALERO, NEW MEXICO
SUMMER 1905

agent couldn't wait. Since the defeat of the Mescalero Apaches' leaders more than twenty years ago, in the 1880s, the Indian agent had made decisions for the tribe. Now, in 1905, the Mescaleros lived on the reservation, in the Territory of New Mexico.

Isabel took her brother's hand and let him pull her to her feet. Together they started down the mountain. Isabel held up her long calico skirt, trying not to get any more rips in it. The trees lower down on the mountain were mostly snaggy and small from logging. "What does the agent want?" she asked, brushing her long, straight black hair from her face.

Jeremy shrugged. "I saw the missionary's wife at the store this morning. Probably the agent wants you to work with her horse again."

"Probably. Don't make that sour face," Isabel said, tugging on her brother's sleeve. "It's not that dangerous for me to work with the horses. And I make good money—we need it." A few years ago, the U.S. Government in Washington had cut off the rations issued to the tribe. Isabel, although she was only fifteen, had to have a job.

"Why don't you work at the school?" Jeremy asked. "Like Mother did. You shouldn't be breaking wild horses—"

"They're not that wild," Isabel interrupted. "The people at the agency or the soldiers have ridden most of them." *And I don't want to work at the school* because *Mother did*, she added to herself. "Don't ever tell Father about the horses," she said. "He will forbid me to ride them, and we need the money. Or he will worry to death and feel even worse than he does already. Promise you won't tell him."

Jeremy looked unhappy. "All right," he said. "I promise."

Isabel dodged the frayed branches of a clump of piñon trees at the foot of the mountain. Before her was the Mescalero settlement on the reservation, baking in the bright summer sun. She kept her gaze forward to see as little as possible of the squalid collection of dirty tepees, old army tents, and dilapidated log cabins where the Mescaleros lived. When her mother died a month ago of scarlet fever, Isabel's father had moved his family from their cabin to three army tents in the settlement. Isabel supposed her father had moved them from the cabin because of his old-time Apache fear of living in a house where someone had died, but at least the cabin had walls to keep out the insects. Isabel had no idea what her family would do when the harsh mountain winter set in.

"Do you work today?" Isabel asked her brother.

"Maybe tomorrow—I may be gone a couple of days with the crew," Jeremy replied. He had a job cutting lumber. "But Isabel, be careful with those horses. You always think you can handle them, but . . ."

"But what?" Isabel frowned.

Jeremy hesitated. He and Isabel spoke English very well because their mother and uncle John had insisted that they use English from an early age, so Isabel knew that Jeremy had the words, he just wasn't sure if he should say what he was thinking to her. "The agent and missionary wouldn't ask you to ride the horses if anyone else could without getting thrown," he said.

Isabel shrugged. "I know." They had reached the edge of the cluster of low, wood agency buildings. With a wave, Jeremy continued on to the tents and tepees, where he would probably spend the rest of the day playing cards or other games with the other young men.

Isabel squished through mud from the last rainstorm toward the agency buildings, ignoring the dark, crouched figure of her father, who was sitting on the fence between the agency office and the trader's store. He had spent most of the last month sitting on the fence, hardly moving.

Mother is dead. Isabel bit her lip hard and forced herself not to think that again. She just couldn't—the pain was huge. That was why she had not let herself cry even once about it. Lifting her skirts, Isabel almost ran the rest of the way to the stable, slowing her steps only so that the mud wouldn't suck off a boot.

In the stable the scent of warm, slightly sweaty horses greeted her. Isabel smiled as five bobbing horses' heads leaned over their stall half doors toward her. She lifted a bridle from the wall for Lexington, the big bay at the end of the row, and let out a breath she hadn't realized she was holding. *It's so good to be back with the horses*, she thought. Jeremy might not approve of her job as trainer, but over the last three weeks Isabel had spent as much time as possible riding.

She had gotten this job only a week after her mother's death. Isabel had been walking through the woods on one of the nearby mountains, thinking that what was in her mind felt like fog, which she didn't see often on the dry reservation. Without realizing it, she had walked quite far. A loud splash in a nearby stream had startled her. Isabel had looked up quickly and seen a sweating, frightened horse. Isabel had quietly approached the trembling animal. The horse still had on a bridle, although the reins were broken. Speaking softly, Isabel had caught the horse, gotten on him, and ridden him to the agent.

It turned out that the horse belonged to the visiting missionary, who had come to teach the Indians Christianity. Surprised that Isabel had been able to stay on the horse, the missionary had promptly hired her to train it for his wife so that she could ride it around the reservation and visit the Mescaleros in their homes. After the story had spread around the reservation, the agent and other agency workers had been quick to ask Isabel to ride their problem horses.

"Hello, Isabel." Daniel Tyndall, the agent's son, greeted her from the other end of the barn. He headed quickly up the aisle, a broad smile on his freckled face.

Isabel smiled back, but she stopped at Lexington's stall without answering. Most of the morning was gone, and if she didn't get started on her ride, the midday sun would practically melt her horse. *I suppose Daniel's taking a fancy to me is a good thing*, she had to admit. *But I don't want to encourage it too much*. She did know that if Daniel hadn't admired her, she would probably be cleaning stalls instead of riding.

Lexington shoved her with his nose. "Pretty boy," Isabel said, reaching for a halter on a peg. "Would you like to go for a ride?"

The big bay eagerly stepped out of the stall with Isabel. She dropped the rope, and Lexington obediently stood while Isabel fetched the grooming box. She could see Daniel standing close by, trying to think of something to say.

"I don't know why Mrs. Aspell had so much trouble with that horse," he said. "I've seen you ride him—"

"And he's a perfect gentleman," Isabel finished, adjusting the saddle on the blanket and tightening the girth. "Lexington's previous owners may not have handled him correctly. He's afraid of people." Isabel knew that horses had to be made to mind, but she didn't understand the white men's brutality with the animals—unless they truly enjoyed being thrown. She didn't think it necessary to ride with huge-roweled spurs and a whip or club. But she decided not to tell Daniel about Lexington's episodes of terror when she had first begun working with him—the horse had plunged away from her hand when she had tried to halter him, and getting him to let her touch his head without flinching was all they accomplished that day. Lexington had made a lot of progress since then, and Isabel didn't want people to dwell on his former difficulties.

"He isn't afraid of you." Daniel sidled closer, resting his hand on Lexington's shoulder.

Isabel saw Lexington eyeing Daniel out of the corner of his eye and knew she was doing the same. "I'll be back in one hour," she said, leading Lexington out of the stable. "I'll ride Captain Pinkham's stallion then."

Isabel mounted up behind the stable so that not too many people would see her riding. Most people, including even the missionary, had given up trying to talk to her father, but she wanted to be very careful that her father did not find out what she was doing. Lexington pranced in place and shook his head, sending his black mane flying. "If I were a soldier, I would yank you down with the reins until you held still," Isabel told him. "But I know that you just feel good this afternoon."

Isabel gave Lexington a quick pat on the neck and let him out into a trot. The missionary's wife would just have to understand that she owned a young, spirited horse and he was full of as much zeal to go fast as she was to convert the Mescaleros from their old native religion to Christianity.

Lexington was a tall horse, just over sixteen hands, and his fast-moving black legs covered ground quickly. The sun, almost directly above, shimmered off the scanty grass, sand, and stumpy cholla cactus in waves of heat. Isabel pulled Lexington to a stop and looked behind her at the reservation buildings and dwellings, now only dots in the distance. She let out a soft sigh, feeling the heavy cloud of the reservation's problems and ugliness rise from her mind.

"I hope Father doesn't find out that I ride," she said to the horse. "Riding horses is a very good way to make money, and if he forbids it, I don't know what I'll do."

Lexington snorted and twisted his head around to sniff her foot in the stirrup. Isabel almost laughed at the alert, interested expression in his big brown eyes. She reached way forward and rubbed the diamond-shaped star on his forehead. A skinny strip ran from the star to a snip on his nose. "You're a pretty enough horse," she said. "Maybe the prettiest I have ever seen." Lexington's dark-caramel-colored coat glittered in the sunlight, and his three socks were perfectly white and clean. "Your coat looks good," Isabel told him. "At least this summer the thunderstorms have made the grass grow better than usual. We must hope it keeps growing so that it can be cut for winter hay."

Isabel sat back in the padded English saddle. Mrs. Aspell had brought it from her home in Massachusetts, and it was made of smooth, well-oiled brown leather. Isabel had looked up Massachusetts on the map in the schoolroom and found out it was a state on the East Coast, about two thousand miles from Mescalero. "No wonder she doesn't understand the horses and people out here very well," Isabel commented. "I think you understand what I say and ask better than she does, even when I speak English. Walk, Lexington." The bay promptly moved out at the requested pace. She rewarded him with a "Very good."

Lexington began to walk faster, but Isabel checked him with the reins. "Slowly," she ordered. Lexington slowed, but almost immediately his pace crept up again. Isabel sighed. "You need a good run to get the energy out of you." Ahead was a long stretch of tree stumps and dead branches from logging. For a moment Isabel was tempted to give Lexington his head and let him jump and zigzag his way through the obstacles. *He could almost certainly do it*, she thought. *He's an agile horse and smart.*

A couple of fleecy, oval-shaped clouds hovered on the horizon, not interfering with the sun, as if waiting to see what the horse would do. Isabel hesitated—but then she let him out into a trot instead of a gallop. "I can't let you run," she explained. "Suppose you did that when Mrs. Aspell was riding you? She would fly off like a sack of oats. You're not supposed to be that kind of horse." *A fun horse*, she added to herself.

Instead Isabel used the field of logs to practice turns. She rode Lexington around the stumps and asked him to step over branches. After a couple of tries, Lexington would boldly push through brush and not startle when twigs snapped against his legs.

Half an hour later, Isabel stopped Lexington again. This time he stood quietly, eyeing her calmly backward. "Good boy." Isabel patted Lexington's summer-shiny dark brown shoulder. She pulled off the band holding her thick hair in a ponytail and shook it back, then gathered the strands that had flown loose during her ride and bunched together a new ponytail. Looking down at Lexington, she evaluated the training session. "You're quiet now, but I think a few parts of our ride might have scared Mrs. Aspell," she said. "I'm not sure you will ever be the kind of horse that stands still for hours, then plods around on the reservation. But that is the kind of horse Mrs. Aspell wants. All she does is look down at people from her horse and talk to them."

Lexington arched his neck and pawed the ground with a front hoof. "You may not be placid enough for Mrs. Aspell, but you are definitely nice looking," Isabel said. "I suppose she chose you for your looks."

Settling her feet in the stirrups, Isabel picked up the reins again. *Lexington doesn't have a skinny, straight neck or a swayed back or awful scars, but I know he is not perfect. I don't think I have ever seen a truly fine horse*, she thought. She remembered the stories her father had told her about a splendid horse he had found in the desert: that horse was beautiful, smart, and magical. The Mountain Gods of the Mescaleros had sent it to him, he insisted. "I don't know if I believe the part about the Mountain Gods," Isabel told Lexington. "If the gods still exist, they must be waiting for something before they show themselves again. I don't see them anywhere on or around the reservation now."

Isabel glanced up at the clouds, which had moved over the reservation buildings and were thicker now. A thunderstorm in the afternoon, common in the summer, seemed possible. *More mud*, Isabel thought. Then she realized that Lexington had gradually turned until they were headed back to the buildings—and his stall. "You have the right idea," she said. "I must get back before I'm missed."

2

"You look like an old crow," Robert Wilkins said to his friend John Chavez, looking up at him on the fence and shaking his head in disapproval.

"I am an old crow," John replied in Apache. "And so I am sure I look like one." He had found a cast-off black army poncho to wrap around himself during thunderstorms. The soldiers weren't around the reservation so much these days now that the Indians were subdued and no longer at war with the ranchers and other settlers, but the soldiers' tents and old clothes were available in the trading store and stashed in odd corners.

"When are you going to get down from that fence?" Robert asked, tugging on his pocket watch chain. He took the watch from the small pocket in his vest and showed John the time: 3:30.

"Where is Isabel?" John asked, reaching for the watch. At least these days, he knew what the white man's trinkets were for. He could tell time from a watch, although sometimes he pretended he couldn't. The sun, which shone brightly almost every day in the clear blue sky over the reservation, was still more reliable.

"I have not seen Isabel all morning," Robert replied, taking back the watch and readjusting it in his vest. He brushed a speck of dust from the knee of his fine black trousers and frowned at John. "I think she may have a job cleaning horses in the stable. I once saw her brushing one there."

"That is not fit work for her," John said firmly.

"So tell her." Robert shrugged. "You haven't spoken to her once this week."

"I have been thinking." From where he sat, John had a good view of his friend's black leather shoes, which were splashed with mud. *He is a headman for the tribe and the agent's favorite, but even he cannot escape the mud of the reservation,* John thought.

"You need to stop thinking," Robert said severely. "You have been doing that for more than a month, since Maria died, while your children work to put food on the table."

John sighed. "You were always like this."

"Like what?" Robert demanded.

John lifted a hand. "A ... stuffed shirt," he said in English.

"And you were always ... an old-timer," said Robert.

"Do you even remember how to speak Apache?" John asked.

Robert shrugged impatiently. "Of course. But now we must speak English as well. Times have changed since we roamed the mountains together as youths, hunting, raiding, and running from the soldiers."

"I know. That is what I have been thinking about." John glanced at the other man, who held a bowler hat in his hand. *Certainly you are Robert now, not Yuu-his-kishn,* he thought, remembering his old friend's Apache name. Robert worked with the Indian police to bring cattle rustlers, murderers, and angry drunks to justice. *I suppose I am John.* His Apache name was Bin-daa-dee-nin, meaning "keen sighted." The agent had chosen the name John for him from the white man's Bible because the agent had said his Apache name was too hard to spell. This new name did not mean much to him.

Two older women in faded dresses, their sleeves torn, walked slowly by, bending their heads under the glaring sun. One of the women limped, and the other held her by the elbow to help her along. The women didn't look at the men—they barely seemed to have the strength to lift their feet from the mire. John watched them pass, then said, "I will send Isabel to school."

"That is good—she and Jeremy have not attended school since Maria's death." Robert nodded vigorously.

"No, I did not mean the school here." John shifted on the fence. Unlike his friend, he had stayed thin, and the rail was not a comfortable perch. "I meant the other school, the one you told me about. The Carlisle school."

Robert's eyes widened. "I also said that the Carlisle school is thousands of miles from here, in the state of Pennsylvania. Did you hear that part?"

"I heard you say that the children are taught well so that they can survive," John said, looking directly at Robert for the first time. "Or do the children die at this school?"

"Sometimes." Robert sighed. "Probably not as often as here. The food is better. I don't think the crops fail in Pennsylvania, the way they have at the reservation for years."

"Isabel cannot survive here." John looked weary.

Robert hesitated. "She seems to be healthy."

"But the women die too young on the reservation. My mother and my wife became worn and tired, then sick." John stared at his shabby moccasin on the lower fence rail. His wife had made the moccasins from the last deer he had hunted successfully. Now both shoes had holes at the big toe. "But even if Isabel can stay alive, her spirit cannot survive here." John struggled to express his thoughts. He had never been a quick talker, like Robert, even in Apache. "She must get skills to survive."

"I agree with that," Robert said quietly. "But you could send her to the boarding school in Albuquerque, with my children."

"No, Isabel must have the best," John insisted. "Albuquerque is also far—but not far enough. The problems of the reservation would also be there."

"Isabel will be too far away to visit in Pennsylvania," Robert warned. "You will not see her for many months."

John said nothing. As usual, Robert was trying to change his mind with sensible arguments, but John did not want his mind changed. He was sure he was right about the faraway school. "I have already gotten the agent to arrange for Isabel to attend the Carlisle school," he said at last. "They are expecting her in a week. Then she will return home next summer. I want her to be gone less than a year."

Robert looked surprised. Then he cleared his throat. "There is one more thing to be said about the Carlisle school."

"You always have one more thing to say," John replied.

"At school the children are taught mathematics, English, geography, art, and many good and useful subjects," Robert went on. "But they are to be 'civilized'—they will learn the white man's ways. You may not know your own daughter when she comes back. And sometimes the children don't come back. They remain in their new world."

"If I could show her the old way to live, I would," John said bitterly. "She would know her grandmother. Her mother would be alive to teach her to make fine clothes and cook. The game would not all be killed off, so I could hunt for food and skins to make clothes."

"I agree that we must look forward," Robert said, his voice gentler than usual.

"There is Isabel." John sat up straight. His voice and mood lifted as he saw Isabel picking her way along the muddy road, as beautiful and out of place as an exquisite butterfly. *She is so much like her mother—tall and elegant, with her beautiful long hair*, he thought wistfully.

Isabel raised her head and looked at him, then dropped her gaze back to the sticky street in front of her.

Her snapping eyes that show her spirit are also like her mother's, John thought. But Isabel did not look happy.

Isabel's throat closed up the moment she saw her father. From outside the cemetery, she had seen that her mother's grave was marked only with a simple wood cross, but her father's lined, weary face was as eloquent in its grief as a granite headstone. *He is always so sad, and nothing I do helps,* she thought. This entire past week, he had not even spoken to her. She stopped just in front of the fence and her father, wondering what she should say to him. To her surprise, he spoke first, right away.

"I have decided you are to go to school in Carlisle, Pennsylvania," he announced.

Isabel stared up at her father in shock. The grief and indecision were gone from his eyes. "Wouldn't that cost too much?" she asked, fingering the coins in her pocket from her pay while she tried to decide what to make of her father's idea. She had vaguely heard of this school—it was back east and said to teach the children many things.

"The school will also give you a scholarship because they want you to come," her father said. "Besides, I have told you many times that I am a rich man." Her father said "scholarship" in English. Isabel had gotten used to these strange conversations where her father spoke Apache and she, Jeremy, and Uncle Robert answered in English.

Isabel saw that her uncle was also looking at John with surprise, probably because her father had taken so much initiative and had to get off the fence to do it. *I've never fully believed Father's story of riches,* she thought. That was part of the story he told about the mysterious horse—while he had the horse, her father had found a wagon full of silver that he had hidden somewhere. But when she had asked him why their family was so poor, he had said that he could not cash in the silver very often or it would all be taken from him.

"Why doesn't Jeremy have to go?" Isabel asked.

"Because my mother and grandmother, women of worth and spirit, died here. That seems to be the way of the reservation. I want you to go away and live," her father said firmly.

Isabel looked down at her shoes. The side was detaching from the toe on one, and the other almost had a hole worn through the bottom. *At a school I wouldn't be so alone*, she thought. *I don't have time for friends, and almost the only people I have here are Father and Jeremy. But will Father survive without me?*

The one person she wanted to ask about this was in the cemetery. Isabel closed her eyes, picturing the crooked crosses and the graves of raw brown earth poking out of the ground there. She had never been in the cemetery, not even at her mother's funeral, because her father and the other older people in the tribe didn't think children should be too close to death. Isabel had come to the funeral anyway, standing outside the cemetery, half hidden by a skinny tree. She didn't remember much about the service, just the priest's droning voice rising and falling as he recited the prayers. Isabel hated that cemetery. Perhaps it was because she was an Apache—Apaches didn't traditionally have cemeteries, and she knew her father hated the place too. Or perhaps the cemetery was just unpleasant because it seemed to demand that you acknowledge that those you loved were in it. They really weren't, Isabel thought. For example, talking to the dead never worked—a blank wall rose up, and no words got through.

Isabel opened her eyes and looked closely at her father. "If I go, you must stay off the fence," she said.

"That will be hard to do," he replied.

"So is going to school at Carlisle!" Isabel tried not to raise her voice.

"She is right," Uncle Robert interjected.

"You are giving bad advice again," John retorted.

"That is what you call speaking the truth?" Uncle Robert demanded.

John was silent. Isabel didn't know what to say either one of them. *What would Mother think of this idea?* she wondered. *But I already know in my heart. Mother would want me to go very much. After all, she worked in a school.* "When will I go to the school?" Isabel asked.

"In three days we leave for El Paso," her father replied. "You will take the train from there to Pennsylvania." He slid off the fence. "I will get the wagon ready for our long journey."

3

The steam engine huffed slowly up the track at the train station in El Paso. Isabel squinted at the sky. Except for the mighty black plume of the engine's exhaust, not one whiff of white cloud touched the searing blue of the morning sky. The sky seemed open to promises and adventures. "Will you be all right?" Isabel asked Jeremy, touching his arm, but she was really asking her father.

"Don't worry," Jeremy said. "I'll take care of things." He was watching the black face of the train approach with great interest.

Isabel looked at him carefully, hoping that he would keep his word. *Jeremy doesn't worry much, even when he should,* she thought.

"I will go back to work," John promised. "I will join the logging crew with Jeremy and spend my time well."

Her father looked better—more alert and like his old self. *All that sitting around can't have been good for him,* Isabel thought. "Does the school know I'm coming?" she asked.

"Yes—Uncle Robert telegraphed the head of Carlisle," John said. "Someone will meet you at the train."

The train hissed loudly, then drew up to the platform and stopped with a belch of exhaust. Isabel stepped back, covering her nose and mouth as a cloud of black smoke overwhelmed the platform. *I'm afraid to get on that noisy beast*, she realized. *But I suppose I must.* Before today, Isabel had only read about trains in newspapers.

At last the train became quiet, and the smoke cleared into the still air. Doors opened in the train cars, and passengers stepped out. Most of the men wore black suits with vests and bowler hats. The women wore dark dresses with tight, trim bodices and long skirts and walked confidently along the platform, carrying cloth or leather travel satchels. A few people had colorful blankets draped around their shoulders, Mexican style.

Those women in tidy dresses are city people, Isabel thought with a quick rise of excitement. *Soon I'll be a city person too! I'll see high buildings and automobiles and read by electric lights. Those things will no longer be stories.*

Several of the passengers headed for a low building with a sign out front that said the R. R. Eating House & Lunch Counter. "Can we go there after Isabel is on the train?" Jeremy asked.

"No, we cannot," John answered. "The food would not be safe in that confined place. I have packed Isabel and us each a dinner."

Isabel touched the big canvas bag of food her father had prepared for her. It was an odd collection of venison, berries, and piñon nuts, but she knew it would be tasty and last her on her journey.

"All aboard!" the uniformed conductor called from one of the doorways to the train. Isabel turned to her father.

"Goodbye, daughter." John hugged her, and Isabel felt the strength in his hands.

"Goodbye, Father. I'll see you next summer." Isabel picked up her bag of food. It was an old army duffel and the only luggage she had. Isabel had wedged her only other dress around the food packet.

"Be careful." Jeremy hugged her too, then looked at her closely, raising one eyebrow. "You're going to have fun. No more wild horses," he whispered.

But I'll miss the horses! Isabel turned toward the train, willing Jeremy's last remark not to make her cry. "No more wild horses," she agreed softly.

She climbed the steep metal steps into the train and sat near the front of the car. Looking out the window, she saw Jeremy make one last attempt to guide their father toward the restaurant. John shook his head and kept walking in the direction of their wagon. Isabel almost laughed at the familiar sight of her father and brother arguing.

The railway car was large but spare, with simple wooden benches. Isabel slid to the side of the bench nearest the window and put her bag beside her feet. *I hope no one sits with me,* she thought. Uncle Robert had warned her repeatedly about the peril of strangers, but Isabel wasn't worried. *If I can handle cowboys, boisterous soldiers, and desperate drunks on the reservation, I'm sure I can handle the passengers on a train,* she thought.

An elderly woman stepped into the car, looked over at Isabel, then sat down on the bench across the aisle from her. Setting a leather satchel on the bench beside her, she took out two books, an apple, and a ball of yarn and put them on top of the satchel. She smiled at Isabel, then adjusted the tortoiseshell combs on either side of her head, smoothing wisps of her white hair back into a bun.

Isabel smiled back, then looked out the window again. With a jolt, the train inched forward. The train's whistle blew loudly, and the wheels began to clack slowly, then faster and faster along the track. Soon Isabel could no longer see her father and brother.

The train thundered by the last low buildings of El Paso and into the countryside. Texas was flat, and a brisk wind across the prairie blew the clumps of tall grass almost flat. Against the empty horizon, a herd of longhorn cattle grazed. Isabel twisted her fingers in her lap. *It's so hard to just sit!* she thought. *And I must do this for many days, until I reach Carlisle.*

Isabel tried to adjust her skirts to get comfortable on the hard bench. She missed home already. *But I'm forgetting what home has become,* she told herself. *Mother is no longer there, and Father is so sad.* Isabel pictured her father and brother alone that night in her family's biggest army tent, silent, eating a simple dinner that might not be enough. *Mother, am I doing the right thing by leaving them?* Isabel wondered.

"Would you like this apple, dear?" the older woman asked, reaching for the apple on top of her satchel.

"Thank you." Isabel slid to the edge of the bench and took the big, shiny red apple. *I might need to save my own food,* she thought. *Maybe I'm being silly, but what if my train goes the wrong way in Chicago and I end up somewhere very far from Pennsylvania?*

"My name is Florence Dixon," the older woman said. She had sharp blue eyes in a pale, unlined face and a bright, intelligent expression.

"I'm Isabel Chavez." Isabel noticed that Mrs. Dixon had set down the book she was reading, by Alfred, Lord Tennyson. *Perhaps after I have studied at Carlisle, I will recognize many books,* Isabel thought. The reservation school had only a few books, and those were mostly about arithmetic and spelling.

"Are you traveling home, dear?" the older woman asked.

"No, I'm going to school in Pennsylvania," Isabel replied.

"How very exciting," Mrs. Dixon said warmly. "You are seeing the world. When I was about your age, I came to El Paso from New York City." When Isabel looked blank, she added, "New York is not so very far from Pennsylvania. I arrived in El Paso in 1860, just before the Civil War."

"Oh." Isabel knew about the Civil War—the war where the North and South of the country had fought over slavery. The Mescaleros had burned down the army fort on their land when the soldiers left to fight back east, but they had just come back after the war was over. Her parents had said that for many years, army drifters from both sides of the conflict had passed through the Mescaleros' lands, causing disturbances.

"When we were living in New York, my husband and I always loved stories of the West. We had heard that you could be a rancher instead of a farmer, with thousands of acres of land and hundreds of animals. So one day we picked up and left New York."

"Do you like El Paso better than New York?" Isabel asked. Mrs. Dixon sounded as if she much preferred El Paso.

"Well, I had five children at our ranch," said Mrs. Dixon. "Then, after a number of years, Mr. Dixon and I opened a store in town that sold ranching supplies. My son Henry and daughter Jane still run the store. But my other three children moved to Chicago. I am on my way to see them and greet a new granddaughter. With the splendid trains that run across the country these days, I have not really had to give up friends or family by living in El Paso. Thankfully, even at my age, I am still able to travel."

Isabel nodded. *It's very nice to meet an older woman who is still fit to travel*, she thought. Many of the older women at Mescalero had serious health problems—tuberculosis, lost teeth, or bones that broke too easily.

"I have seen so many wonderful new things in my long life," the older woman said. "My goodness, now people ride around in horseless carriages—in automobiles! And they talk over wires on the telephone."

"I have not seen any of those things," Isabel admitted.

"You will," Mrs. Dixon promised. She reached across the aisle and patted Isabel's hand. "You will see many marvels in your life."

4

John awoke to a blue-violet dawn. He lay on slanting, rocky ground at the logging camp, halfway up White Mountain and two miles from the reservation settlement. A sharp pain shot through his side and down into his right leg. The next pain, the one in his mind, would come next and would be worse, he knew. Patiently John dropped his head, waiting for the rush of grief. *Isabel has been gone for three days, and it is always the same,* he thought. Still, he got to his feet, although slowly, and tried to stretch out his aches. Some of them could not be stretched out— they were from badly healed broken bones and wounds from the old days of battle against the soldiers, before the Mescaleros were put on the reservation for good.

The mountain did not look in any better shape than he was. The biggest and finest trees were felled in a large circle around him, and the ground was bare except for gray rocks and brown dead pine needles. "How can sacred White Mountain look so?" John muttered. "The Mountain Gods are surely angry, wherever they are. If only they were in Pennsylvania with Isabel. But that seems a foolish thought. Rather than expect the gods to travel, perhaps I should go to the school myself."

When he had returned from El Paso, the agent's wife had told him that some parents camped around the boarding schools their children attended in case the children needed them. John sighed deeply. "It is much more likely that the parents need the children," he said softly to himself. Isabel was so strong and smart—she was a very great gift to Carlisle. He knew he had done the right thing, although he did not feel good about it just now. But he could not imagine camping in the East by the school. The settlers would run him back to the reservation, just as they had in New Mexico.

Jeremy still slept, lying on his back with one arm flung over his eyes. John bent down and shook his son's shoulder.

"Let us take a walk," John said. "The other men will not wake for work for some time."

"Why should we take a walk?" Jeremy asked groggily.

"To feel better." John had gotten his legs and arms to move fairly well. Now he needed to work on his mind.

Jeremy turned over, burying his face in the shirt he was using as a pillow. "I feel fine," he mumbled.

"Up!" John commanded. "Or I'll send you to Carlisle!"

"Couldn't be worse than this," Jeremy said into the shirt.

"Yes, it could. They will get you up even earlier in the morning." John wondered if this was true. *I hope Isabel is getting her rest*, he thought.

Jeremy slowly sat up and rubbed his eyes. His short hair was standing on end like a bluejay's crest. Almost all the young men on the reservation wore their hair short. John still found it difficult not to think of a man with short hair as being in mourning, but he'd had to cut his own hair a few times when one agent or another had made all the men cut their hair to look civilized. At the moment John's hair hung to his shoulders.

John nudged Jeremy with his toe. *I do not know if that school really could get him up*, he thought. *Jeremy does not obey rules well.*

I made the right choice to send Isabel, he reminded himself. "Get up—the sun will rise soon."

"When will we eat breakfast?" Jeremy asked, yawning.

"We will eat when we get back to the camp. This will be a short walk." John began to climb the steep slope behind the logging camp. The twenty other men were still asleep around the remains of last night's cook fire, their heads resting on a change of clothes. John was not sure Jeremy would follow him, but when he looked around, Jeremy was bounding easily up the hill, then past him.

"I must return to El Paso to get a waffle maker—then we could have waffles for breakfast!" Jeremy called down. The mountain above him lay in deep purple shade, but a rim of gold brightened the jagged edge at the top.

Waffles. John squinted up at Jeremy, who had started moving again and almost disappeared into the dark side of the mountain. After much effort, Jeremy had finally persuaded him to enter the restaurant at the train station. Many people were passing through the doors, and John's curiosity to know what was inside had at last outweighed his concerns for his and Jeremy's health. While John was looking at the spattered, dirty floor of the restaurant, Jeremy sat down at the nearest table and ordered a breakfast of bacon, fried eggs, and several square objects he called waffles from a big woman in a white uniform. John had tasted a waffle at Jeremy's urging. He had to admit it was very good, especially doused in maple syrup. John had been fascinated by the perfect square shapes that the waffle machine could make.

Perhaps Jeremy does not have to go to school to have new experiences, John thought as he grabbed a tree root to hoist himself along, struggling to keep up with his fleet son. *Even waffles may come to the reservation.* The reservation did not have many machines right now—mules and horses pulled the logs down from the mountains—but in El Paso, John had seen not just a waffle maker but telegraph lines to bring messages from unseen people and a box on wheels that had been traveling down the street without a horse or a push from anyone. The box had been stuck in a rut and the owner was swearing at it, but before that, John had seen it rolling quickly along. He knew from Robert that it was an automobile—his friend and the agency workers talked about those miracle machines all the time. Robert, John was sure, would be one of the first to own an automobile.

Suddenly the sun's first crescent popped over the top of the mountain, blazing a line of gold across the pale blue sky. Shielding his eyes, John continued his climb, trying not to gasp for breath.

Jeremy already stood at the top of the ridge, looking into the valleys below. At the end of the gentler slopes to the south, the desert of white sands glistened. As John joined his son, the full searing ball of the sun rose, burnishing the mountaintops and valleys with orange.

"Look, a herd of horses." Jeremy pointed into one of the valleys. "I've seen them before."

John squinted. His eyes were not so keen as they used to be, but he could see about ten horses grazing. "Whose are they?" he asked.

"I don't know." Jeremy shrugged. "That probably means nobody's. I think they're wild."

John pushed his headband down to rub sweat from his face, then retied it. Jeremy, he noticed, was not sweating at all. "Let us go look at them," he said.

Jeremy groaned. "I knew you'd say that. I hope the crew saves us some breakfast."

"They will." John started down into the valley. Over his shoulder he could see the new sun following him, casting its light and dispelling the purple shadows. He could hear Jeremy behind him, stepping on twigs, and the slip of his work boots over the mountain's coat of dead piñon needles. Jeremy's steps were slow. John knew Jeremy hoped he would change his mind about going to the horses and return to the camp and breakfast.

The horses flung up their heads as the two men approached,

staring at them with a mix of expressions. Some of the horses seemed curious, as if they hoped the people would feed them, and one horse nodded and whickered softly. Others backed away fearfully. The horses were mares, John noticed, guarded by an old white stallion with a fierce air. The stallion whinnied, then snorted. He glared at the two people and pawed the ground threateningly with a front hoof.

"You are all right," John murmured, looking over the other horses carefully. "Most of you know we will not harm you. Only this stallion seems quite wild."

All the horses were plump and well fed. John had seen small herds of wild horses before in the valleys—they were runaways from ranches and often stayed near their old homes, eating hay put out for the cows. The longer they were free, the more skittish they became.

The newborn sun caught up with the horses, sweeping over them and brightening the coats of a black horse, several bays, two pretty red chestnuts, and a speckled gray and shining into the cold blue eyes of a brown-and-white pinto with a white face. A pale yellow horse stood apart from the rest, nibbling at cottonwood leaves stuck high in the branches of a juniper.

Suddenly the sun's fire lit up the yellow horse's coat, exploding it into countless sparkles of gold. At that moment the horse turned and looked at them.

John almost gasped aloud. He had never seen a horse of such perfect beauty. *How can this be?* he thought. *Where can such an animal have come from?*

The horse was slender but well muscled on her shoulders and hindquarters. Her gold head, with small, black-tipped ears, tapered from a broad forehead with a star to a dark gray muzzle. Her thick mane and tail were also golden, slightly paler, and lifted in the morning breeze. The horse began to walk toward them with a bold, energetic gait.

"I have found another horse," John said, smiling broadly. "Is this not sacred White Mountain?"

Jeremy looked at him out of the corner of his eye and shifted from one boot to the other. He said nothing.

"I have," John insisted, stretching out his hand to the horse. John knew that even his children thought he was superstitious, but he felt almost sure the gods were giving him another horse as a present. *This horse is to replace Moon That Flies*, he thought. *But I will not lose her to ranchers. I will keep her and in this way break with the past. Not only that, I will keep this new gift for Isabel.*

John walked toward the horse to greet her. The horse stopped a few paces away and dropped her head. She sniffed.

"She's going to run," Jeremy predicted.

"I will go slow." The mare watched John with her large, dark brown eyes. She seemed to be thinking about running, but then her curiosity won out, and she let him come up beside her. John ran his hand down her shoulder, and the mare arched her neck and twisted her head around to sniff his fingers. *If I bring her an apple treat every time, she will come easily to me*, he thought.

The mare yanked her head away and huffed out an impatient sigh. She seemed to be saying, *Where is that apple now?*

The mare had expressed her thoughts so clearly, she might as well have spoken. John laughed, then caught himself and stopped. *When did I last laugh?* he wondered. Laughter felt like the sparkles of the sun, golden and carefree.

"She seems young," Jeremy said. "Maybe not even full grown."

"I think so too. Once we know each other better, I will open her mouth to look at her teeth and see exactly how old she is." John patted the horse's neck. She bent her neck again to look around at his hand and accepted his caress with a little toss of her head. She seemed content to stand with her new companions.

"How are you going to get to know her better?" Jeremy asked, turning back toward the mountain. "Will you walk out here every day? We can't take her back with us—the agent won't let us keep riding horses anymore."

"I will come out here when we have work and other times

when I can get away," John replied. Not long ago, all the Mescaleros' fine horses had been rounded up and sold to buy draft horses to pull the plows for farming. Perhaps this one had escaped—she might even be a Mescalero horse.

"But why?" Jeremy looked bewildered. He bent to touch the purple flower of a thistle. John drew in a sharp breath.

Almost every day, John saw his son gathering flowers to put them on his mother's grave. He had walked into the cemetery at the funeral, as was perhaps right for a young man. Often Jeremy brought his mother sunflowers—Maria's favorite. All across the reservation, those flowers nodded in the wind, their beautiful yellow petals and dark eyes like life and Maria herself.

John would watch Jeremy leave the colorful bunch of flowers on the fresh mound of the grave, then brush the dirt from the small wood cross. John did not know how his son found the courage to stand by the grave. He could not bring himself to go there and imagine that his wife was under a mound of mud and a cross. Jeremy's courage was that he found comfort in visiting Maria's grave. That was all that was left of his mother, and he grieved but accepted it.

Isabel did not go to her mother's grave either, although John had seen her watching the funeral. Neither he nor Isabel had cried then, but her expression, so vacant and lost, frightened him. Good that she was away from this place with its constant reminders of sorrow.

Now that Isabel is gone, the sun in my life is out here, John thought, admiring the pretty mare again. He had no wish to bring the horse back with him to the reservation settlement, empty of Isabel, even if that were possible.

The little horse pushed his fingers, tickling them with her soft gray muzzle. John rubbed her nose, then her forehead. He would have to find out exactly where she most liked to be petted so that she would look forward to being with him.

"Together we will train this horse, Sun That Rises, for Isabel," John said. "When she returns from school, Isabel will not clean horses but will ride an excellent one—this fine horse will be waiting for her. We will have good times again."

Jeremy turned and looked at his father closely. Suddenly he seemed very interested in this trip over the mountain. "Training the horse for Isabel is a good idea," he said. "I think Isabel will like to have a horse of her own very much."

PART II

THE INDIAN INDUSTRIAL SCHOOL,
CARLISLE, PENNSYLVANIA,
SUMMER 1905

5

The train carrying Isabel to Carlisle rattled on for five days and nights, journeying steadily through the flat states of Kansas, Missouri, and Illinois, blowing a long plume of smoke behind it. The train whistle wailed at crossings, and sometimes when Isabel looked out the window, townspeople or farmers would wave at the train. Isabel waved back, wondering about the lives of those farmers in their blue overalls and girls in their gingham dresses. She had seen tidy white wood farmhouses and red barns in the middle of fields planted with wheat, corn, and barley. *Perhaps the farm families have come into town to shop or go to church*, she thought. *Then they go home and feed the livestock.*

Mrs. Dixon had gotten off the train in Chicago, leaving Isabel with many warm wishes and giving her the book by Lord Tennyson. Isabel had watched her go, adjusting her small straw hat with its nodding cloth flowers, and imagined Mrs. Dixon greeting her sons and gathering her grandchildren in her arms. In Chicago the train had made a long stop of several hours. The smoke did not blow away as it had in El Paso but lingered over the train, mixing with many smells: flowers from a stand selling bouquets next to the tracks, the sweet scent of passengers' perfumes, and a strong undercurrent of rotten meat from the city's meat-packing plants. Although all the other passengers got off to eat at the station and stretch their legs, Isabel was afraid the train would leave without her if she followed them. She stayed in the car, eating the food her father had packed. One of the passengers in her train car, a gray-haired man carrying a small black bag like a doctor's, brought her back a spicy, delicious sausage from one of the restaurants.

After the train left Chicago, the states of Indiana and Ohio clacked by in a black, expressionless night. Time and again the glow from small train stations grew rapidly bigger, illuminating faded billboard signs for tobacco and tonics. Isabel would watch out the window until the anonymous, deserted stations made her feel alone and adrift. She glanced several times inside the book by Tennyson, which turned out to be poems, but the constant swaying and noise of the train was too distracting for her to concentrate on reading. After two more days of travel, near sunset, one poem did catch her eye:

Ask Me No More

Ask me no more: the moon may draw the sea;
The cloud may stoop from heaven and take the shape,
With fold to fold, of mountain or of cape;
But O too fond, when have I answered thee?
Ask me no more.

Ask me no more: what answer should I give?
I love not hollow cheek or faded eye:
Yet, O my friend, I will not have thee die!
Ask me no more, lest I should bid thee live;
Ask me no more.

Ask me no more: thy fate and mine are sealed;
I strove against the stream and all in vain;
Let the great river take me to the main.
No more, dear love, for at a touch I yield;
Ask me no more.

Isabel swallowed and set the book gently aside on the seat beside her. *I don't know if I have the courage to reread that poem just now*, she thought. Clearly it was about the acceptance of death for someone who was very sick. She was too tired to read anyway. The past three nights she had spent on the short, narrow wood seat, and she had barely gotten a catnap, curled up with her head on her duffel.

I miss Mrs. Dixon, Isabel thought, looking at the empty bench across the aisle. *She made this trip fun and the time go by quickly. Now I'm just scared.*

The train car was empty. The unoccupied benches were a strange presence, as if ghost people sat in them and might rise at any time and approach her. Isabel found herself glancing back at them nervously. She felt as if she had been traveling forever and could never stop.

I'm completely alone now, and I don't really know where, Isabel thought. She shivered, although the air in the car was warm and stagnant, smelling of cigarettes. Isabel found it hard to breathe. "Mother?" she whispered, burying her head in her hands. As always, she got no answer.

The train stopped with a jerk and a shudder, and Isabel peered out the window into blackness. "Is this Carlisle?" she asked herself softly.

"Carlisle station!" the conductor called outside the train.

Isabel stood resolutely and picked up her duffel. The agent had told her that the train would let her off right at the school and a representative of the school would meet her there. *Hurry*, she told herself. If the train left before she got off, she had no idea what the next station could be. She quickly descended the train's metal steps and looked around. The dim shapes of very large trees rose out of short-cut grass, and farther away she could see hazy lights shining from what must be tall buildings.

"Isabel?"

Isabel let out a quick breath of relief. She turned and saw a young woman wrapped in a light plaid cloak approaching her.

"I'm Miss Alice Hayes, one of the teachers here," the woman said, smiling. She had a lovely mother-of-pearl choker around her neck, and her hair was done in a simple but elegant twist. She held out her slender hand, and Isabel took it. "Welcome to Carlisle, Isabel."

"Thank you," Isabel replied, smiling back.

She had expected to be frightened and overwhelmed in this strange place, the way she was in Chicago. But the school wasn't noisy with the shriek of many train wheels on tracks, or crowded with unfamiliar, bustling crowds of people, or garishly, unnaturally bright with smoke-clouded lights. The air here was thick and sweet, like an unimaginably soft blanket. No one else was around.

"Come with me," Miss Hayes said. "We'll go to the administration building and get you checked in, then we'll introduce you to your roommates. Have you eaten?"

"Yes, I have," Isabel said politely, although she had been too nervous to eat any of her food tonight. Miss Hayes set off across the broad school lawn, and Isabel followed, gripping the handles of her duffel tightly.

What enormous trees! she thought, lifting her feet high as she walked through the damp grass. *Even in the mountains on the reservation, no trees are so tall.* The trees stretched up into the night, their long branches disappearing into the dark, blurry sky. All of these trees had leaves, Isabel noticed, not needles like the familiar piñon pines and junipers on the reservation. As she and Miss Hayes stepped onto the school grounds, Isabel could see that the buildings were set up in a vast rectangle, all around a lawn of short grass. Right in the middle of the lawn was a funny little round structure with a roof, but Isabel didn't know what it was.

"I will be your English teacher," Miss Hayes said, turning and touching Isabel lightly on the shoulder. "I'll have to recruit you later for one of our literary societies."

"I'd like that," Isabel said, although she couldn't imagine what a literary society was. She felt a sharp nervous pain in her stomach and was glad she hadn't eaten on the train after all. *There's so much I don't know about this place!* she thought. *So I will have roommates—what will they be like?* Isabel prayed the other girls would be nice and not feel superior to her because they had been at the school longer.

"You will be assigned a grade here based on the schooling you have already had at home," said Miss Hayes. "I think we will try you out in the ninth grade. That should work well because one of your roommates, Lily Monroe, is also in ninth grade. Lily will meet us at the administration building and take you to the girls' dormitory so that you can settle in and get acquainted."

"How very nice," Isabel said politely, but she could feel her heart begin to beat fast. *I'm not really used to the company of other girls,* she thought. *This Lily may not like me at all.* At the reservation, not many girls were Isabel's age, and none of them had much time for socializing or fun: all of them had to work, and care for sick relatives, and keep the household going. Isabel's constant companion had been her mother. They rose together every morning and walked to the school, where they lit the fire in the winter, swept the floor, and prepared the lesson books and other materials for the day's lesson. When the teacher arrived, Isabel would take her place with the other students.

My experience will be very different here, she realized. The pounding of her heart made her stomach ache even more. Brushing away a strand of hair that had fallen in her face, she could feel the dampness in it. The low clouds had come down from the sky as light fog. She had seen wreaths and tongues of fog in the high mountains at home, but never across flat land. *Do the clouds stay on the ground often here?* she wondered.

Miss Hayes opened a tall, white-painted door, and Isabel followed her across a gleaming, well-polished dark wood floor to a desk piled high with papers. Standing beside the desk was a slender girl in a long, high-necked dress. She stepped forward, holding out her hand. "I'm Lily Monroe," she said, smiling.

"I'm Isabel Chavez." Isabel shook Lily's hand, smiling back at her. *Lily is so very lovely*, Isabel thought. The other girl was about Isabel's age and height and wore her dark hair pulled back in a neat chignon. Lily's smooth, perfect complexion set off her straight long nose and full lips, but it was the sweet expression in her brown eyes that made her stunning.

Miss Hayes sat at the desk and wrote quickly on a sheet of paper. "There," she said, setting the paper on top of a stack in a low box. "Now you are officially enrolled at Carlisle, Isabel. We'll fill out the rest of the paperwork tomorrow." She opened a drawer, then handed Isabel a small, neatly wrapped brown paper packet. "Here are a sandwich and cookies to last you through tonight, just in case your dinner on the train was inadequate. Tomorrow Lily will take you to breakfast and show you our dining room. Now, Lily, why don't you and Isabel retire for the evening? She must be exhausted from her very long trip."

Lily took Isabel's hand. "Tomorrow we'll go to the schoolrooms as well. Miss Hayes told me we have the same classes."

"Thank you, Miss Hayes," Isabel said. "Good night."

"Good night, Isabel." Miss Hayes smiled warmly. "I'll see you in class tomorrow."

Outside the administration building, Lily pointed across the manicured lawn to a wide, three-story building lit by gas lamps. "That's the girls' dormitory, where all the girls at the school stay. We're going there."

"So many girls must attend the school," Isabel said. She could hear how stiff her voice sounded and tried to relax, but it was difficult when she was so tired and nervous. Examining the huge dormitory building, she tried to imagine that it was her new home. The outside of the building was divided into squares, each with its own porch behind a low railing. *Those squares must be the rooms, with several girls in each*, she thought. *More than a hundred girls must go to school at Carlisle.*

"Don't forget the boys," Lily said. "They have their own dormitory across the square. We have classes with them, but we're separated for domestic arts and activities." Lily waved her hand at the broad lawn around them. "Sometimes we have outdoor assemblies here or play games, like croquet."

Isabel nodded. She had no idea what croquet was, but she didn't want to admit it. *It's tiresome that I don't know anything about this new place,* she thought.

"How was your trip?" Lily asked, turning to Isabel as they walked along. Again Isabel was struck by her warm, gentle expression. "I hope it wasn't too strenuous," Lily added.

"Oh—" Isabel tried to gather her thoughts. "It was all right. But I didn't get much sleep."

"Miss Hayes told me you traveled alone," Lily said. "You're lucky—I rode the train with ten other Indian children, and people stared at us everywhere we went. At one station they even threw money at us, and when we tried to eat at the restaurants in the train stations, they peered in the windows. We had to take our food back to the train cars to eat." Lily shook her head.

"Are the people in this town strange like that?" Isabel asked cautiously. Although the agent and his staff at the reservation didn't treat the Apaches as their equals, at least they had lived among them for many years and didn't find them bizarre.

"The townspeople are fine," Lily said seriously. "They like the school. The first headmaster, Colonel Pratt, went around to the townspeople before he started the school and asked them if it was all right. They said yes. And thousands of children have been at the school since it started in 1879, so they are very accustomed to us."

Lily opened another white wood door and ushered Isabel into the dormitory. "I hope you don't mind that we are on the third floor," she called over her shoulder. "I suppose it's good for our leg muscles."

Isabel easily climbed the stairs after Lily. The air in the dorm was warm and close, with the same dampness and heaviness as outside. The smell of starch and soap lingered in the stairwell, mixed with the pungent, slightly decayed scent of polished old wood.

"Here is our room." Lily opened a door off the long corridor and stepped inside.

The room was painted white, with three beds each against a wall. Above each bed was a row of shelves, and in the corner stood a small square table with a yellow tablecloth and three chairs around it. One of the walls was almost covered with photographs and drawings, and the top shelf on that wall was stacked with books. The bottom two shelves were full of knick-knacks: a dried bunch of flowers, photographs in frames, and a small ceramic teapot.

"This is my part of the room." Lily waved her hand at the side of the room with all the decorations tacked to the wall. "And that's yours." Lily pointed to a bed under the window, neatly made up with a white blanket and pillow.

Isabel sat down gingerly on the bed. Her clothes were so grimy from the train, she almost didn't want to touch the clean bedclothes.

"You'll get new clothes tomorrow," Lily said understandingly. "I know, looking like a blanket Indian isn't enjoyable."

Like Father, Isabel thought, and immediately felt bad. Most of the people on the reservation wore the blankets from their beds around in cold weather because their clothes were thin and worn. Isabel had tried to clean and patch the blanket her father had walked around in last winter, but he still looked shabby and poor. And now he had taken to wrapping himself in that awful old army poncho. "I'd like some new clean clothes," Isabel admitted. "I'm covered in train smoke."

"Your English is very good," Lily complimented, sitting on her own bed.

"Thank you. I learned it from my mother and uncle." Isabel

looked at the third bed, across the room. The wall above it was undecorated, and only a dress laid out on the bed indicated that part of the room was occupied. "Who is over there?" she asked.

"We have another roommate. She just moved in, when the last girl who lived here went home. She's—" Lily bit her lip and shook her head.

"Is something wrong with her?" Isabel asked bluntly.

"Well, she's a Sioux," Lily said hesitatingly. "I'm Kiowa, and I saw on your registration papers that you're Apache. So the third girl in here has to be from a different tribe from us since no girls from the same tribe are allowed to room together—the school authorities want us to speak English, not our own languages in secret." Lily giggled. "I suppose it would undermine our morals or something to speak Kiowa or Apache. No, really we're supposed to assimilate—become like white people by speaking English. So that's how we got Frances."

"What's so bad about being Sioux?" Isabel asked. She curled her toes in her shoes. *It won't be much fun to be in this small room with a disagreeable girl,* she thought.

"Nothing, I guess, if Frances didn't have to fight the Battle of the Greasy Grass every ten minutes—you know, that battle the Sioux fought against General Custer? Everybody but Frances calls it the Battle of the Little Bighorn, which is some river in Montana." Lily laughed, then sobered. "The Sioux won the battle, and Frances is very proud of that. I mean, I guess it's all right that Frances is always talking about her ancestors. All of us here are proud of our ancestors, though, so it's annoying when Frances acts like she's better than the rest of us."

Isabel was silent. She remembered her father's stories of riding long ago with Victorio, the Apache chief who defied the soldiers and lived for many years in the mountains of New Mexico and Old Mexico. Then Victorio had been killed, and her father, Uncle Robert, and another boy had tried to stay off the reservation, raiding ranches and hunting. That was when her father found what he thought was a miracle horse from the gods, who had helped the boys live free. But in the end, one boy was killed by the soldiers and Uncle Robert and Isabel's father ended up back on the reservation, this time for good. Before the reservation times, the Mescaleros had hunted and moved around their lands, but that was long ago, and even Isabel's father had no memory of life without soldiers.

Does Lily have a similar story? Isabel wondered. "Where are you from?" she asked.

"The reservation at Fort Sill, Oklahoma," Lily said. "Times are very hard there," she added softly. "The other girls have told me that all the other reservations are this way."

Isabel nodded. *What are Father and Jeremy doing now?* she wondered. They were probably sleeping in their tattered, dirty tents, surrounded by tepees and shacks that people got to by walking along the muddy paths at the reservation. *I hope Father is all right and doesn't slide back into despair*, Isabel thought. *He doesn't have a bright clean room or a good new friend or studies to look forward to.*

Lily glanced at Isabel and furrowed her brow. Isabel tried to smile, but she felt on the verge of tears.

"So let's talk about that battle of the Sioux—" Lily began, standing.

Suddenly the door to the room whipped open and a stocky Indian girl strode into the room. She dropped an armload of books on her bed, then ran a hand through her curly black hair. Swinging around, she stared at Isabel. "Who are you?" she asked.

"Isabel Chavez, meet Frances Twiss," Lily said. "Frances, this is our new roommate." Lily sat down beside Isabel on her bed and looked warily at Frances.

"How do you do?" Isabel said. She heard her voice stiffening again and reminded herself to use the good manners her mother had taught her. But the very sight of Frances was irritating. *Perhaps Sioux people are tough and proud, but Apaches won't be pushed around either*, she thought.

"So what tribe are you?" Frances asked. She was a good-looking girl, not beautiful like Lily, but with full lips and arched eyebrows over deep-set brown eyes. Her eyes looked strangely soft, as if she often had a warm expression.

But right now, she looked downright hostile, Isabel thought. "I'm a Mescalero Apache," she said. "From the New Mexico Territory."

"I already told her about you," Lily said quickly to Frances before the other girl could speak. "So what domestic art did you pick?" Lily asked Isabel.

"Domestic art?" Isabel asked. She heard Frances mutter something, then she started stacking her books on the shelves above her bed, turning her back on the other girls.

"I guess Miss Hayes didn't want to overburden you with information before you had a chance to rest. The girls at the school spend the mornings in class, then the afternoons learning a domestic activity, which is a useful trade of some kind," Lily explained. "I work in the school hospital as a nurse. When I go back home, I can use my nursing skills on the reservation."

Frances looked over her shoulder. "I work in the print shop."

"Why?" Isabel asked after a moment. It took her a few seconds to register what a print shop could be.

"I like it." Frances stared at her again.

"But what do you do there?" Isabel asked, locking eyes with the other girl. Isabel had a feeling they were talking about more than Frances's work.

"The print shop publishes the *Red Arrow*—that's the school newspaper—and prints invitations, visiting cards, circulars, and many other materials," Frances said in a superior tone.

Isabel raised her eyebrows at Lily. *I don't want to argue with Frances, but the poor, hungry people at the Mescalero reservation would have little use for visiting cards, and I imagine the Sioux reservation is the same*, she thought. *Didn't Lily say we're supposed to learn useful trades at school?*

"I'm sure Miss Hayes will talk to you about domestic activities tomorrow," Lily said in a conciliatory tone.

"My mother was a teacher," Isabel said, although she doubted already that the teachers here would consider her one. After all, her mother had really only helped the official teacher on the reservation. "So I thought I might study to be a teacher as well," she added.

"Of course—that would be a very good thing to learn," Lily said quickly.

"If you're smart enough." Frances looked Isabel up and down. "The Sioux are smart and have proved it by winning battles."

Isabel felt like snapping back, but she saw Lily shake her head slightly. "I like your drawings," she said to Lily. At the center of Lily's wall was a very large drawing of three horses: they were green, red, and a brilliant shade of turquoise. *Obviously horses aren't those colors, but somehow, when horses are very beautiful, they are striking like that,* Isabel thought.

"Thank you," Lily replied. "I drew all of my pictures in art class. Except for—" Lily pointed to a drawing of a tepee with people clustered around it. "My grandfather drew that one."

Isabel got up to examine the drawings more closely. Out of the corner of her eye, she could see Frances watching her, but Frances didn't say anything else. *Perhaps she will drop her arguments after one try if I don't argue back,* Isabel thought. *I don't want her to win or overwhelm me, but I also don't want our room to be full of shouting all the time. I guess Lily and I are stuck with her, and so we must make the best of it.*

Several of Lily's drawings were of brightly colored horses and antelopes. They had swooping, indistinct lines and seemed more about the effect the animals had on the viewer than copying the exact shape. Other drawings of fruit, vases, and rooms were as real looking as photographs. "You have many drawings of horses," Isabel said.

"I love them," Lily replied. "In the past, my family owned many horses and used them to hunt buffalo. We don't have any horses now, but my grandfather taught me to draw them."

"Why draw them if you don't even have any?" Frances asked, dropping down on her bed and bouncing slightly.

Lily shrugged. "Because horses are beautiful, and my grandfather says Kiowas always draw. It's just something we do. In the old days, we painted designs on big tepees, on our horses, and even on ourselves. But paper is fine to draw on. And I can sell my drawings to the townspeople. I've made good money that way."

"Why are your drawings so mixed up?" Frances asked. "Some look right, and some are—"

"Very different," Isabel finished, since she feared Frances would say something unkind or even insulting.

"Yes, they are," Lily agreed. "Just recently, the school changed its position on Indian art. When I started here, the students drew in the classical style—those apples and oranges in the frame are a still life"—she pointed—"and I drew my horses only after class, for myself. Now we are sometimes allowed in art class to make Indian art. You'll like our class, Isabel—it's fun."

"I can't draw very well," Isabel said doubtfully.

"Me either." Frances shook her head. "And I've been going to that art class for six months. But Lily keeps telling me my buffaloes will stop looking like antelopes someday."

Isabel looked at Frances, whose soft eyes definitely had a twinkle in them. Suddenly she and Isabel burst out laughing.

"Come on, you two," Lily protested. "You can learn—I know you can!"

Isabel and Frances just laughed harder. Gasping, Frances fell off her bed with a thud.

Lily gave her a push with her foot. "Frances, stop it. We'll get in trouble if we make too much noise."

Frances sat up. "I've lived in this room for three whole days and I haven't gotten in trouble yet," she said, wiping tears from her eyes. "But we'll all be right here until summer, so we have lots of time yet."

6

Isabel turned over uneasily in bed, pulling away from a bad dream. She had dreamed that she was in a train car, gazing out the window as she had so many times on her trip to Carlisle. Hundreds of people were outside the window, and Isabel thought she might be in the Chicago train station, except these people weren't strangers—she knew them somehow. They were looking in the window back at her and seemed to be motioning her to get off. Somewhere in the crowd, unseen, were Isabel's father and brother. "What should I do?" Isabel asked as the train whistle sounded.

Isabel opened her eyes and found herself staring at the smooth white ceiling in her room at Carlisle. She knew instantly where she was: this ceiling wasn't the sloping canvas of her tent at home, and the even, soft surface under her back wasn't the lumpy mattress stuffed with pine needles she usually slept on.

But the train whistle kept blowing, even though the dream was over. Then she realized that the blast wasn't actually from a train. Someone was blowing a tune with a device that sounded as if it were right in Isabel's head.

"It's a trumpet," Frances said. She already stood at a washbasin set on a small cabinet between her and Isabel's beds, pouring water into it from a pitcher.

Next to Frances, Lily was looking in the mirror and pinning up her hair. She was already wearing a neat dark skirt and a crisp, long-sleeved white shirt with ruffles down the front. "Every morning, one of the boys plays reveille," Lily explained. "That means it's time to get up. Frances and I get up before then so that we have more time to dress."

"Hurry," Frances urged, flinging open the door to the room. "Breakfast is in fifteen minutes, and you have to be ready. All the girls walk over to the dining room together."

Isabel swung her feet to the floor and flipped her hair behind her shoulders. She touched her new long white nightgown, which had been folded on her pillow last night. *Am I to dress in front of the other girls?* she wondered. *That will feel strange.*

"We'll wait for you downstairs," Lily said in an understanding tone.

"But not for long," Frances added.

Isabel poured water in her own basin and splashed water on her face, drying it with a towel set beside the basin. She took her only other dress out of her duffel and plaited her thick black hair into a braid. Glancing in the mirror, she was mostly satisfied with what she saw. She didn't look sophisticated and perfect like Lily, with her pretty dress and complicated hair arrangement, but Isabel's smooth skin glowed from the cold water washing and her dress, the last one her mother had made for her, was neatly sewn though worn.

"If I fuss with my appearance any more, I might miss breakfast," Isabel murmured. She realized she was very hungry, even though she and her roommates had eaten all of the food package from Miss Hayes last night.

Isabel hastily made her bed since Lily and Frances had made theirs. She eyed her duffel, which sat by her bed, still mostly unpacked. The shelves over the foot of her bed were empty except for the Tennyson book from Mrs. Dixon. *I'll enjoy arranging my things later*, Isabel thought. She didn't have much, but maybe Lily would loan her a drawing or two.

Not wanting to be late for breakfast, Isabel flew down the stairs. Frances and Lily were waiting in front of the dormitory, at the back of a very long line of girls of all ages, from almost grown to tiny. The line began to move. On the other side of the big square of grass, Isabel saw a similar line of boys. The boys wore blue military uniforms and had short hair, and they walked in an orderly way.

The morning sun caressed Isabel's face through the sweet, thick air that brought the scent of flowers and grass and the warm smell of eggs, toast, and bacon cooking for breakfast. Out of habit she looked at the morning's clouds. They were smudged around the edges and floating in small groups, and the summer sky had a soft blur of haze. The sky was blue but not the brilliant, deep turquoise of the sky at home; it was a gentler, lighter shade. Near the horizon the sky became white, touching the tops of the trees and green of the fields and blending in with them. At the far edge of the grass square in the center of the school, a thick band of fog wrapped itself around the base of the trees, rising in streamers to the sky as the day warmed.

I don't understand these clouds at all, Isabel decided. *Will it rain later or not? Perhaps I will come to understand them, as I will this whole school.* She drew a deep breath.

The girls walked across the lawn to a large building that looked much like the girls' dormitory, with a peaked roof and long windows. Inside the building, the huge dining room was mayhem. Hundreds of boys and girls streamed around dozens of tables set with many bowls and plates and surrounded by low stools. Isabel stood just inside the door, unable to move. So many people! She checked quickly to make sure Lily and Frances were close by. She cleared her throat to ask them what to do but realized they wouldn't be able to hear her.

The two other girls took seats at a nearby table, and Isabel sat next to Lily. Frances leaned around Lily. "Now we'll be served!" she yelled, or that was what it sounded like.

Within moments older Indian girls were setting big bowls of oatmeal, plates stacked with toast, and pots of jam on the tables. The food smelled rich and heavy. Isabel tried to eat, but she was too nervous to get much down. So many other children were eating and talking, in English, that the room buzzed like a thousand hummingbirds. Isabel took a couple of deep breaths and tried to calm her stomach.

"There's Major Mercer," Lily said, pointing across the room. "He's the head of the school."

Isabel saw an older man with a graying mustache and hair and the erect soldier's bearing she had often seen on the reservation. Major Mercer seemed to be conferring with a couple of teachers.

"We don't see much of him," Frances said, leaning around Lily again. "I've never even talked to him, except he shook my hand when I started school here. But he's in charge."

"Eat something," Lily advised, pointing at Isabel's full plate. "You'll be starving in an hour if you don't."

Isabel forked up a bite of scrambled egg and popped it into her mouth. The eggs were warm and buttery and tasted delicious, but her stomach was firmly saying no. Ignoring it, she tried a bit of egg on a piece of toast with jam, but this time her stomach fluttered, then heaved. Isabel dropped her fork.

Lily and Frances rose from the table along with all the other students. "Now what happens?" Isabel asked, hastily getting up.

"You and I have mathematics together," Lily replied. "Frances isn't in our class."

Frances opened her mouth to say something, but Isabel couldn't hear her over the loud talk of the other students. Lily said in Isabel's ear, "Frances was just trying to tell you that she's in a more advanced math class than we are."

"You could hear that?" Isabel asked, raising her own voice.

"No, I just know that's what she'd say." Lily laughed.

Waving, Frances joined two big boys near the door of the cafeteria. "Those are her cousins," Lily yelled. "Frances has a lot of relatives at the school. But just boys—she was the only girl her family would send. Come on." Lily took Isabel's arm.

Isabel was glad Lily kept a firm grip on her as the other students swirled around like a swarm of grasshoppers. In the classroom, Isabel slid quickly into an empty bench. In front of her was a flat desk. She was aware of a blur of other people in the room, but at first she was too nervous to look up. The door closed, and a rather severe-looking, stout woman with a long face and wearing a black dress with high shoulder ruffles swept into the room. She immediately spotted Isabel.

"I am Miss Kingsley," the teacher said with a smile. She handed Isabel a slate and a piece of chalk. "You will use these to do your work in this class. You may sit at this desk every day."

"Thank you," Isabel replied. While the teacher checked attendance, she looked around at her first classroom. A blackboard stretched the length of an entire wall and had circles divided by lines to show fractions. Isabel felt a quick burst of relief that Uncle Robert had taught her about fractions when he was explaining land ownership to her father one day. Above the blackboard was a row of papers showing the students' work. Glancing at her teacher's earnest face, Isabel felt a surge of excitement. *I'll learn so much here*, she thought. *When I'm home, I'll share it.*

Miss Kingsley moved to the blackboard. "George, please come up to the front of the class and write on the blackboard the answer to the first problem in the homework assignment."

Isabel was surprised by the look of frank interest that the big boy, George, gave her as he passed her on the way to the blackboard. Then she realized that most of the boys in the class were staring at her. Isabel looked back. The boys' military uniforms

were navy blue with high-necked white collars and a row of but-
tons down the front. Their hair was cut very short, like Jeremy's,
and they sat quietly among the girls, except for three boys at the
back, who were talking.

It's odd to have so many boys looking at me at once, she thought.
I hope they aren't examining my shabby dress! She dropped her
gaze to her hands.

On the reservation, the boys, like everyone else, were too
busy working for their next meal to have much time to look at
the girls. Isabel remembered her father telling her about the old
Mescalero ways of courtship and the long, joyful ceremony that
was held for each girl to celebrate her becoming a woman. Now
the Mescaleros had no time for celebrations or courtship.

Isabel looked around the class out of the corners of her eyes.
All the students seemed to be about her age or older. She counted
seventeen students in the class.

"Very good, George," Miss Kingsley said approvingly when
George had finished drawing on the blackboard. "Let's move on.
William?"

Isabel noticed that although Lily was sitting at the desk
right next to hers, she didn't talk to Isabel or even look at her. In
contrast, the three boys at the back couldn't seem to sit still, and
they were talking nonstop, not paying attention.

What is the punishment for that? Isabel wondered. *Will they
be sent back to the reservation? That won't reflect well on their
families.*

Bang! The teacher rapped her desk with her ruler. Isabel
jumped. "Frank, Thomas, and Albert, you are to stop talking immediately or I shall send you to Major Mercer's office,"
Miss Kingsley said. "He will not be pleased to see you again this
week." She didn't sound nice at all now. Lily grimaced and shook
her head slightly.

The three boys settled down after that, although Isabel
thought she heard a soft laugh when one of the girls tripped
on her way to the blackboard. Isabel didn't turn around to see

who it was. *I'll pay them no mind*, she vowed. *I can't learn and laugh at the same time. Besides, I have no wish to be disciplined by Major Mercer. It would be like punishment by the agent back home, and you never know what the outcome of that will be.*

After math, Isabel caught up with Lily again to be taken to her next class. "I was so worried that Miss Kingsley would whack her ruler on a desk again," Isabel said as they walked down the hall of the academic building. "Do those boys always cause trouble?"

"Pretty much," Lily answered, dodging to avoid a group of giggling younger girls. "But you get used to it."

"What would be the worst punishment the boys could get?" Isabel asked.

"Well, being sent to Major Mercer for a lecture isn't pleasant, or so I've heard. But those three boys have been in his office so many times, I guess they don't care." Lily shook her head. "Getting put in the guardhouse is the worst punishment here. It's damp and awful, and you don't get much food. I've never heard of a girl having to stay in the guardhouse, though."

"Do the authorities ever make anyone leave the school?" Isabel asked.

"I don't think so." Lily smoothed her skirt. "The school has been going a long time, and the people who run it know how to enforce discipline without drastic measures. But we all need to be careful to behave."

"Frances doesn't seem to care," Isabel said.

"She just says she doesn't," Lily replied. "But I haven't seen her actually do anything wrong. Here we are—this is our English classroom." Lily ducked in the doorway of another classroom.

Isabel looked across the rows of desks and was happy to see Miss Hayes's familiar, kind face.

"Good morning, Isabel and Lily," Miss Hayes said warmly. "Why don't you have a seat right up here at the front, Isabel? Lily, you may change your assigned seat to sit next to her."

"All right," Lily said, sounding a little reluctant. As she

sat down next to Isabel, she whispered, "I'm not very good at English, so I hide in the back and hope I'm not called on."

"Sorry!" Isabel whispered back.

"It's okay." Lily sighed. "Miss Hayes always calls on me anyway, as much as anybody else."

The rest of the class came in, chatting in small groups and pairs. Miss Hayes looked up from her desk. "All right, students. Please take your seats and open your books to page 21." The teacher stepped around her desk and handed Isabel a small yellow paperback book. "We have been discussing the poetry of Henry Wadsworth Longfellow, an American poet of the nineteenth century. Today's assignment was to write down our thoughts about the meaning of Longfellow's poem 'The Tide Rises, the Tide Falls.'"

Lily rolled her eyes and dropped her head onto her hand. Isabel opened her book to page 21 and read the short poem.

> *The tide rises, the tide falls,*
> *The twilight darkens, the curlew calls;*
> *Along the sea-sands damp and brown*
> *The traveller hastens toward the town,*
> *And the tide rises, the tide falls.*
>
> *Darkness settles on roofs and walls,*
> *But the sea, the sea in the darkness calls;*
> *The little waves, with their soft, white hands,*
> *Efface the footprints in the sands,*
> *And the tide rises, the tide falls.*
>
> *The morning breaks; the steeds in their stalls*
> *Stamp and neigh, as the hostler calls;*
> *The day returns, but nevermore*
> *Returns the traveller to the shore,*
> *And the tide rises, the tide falls.*

Isabel furrowed her brow. *I think this poem may be about me,* she thought.

"You think this is difficult," Lily whispered, misunderstanding Isabel's expression. "We just finished 'Hiawatha's Childhood,' also by Longfellow, which is about an Indian tribe in the East. They must not be like us, because I couldn't understand the poem at all. But I hardly ever do—"

"Lily, please don't whisper in class," Miss Hayes reproved. "That is unlike you." She looked around the classroom. "Would anyone like to share his or her thoughts about 'The Tide Rises'? Yes, Sandra?"

A tall girl in the middle of one of the rows stood up. "It's about change and the sameness of things. Travel is change, but the tide in the ocean is constant. But you can turn that around and say that the ocean changes, but travelers coming and going from an inn don't change."

"Very good, Sandra," Miss Hayes said approvingly.

Isabel looked at the poem again. *I agree*, she realized. *How amazing to say so much in so few lines. But I wonder what the tide is?*

Miss Hayes closed her book. "I'd like everyone to write a paragraph on his or her impressions of the poem. You can relate it to your life at home or write a general description."

Isabel picked up her chalk and gently touched the slate in front of her with it. *Time to learn again*, she thought. For a moment, Isabel closed her eyes and imagined herself back in her mother's classroom at the reservation. *Mother would be so pleased that I'm back in school.*

"Write something about the poem," Lily whispered. "Don't worry too much about what."

Isabel opened her eyes and looked at the blank slate. *What can I say about this poem?* she wondered. She frowned and glanced over at Lily, who was writing quickly and then made several swooping strokes with her chalk.

Isabel read the poem again. *So I'm a traveler, just like the person in the poem*, she thought. *And others will follow me to the Carlisle school. I don't know what the tide is, but it comes and goes, I guess forever. Will travelers come here forever?*

Frustrated, Isabel looked up from her book. She saw that

Lily had written a few sentences, signed her name, and finished with a picture of a galloping spotted horse with a girl riding it. Isabel covered her mouth, trying not to laugh.

"All right, class, work on your assignment a bit more tonight, then we'll read a few of them tomorrow," Miss Hayes said.

Isabel let out her breath. *Thank goodness I'll have more time to write something*, she thought. *Tonight I can figure out what.*

Miss Hayes led the class in a discussion of several more poems, all by the poet Longfellow. At the end of class, Isabel felt she had understood most of the poems, with their odd cadence and condensed meaning. She still didn't know what some of the words meant, but she'd ask Lily later. Then Isabel noticed that Lily was running her hand over the iron filigree design on the end of her bench and didn't seem to be attending to the classroom discussion in the least. *Maybe I'll ask somebody else*, Isabel amended.

She stood up with the rest of the students after Miss Hayes dismissed the class and put the Longfellow poetry book on top of the math book in her arms.

"Wait a moment, Isabel," Miss Hayes called. When Isabel turned, she said, "Let's spend a few minutes getting your schedule and clothing sorted out. Ordinarily you would have art class next, but you can begin it tomorrow."

"All right," Isabel said gratefully. She was in no hurry to try her hand at drawing antelopes in art class.

"Let's find you a few dresses first," said Miss Hayes. "We'll go to the dressmaking shop in the industrial building for that. But wait—"The teacher returned to her desk and opened the big drawer in the bottom. She handed Isabel a thick book. "Here is a dictionary," Miss Hayes said. "You can look up the words you don't understand."

"Thank you," Isabel replied, carefully fitting the big book at the bottom of her stack. Miss Hayes looked so kind, Isabel almost asked her what the tide was. *But suppose it's something very simple, like an apple or a tree?* she thought. *I don't want Miss Hayes to think me very ignorant right from the start.*

"The dressmaking classes are held in the industrial hall," Miss Hayes said as she and Isabel walked across the green. "We have a darning class for the small girls and beginners. Next, students progress to clothes repair, then to making simple items—shirts for the boys, aprons, curtains, and the like. The most advanced class is dressmaking. While we are on the subject of domestic activities, you will need to pick one. Then you will spend each afternoon during the week perfecting your skills."

"I—think I want to be a teacher," Isabel said shyly. "How do I do that?"

"The best thing would be to join one of our literary societies," Miss Hayes said, opening the door to yet another tall, white-painted building with a pitched roof. "We meet in the evenings and discuss a work of literature. How about I sign you up for the Susan Longstreth Literary Society? The girls call themselves the Susans."

"That sounds good," Isabel said. *I'll have to learn what to say at such a meeting, though*, she thought.

"The domestic activity you select will certainly be useful to you in later life as well as the teaching skills you learn," Miss Hayes continued. "I will give you a list of the choices of domestic activities. Here we are at the fitting room. You may select three dresses, and the advanced dressmaking students will fit them for you."

Isabel stepped into the room. Two girls stood on top of low tables, and in front of them other girls were hemming their long white skirts. On a square rag rug, another girl knelt, reaching up to fit the waist of a dress. A mannequin in a complete, elegant white dress had been placed along the wall, out of the way, and a full-length mirror was propped in the corner. The girls acknowledged Isabel's and Miss Hayes's presence with smiles, then went back to their work.

"That white dress on the mannequin is available," Miss Hayes said. "Do you like it?"

"Very much," Isabel said promptly. *I'm actually glad that I waited to get this dress until I had seen something of the school*, she thought. *On the reservation, this dress would stay white exactly one step on the muddy paths, and I would have refused it if offered it, but here I can stay clean all day long.*

"Let's get you two dresses today, and one of the girls can make you a third." Miss Hayes touched the white dress on the mannequin. "You can pick out the cloth and style for the third dress."

"I'd like a striped dress like Lily's," Isabel said.

"That can be done." Miss Hayes nodded. "Emma, would you help Isabel?"

One of the girls who had been sewing ruffles on a shirt got up from her chair and came over to them. "Emma, meet Isabel," Miss Hayes introduced. "She needs to be outfitted in new clothes. Isabel, Emma is our head dressmaker."

Emma, a short girl with slanting black eyes, walked slowly around Isabel. "Let's start with fitting the white dress," she said. "Take it off the mannequin, and it's yours."

Isabel smiled. "I'd like to very much." In a back room, she changed into the lovely dress. When she came out, Miss Hayes was still waiting. "I don't want to take too much of your time," she said to the teacher.

"This is my job, and one of the fun parts of it." Miss Hayes laughed. "That dress suits you perfectly, Isabel."

"It almost fits." Isabel touched the waist. "It only needs to be taken in a little here."

"Do you sew?" Emma asked.

"Yes, a bit," Isabel replied. "But I never had a sewing machine." *I've made many clothes, but not out of beautiful cloth such as this,* she thought. *The purpose of the clothes I made was to keep my family warm, and those clothes had to last through hard work. That was all.*

Emma nodded, and Isabel knew that the other girl understood. She had probably begun sewing in the same way at the reservation. "You'll like using a sewing machine," Emma said. "The stitches are even and perfect, and the machine is so fast!"

"I can't wait to try," Isabel said eagerly.

"I think I can guess what domestic activity you would like to do." Miss Hayes smiled. "Or should I run down the list of possibilities?"

"Dressmaking," Isabel said promptly.

"Done! You can start tomorrow," Miss Hayes said. "Why don't you take this afternoon off, Isabel, and get acquainted with the school? Then tonight write a letter to your family. They will want to hear that you have arrived safely and your initial impressions of the school. All the students are required to write one letter home a month, but I'm sure the families would like to get news more often."

"Thank you, I will." Isabel noticed that Emma's quick, dexterous fingers had already almost finished pinning the waist of the new dress.

"I'm going to look over my plans for tomorrow's classes now, but I'll see you at dinner tonight, Isabel," Miss Hayes said. "Here are a pen and a few sheets of paper for your letter. When you're ready to mail it, bring it to me and we'll address the envelope."

Isabel took the thick, cream-colored paper and black pen. "Thank you so much. I'll enjoy this."

"Excellent." Miss Hayes smiled and with a wave took her leave.

A short time later, Isabel stepped out of the dressmaking classroom onto the lawn and twirled in her new white dress, admiring the way the long, full skirt lifted around her. The big lawn in front of the buildings was deserted. *I wonder what time it is?* she thought, looking at the angle of the sun. Strangely, this didn't hurt her eyes. Although the sun must be the same one that shone right now on Mescalero, here at Carlisle it was subdued and gentle.

"Isabel!" Lily called. Isabel saw her roommate hurrying toward her from the academic building. "That's a wonderful dress," she gasped when she reached Isabel, trying to catch her breath.

"Thanks. I hope to learn to make dresses," Isabel replied.

"My domestic activity will be dressmaking."

"Oh, that will be wonderful for Frances and me," Lily said, smoothing back escaped tendrils from her chignon. "You can make us all dresses!"

"I'd like to," Isabel said. *Lily is such a pretty girl, I'll enjoy making her the perfect dress,* she thought. *I can already imagine just the right shade of blue.*

"I'm off to the school hospital," Lily said. "Speaking of clothes, we nurses look very sharp in our uniforms." She giggled.

Isabel tried not to shudder visibly at the thought of the hospital, with all those people crammed together into a building full of illness. *I can't imagine working with sick people,* she thought. But at least here at the school, there was a place for them—on the reservation, very sick people were everywhere. "Aren't you afraid you'll fall ill?" she asked. "And don't a lot of sick people all together just make each other worse?"

"No, we separate them into different wards," Lily said. "And we're careful to wash our hands and put on a clean uniform every day, so we don't usually get sick ourselves. You should come over and see the hospital. It's quite nice."

"I will soon," Isabel said, although she had no intention of ever setting foot in that place. "I think I'll just walk around for a few minutes now and get to know the school. Miss Hayes said that I can take the afternoon off."

"All right," Lily said. "I'll see you at dinner. Lunch is in about half an hour—don't forget that. It's at the same place we had breakfast; we get all our meals there. I eat lunch at the hospital so I'll be around if the patients need me."

Isabel set out on her walk. Out of habit, she glanced at the sky and stopped in surprise. *The sky is completely white,* she thought. *It's as if the blur on the horizon this morning has overtaken the blue. Perhaps this means rain?*

She planned to walk around the long rectangle of buildings, stopping occasionally to go between them and see what was out back. *First I must take a look at that strange little house without walls in the very center of the lawn,* she thought. She walked up the steps, lightly holding the wood rail that circled the building's porch, and looked out at the school through the open sides. Nearby, a group of laughing, jostling boys tossing a ball to each other pushed through the double doors into one of the buildings.

"What *is* this?" Isabel called over to a passing girl, pointing at the wood floor.

The girl laughed. "I asked that too when I first got here. It's a gazebo," she said. "It's just like a little covered porch in the middle of the lawn. Sometimes the school band plays concerts in it. I guess mostly people sit in it and enjoy the day."

"Thank you," Isabel said. "Just one other question—where did those boys go?"

"The gymnasium," the girl answered. "They're going to play a basketball game. Girls have their own teams too, so you can play if you want."

"That is my last question for today," Isabel murmured as the girl walked on. Isabel crossed the lawn to the gym and opened one of the heavy double doors. At the end of a long hallway, she could hear the shouts of the boys. In glass cases along the walls were many trophies of all different sizes in gold, silver, and bronze.

I might as well find out what basketball is, she thought, opening one of the doors in the next set of double doors at the end of the hall.

Inside, about thirty boys were running fast around a wide, highly polished wood floor, throwing a big round ball to each other. The boys still wore their long-sleeved white shirts and navy blue pants from their uniforms, but they had taken off their coats. Isabel covered her ears for a moment as the boys' loud calls echoed off the high ceiling, rising into yells as one boy tossed the ball through a stiff hoop at one end of the gymnasium. Then the boys all ran the other way across the floor.

Isabel made her way down a narrow raised platform along the length of the gymnasium so that she was at the center of the room and could see both ways. *I hope I'm allowed to be here,* she thought. *But even if I'm not, people have been kind to me, a new girl, so far. I'll probably be asked gently to leave if I must.*

The pack of boys galloped by her again. Isabel watched the leader, who was bouncing the ball in front of him. Oddly, although the boy had managed to snatch the ball from the other boys and get away out in front of them, he was much smaller than the rest of the players. As the boys thundered by her, Isabel recognized the first boy as one of the troublemakers from her mathematics class. Short as he was, he managed to elude the reaching hands of the other boys and throw the ball up at the hoop. It banged the metal rim, then dropped through the net.

About half of the boys cheered—the short boy's team, Isabel supposed. The boy took the ball to the side of the gym, and then he saw her. Now that Isabel could get a better look at him, she realized he wasn't as young as she'd thought. He looked about her age.

The boy winked at her. Then he threw the ball to one of his teammates and hurled himself into the fray. Isabel smiled slightly. *Basketball does look like fun,* she thought. *Jeremy would like to play such a rowdy sport with other boys. Perhaps he should come to school here too. But then Father would be so lonely. I must write them.*

Isabel made her way out of the gym. She glanced at the sky with its odd pale clouds, but she could tell from the light that although the day had gotten later, no new weather was approaching. Her father had said he understood her fascination with clouds, although no one else did. "In the old days, when the Mescaleros were hunters, we had to watch the clouds and sky," he told her. "The animals are found in different places when the sky is cloudy or it rains."

Isabel didn't know if that was why she watched the sky or not. She had never hunted for food or been a part of that old-style life—the Mescaleros had already been on the reservation a long time when she was born. "She's not a hunter—she just likes lying around and looking at the sky," Jeremy had said, and to Isabel that had felt more like the truth. But now that she was at Carlisle and the clouds didn't mean what they had, she felt unsettled. She wondered if her father had been right after all.

Abruptly Isabel stopped, her hand to her mouth. She had almost walked into a little cemetery. The cemetery was neatly kept, with trimmed grass between the rows of headstones. The dates of birth and death carved on the headstones were close together. *These must be the graves of children who died at Carlisle,* Isabel realized. The headstones had the names of many tribes: Apache, Sioux, Kiowa, Hopi. One child had been only nine years old.

The bell rang for lunch, startling Isabel. But tempting as the thought of another warm, good meal was, she didn't think she could face the crowd of students again so soon. *I'll write my letter home,* she thought. Quickly she crossed the lawn to the girls' quarters and climbed the smooth wood steps to her clean, quiet room. Sitting at the square table, Isabel set down the paper Miss Hayes had given her and began to write.

> *Dear Father and Jeremy,*
> *I have safely arrived at the Carlisle school and went to classes today for the first time. I enjoyed mathematics and English. My teachers are very good.*

Isabel nibbled the end of her pen. She had a quick, clear vision of her father and brother right at that moment, boiling water in an old can over a fire before their tents. What else would interest her family about her Carlisle experience? Probably she shouldn't brag about the good meals here—Jeremy would be envious. Her father didn't know anything about English class or mathematics, and Jeremy did know but didn't care about them, so she shouldn't go into details about her classes. Uncle Robert would be pleased that she was learning mathematics—before Isabel had left for Carlisle, he had emphasized the importance and usefulness of the subject in business.

--- ❖❖ ---

Isabel frowned, then realized that of course her father would want to hear about her new friends.

> *I live in a nice room with two other girls. One is Kiowa and the other is Sioux. The Kiowa girl, Lily, is very pretty and nice, and she is a fine artist. Frances, who is Sioux, works in the print shop on the school newspaper.*
> *Please write back, Jeremy, and tell me what you and Father are doing. Are you both working in the logging camps?*

Isabel sat back. She wanted to tell her father and brother to be careful when they cut down the trees—several men had been badly hurt or killed when the saw slipped or a tree fell the wrong way and crushed them—but what choice did they have in their work? Isabel remembered how annoyed and exasperated she felt when anyone told her to be careful with the horses at the reservation. "I'm always as careful as I can be, but I still must train whatever horse I am given," she murmured.

Isabel felt a pang at the thought of Lexington and the other horses on the reservation. She missed the big animals' sweet, trusting eyes and their warm, hay-scented breath tickling her hands and face. After this long day struggling to understand her new school, Isabel knew a fast gallop would be just perfect to ease her tension. "I doubt if anyone else is continuing Lexington's training," she said aloud. "I hope some old soldier hasn't taken him over. How can I ask Jeremy about the horses at the reservation without Father guessing that I've been riding them?" she asked the ceiling.

Isabel hesitated, holding the pen above the paper. She wanted very much to write *I miss you*, but then her father and brother would think that she was unhappy at the school and worry. Her father would think that his sacrifice in letting her go to Carlisle wasn't worthwhile.

I like school very much, Isabel finished. *I will write again soon. Love, Isabel.*

7

The late summer morning was already hot on the mountain. John could feel it burning through his shirt as he bent over the tracks on the damp ground near the stream. "The horse went this way," he said to Jeremy, speaking quietly because the tracks were soft and fresh and the horse probably had not gone far. He had started tracking Sun That Rises at this small stream because the horse would go for water and it was near where he and Jeremy had seen her last.

John studied the tracks again. He could see the marks of the mare's small hooves digging into the mud near the water, then moving up the bank along with the much bigger tracks of the other horses. The biggest tracks of all were probably the white stallion's.

"There she is," Jeremy said, also keeping his voice low. He pointed up the bank, where the palomino mare was vigorously pulling leaves off the low branch of a cottonwood. In a small gully nearby, two mares and a couple of foals were grazing. "Now what?" he asked.

"We must catch her." John held up an apple in one hand and a rope and halter in the other. "You stay here, and we will hope she goes for this apple."

"I still don't see why I had to come along," Jeremy grumbled, sitting down on a dry pile of leaves.

"I told you, I need your help to train the horse for Isabel," John said patiently. That was true, but he had also discovered that Jeremy had no work for another week and intended to play cards all day with the other young men. Now that Jeremy was almost grown up, John had learned that he could not directly confront him about wasting time in such ways, but he still hoped to keep him focused on important matters, like preparing a fine present for his sister.

Isabel had already been gone almost a month, and work at the logging camps and repairing buildings at the agency had kept John from returning to the horse. He almost wished he had not promised Isabel that he would work, but because he had, he could not bring himself to do the enjoyable task of horse training while Jeremy supported the family. *Now that I am thinking properly again, not merely a rock of grief from Maria's death, I see that I should never have expected Jeremy to work so hard*, John thought. *Even Isabel, who loved her mother so, did not sit on that fence with me. I behaved very badly to my children.*

Right after Isabel left, John had started to wonder what she had done all that time after Maria died in the early summer. Perhaps she had gone for walks. *I am lucky to have such fine children who did not get into trouble while I mourned*, he told himself. *I must never treat them so again.*

John walked up the low rise toward the horse. He kept his steps steady and even so that he would not remind her of a wolf or mountain lion about to spring.

"She doesn't seem to mind you getting close," Jeremy called.

"No, not yet." John stopped a few paces from the horse and looked up at her. Sun That Rises was calmly looking back, finishing her mouthful of leaves. She seemed to have been listening to the conversation—she had a very aware expression in her eyes. *Either you were listening or you are thinking what to do about me,* John thought. *Well, I will find out.*

The mare watched him closely, but she didn't run away. "She isn't afraid—this is good," John called back to Jeremy.

John slowly held out the apple. Sun That Rises stretched her neck and took the apple in her teeth. She crunched it, bobbing her head and seeming to enjoy her treat. John carefully slipped the rope around her neck, then eased the halter onto her head. The mare seemed to accept this as payment for the apple and didn't move away.

"So far, so good," John said. "I think she is used to being caught. Now we have to hope that she does not have vices when a rider gets on."

At least this horse does not think of people as enemies, he thought as he led the mare to a clearing. She followed him willingly and even nibbled his back pocket, looking for another treat. John tied her to another cottonwood tree. Many horses feared people, he knew, and with good reason. The soldiers in particular usually did not treat their horses well, and a horse that had belonged to a soldier often would bite or buck off its rider any chance it got. John knew that the soldiers' horses became rank because the soldiers did not have time to train them and sometimes broke them to ride in one severe session over one afternoon. Isabel would not be home until next summer, and so he intended to take whatever time he needed for the mare to feel that being ridden was a pleasure.

Jeremy pushed through the brush on the stream bank and joined him. "She already is nicer than a mule," he said, studying the horse. "What will you do with her now?"

"We will see what kind of a horse she really is," John said. "I will go for a ride."

"Are you going to ride bareback?" Jeremy asked, patting the horse's shoulder. She swung her head around and nudged him gratefully.

John pointed at a creosote bush. "I hid a saddle there yesterday," he said. "I did not want anyone to see me bringing it out here." He also did not want the horse to see it. Either she and the other horses were wild enough to want to avoid saddles or anything else that reminded them of people, or the mare would understand that the saddle meant she would have to work. John felt a little foolish thinking this horse was so intelligent, but he had the firm impression that she was thinking right along with him.

"Good planning." Jeremy sighed. He walked over to the creosote bush and picked up the saddle and blanket.

The horse watched with interest, but she made no move when Jeremy set the blanket and then the saddle on her back. "Very good," John said approvingly.

Jeremy removed the bridle from the saddle horn and handed it to his father. John approached the mare cautiously, but she easily accepted the bit and even dropped her head so that John could pull the headpiece over her ears. "I may not have to train her much at all," he said, trying to contain the excitement he felt about the horse's cooperation. "Isabel is not an experienced rider, but this horse may be right for her already."

"Huh," Jeremy said noncommittally. "Maybe."

"Isabel may become a fine rider if she has such a horse." John unclipped the rope from the mare's halter. "We will see."

Jeremy didn't meet his eyes. "I bet she will," he said. He leaned against the cottonwood and folded his arms.

"Hold the horse while I get on," John said. Although he trusted Sun That Rises more and more with each step of the training process, mounting always left a rider vulnerable. He had no wish to feel a saddle horn in his gut or break a rib; he had enough aches and pains.

Jeremy stepped up to the horse and held the reins under her chin. The mare pulled the reins a little through his hands so that she could turn her head and watch while John quickly swung into the saddle.

"Very good," John said, smiling broadly. He settled himself in the seat of the big cowboy saddle, stretching out his legs in the stirrups. They seemed the right length—his legs were almost straight. *When did I ride last?* he wondered. *Once, years ago, I rode to carry a message to workers at a logging camp—but the last time I rode a fine horse was Moon That Flies, when I lived in the mountains, fleeing the soldiers.*

"Where will you ride?" Jeremy asked.

"I think I will try her in the meadow." John nodded in that direction, not taking his hands off the reins. "Although she may rush across it to join the other horses, that is still better than a fight with her in the trees." John realized how very much he did not want to get hit with the sharp points and heavy weight of branches. *I have grown old*, he thought.

Jeremy nodded and moved away. John cautiously urged Sun That Rises forward with his legs. She hesitated, then stepped out briskly. She did not arch her back or falter in her steps, and John could feel some of the tension leaving his shoulders. Apparently the mare was neither a bronc nor unbroken.

At the edge of the meadow, John could see several of the other horses in the herd, although not the stallion. They raised their heads, as if watching the show. Sun That Rises glanced at the other horses, then looked back at the grass, which almost reached her knees. "No eating right now," John commanded. "We must work a little." He touched the left side of the mare's neck with the rein, signaling her to turn right. After a moment's hesitation, Sun That Rises obediently turned and walked in the direction he had indicated.

"She does not seem to mind being apart from the other horses," John called to Jeremy, who was watching from the edge of the meadow.

"That's good," Jeremy called back. "The mules don't like it when we separate them. One time at the logging camp, we took one of the mules over a creek by itself and the rest of the team charged after it. Two of them ended up overturned in the creek."

John walked Sun That Rises around the edge of the meadow twice, making her weave to practice turns. "Do you see this, Maria?" John whispered. He could not get out of the habit of talking to his beautiful wife, although he had learned not to do it aloud in front of other people. He had talked to her so much when she was alive, he simply could not bear that she no longer shared the important times of his life.

He turned Sun That Rises down the middle of the meadow. The mare's yellow ears pricked, and she strained her head against the reins.

The next moment Sun That Rises leapt forward. The back of the saddle hit John hard on the spine. Before he could sit up again, the palomino threw a huge buck.

John caught a glimpse of her heels flashing in the air, up above his ear, and he could feel himself slipping to the side. *I'm going to fall—very hard*, he had time to realize. In desperation he grabbed Sun That Rises' thick white mane to try to steady himself. That helped him to not slip farther, but then the mare threw in a whole series of bucks, each one higher and harder than the last, and he could not regain his seat.

Suddenly, at the far edge of the meadow, the mare stopped bucking and slowed to a trot. She halted abruptly in front of the line of trees bordering the meadow. Immediately John hitched himself back upright in the saddle and shortened the reins so that he had contact with the horse's mouth again. He was breathing heavily, and sweat was running down his face. Sun That Rises snorted loudly, then tossed her head.

Jeremy ran across the meadow to them. "I can't believe you didn't fall off," he said.

"What could have spooked you?" John wheezed. He bent over, trying to pull air into his lungs.

Sun That Rises rolled her eye back to look at him. She was breathing quickly but did not seem otherwise the worse for her long run.

John leaned back, studying her. "Do you want to see something in these woods?" he asked. For all his experience with horses, this one had surprises.

"She just wanted to have some fun." Jeremy reached out to touch the mare's slightly sweaty gold neck. "You kept turning her and making her walk, and she got tired of it."

"That is no reason to try to kill me." John managed to catch his breath and bent down to adjust his stirrups. "She must learn to behave, whether she wants to or not."

Sun That Rises abruptly turned and moved back toward the meadow. John pulled her up hard. The mare stopped, looked around at him, then pawed the ground with one front hoof. John tugged on the reins again, and she finally stood still. "Sun That Rises is like a different horse now, when she does not listen," he said. "But you are right, Jeremy—I do not think she is acting wild, just stubborn. I hope I can ride that out of her." He could hear the doubt in his voice. No matter how much he rode this young horse, she would always have more energy left than he did. A very spirited horse would be fine and even fun for an experienced rider, but he did not want Isabel to be frightened or hurt if the horse treated her in this way.

"Perhaps it's good that I'm here," Jeremy remarked. "To catch the horse if she throws you and to pick you up."

John frowned. He did not look forward to any more rides like this one. *I can only hope that with much patience and work, she will be as well behaved as she is beautiful*, he thought, dismounting.

Sun That Rises stretched her neck, sniffing Jeremy's hand. He tickled her muzzle, and she rested her head on his shoulder. John could not help smiling. The palomino's pale gold coat was as warm and bright as the day. "You will bring the sun to my Isabel," he said.

8

The clouds trailed in thin, hazy lines across the whitish Pennsylvania sky, like the scribbling of an unknown language. *The clouds are neither friendly nor knowable here,* Isabel thought. *They are never animals, the way they are at home. I miss seeing roadrunners and fish crossing the sky. And here the clouds just poke along. At home they fly free across the sky, galloping like horses.*

Isabel picked up a leaf from the school lawn. It was green in the middle but edged with yellow and curled. Just this past week, all of the trees at Carlisle had begun to turn fall colors of yellow, orange, red, and brown. Isabel twirled her leaf by its stem. *I don't have sky horses or real horses here at Carlisle,* she thought. *It's October, and I haven't ridden a horse in months. I don't suppose I will be riding a horse here anytime soon.* She sighed, then looked across the lawn at the academic building, where art class would begin in a few minutes. Isabel had already had a full morning of classes, and she had come out into the fresh air to stretch.

A gentle, cool breeze touched her face and lifted the tendrils of hair that had escaped from her braid. "The clouds don't form shapes here because the wind isn't strong enough to push them," she said aloud. At home, the clouds often blew answering a wind of their own, far up in the sky, and moved wherever they were going faster or slower than the swaying tree branches below. Sometimes the clouds chased one another but never caught up with the lead cloud, and sometimes they did catch up and blended, streaming across the sky together in a new shape.

Isabel shook her head hard, trying to clear her scattered thoughts. *I must be feeling melancholy*, she said to herself as she started walking toward her art classroom. *I guess the coming of fall, when I see all around the preparations for the winter, is doing this. Winter is really just death.* She began to run, covering the ground easily with quick strides. *The shorter dress works for running*, she noticed. Isabel had sewn this dress slightly higher off the ground than most, allowing her to run fast.

In the classroom, Lily looked up from her easel and gave Isabel a quick smile. "There you are!" Lily greeted. "Come show me your drawing."

Isabel stepped over to her easel, then folded back the sheet of paper covering her charcoal drawing of a horse. She had been working on it for several days. "How does this look?" she asked hopefully.

Lily leaned over to look at Isabel's easel and frowned. Isabel held her breath. After two months of art classes, Isabel knew her drawing and painting skills had improved, but she would never have Lily's artistic talent.

The other students were working hard on their own drawings, mostly still lifes. At the front of the classroom the teacher had positioned vases, a bowl of fruit, busts of the Roman Caesars Julius and Augustus, and a statue of a horse for the students to use as models. Lily had urged Isabel to draw the horse because Lily had found out that Isabel was very interested in horses. Isabel had tried to make her horse as much like the statue as possible, which was what the teacher, Mrs. Stemple, had instructed them to do.

Frances came over from her easel next to Lily's and stood on the other side of Isabel, tapping her foot and frowning in imitation of Lily. She folded her arms, cocked her head, and hummed disapprovingly. "I'm sorry, Isabel, but that horse won't do at all. It's not in the classical tradition of any . . . classic."

"Stop it, Frances," Isabel said, laughing. "Or I'm going to critique your vase."

Frances wrung her hands in mock despair. "Uh-oh. All right. So your horse is a work of genius, not a funny-looking thing that's smudged across its nose and has one leg that's too short," she said. "That horse is almost alive—it's ready to limp off the paper."

Isabel picked up a loaded paintbrush from one of Lily's paint pots and aimed it at Frances. "I think your nose would look better blue."

Frances jumped back before Isabel could swat her. "I surrender!" she said. She returned to her easel and began busily mixing paints.

Isabel studied her drawing. *Oh, dear, Frances is right about the horse's nose and leg*, she thought. *Why didn't I see that? It's so hard when drawing to make any part of the animal even close to the right shape.* Isabel picked up her worn eraser to try to fix the horse.

"Just add a couple of lines to his shoulder, Isabel," Lily said. "Then he'll look like he's running, not like his leg is too short."

"Show me how," Isabel pleaded, holding out the piece of charcoal.

Lily took it and deftly sketched in several lines. "There," she said. "You're really getting good, Isabel."

"Hey, it doesn't even look that much like a buffalo," Frances said, leaning around Lily, paintbrush in hand.

"That's because I've never seen a buffalo." Isabel smiled. She looked at her horse drawing again. She had drawn a black-and-white horse, like the one her father talked so much about, the one he'd had as a boy. *I'll send the drawing to him*, she thought.

He'll be pleased with my new skill and that I am thinking of him. In her last letter home, she had written her father and Jeremy that she could now speak a little French. Before that, she had told them that she had improved her reading and writing and was learning history and geography. *My teachers say they are very pleased with me,* she had finished.

Isabel took the most recent letter from Jeremy out of her pocket and quickly read it. She was impressed that her brother had actually written her two short letters in the time she'd been at Carlisle. She knew he didn't like to write.

DEAR ISABEL. WE ARE HAPPY YOU ARE
DOING WELL AT SCHOOL. WE ARE FINE HERE.
FATHER AND I ARE WORKING A LOT CUTTING
TREES. MRS. ASPELL IS RIDING LEXINGTON
ALL OVER THE RESERVATION AND SHE SAYS
HE IS THE BEST HORSE SHE EVER HAD. I
THOUGHT YOU MIGHT WANT TO KNOW.
FATHER SAYS HE IS VERY PROUD OF YOU.
LOVE, JEREMY AND YOUR FATHER

Isabel folded the letter and put it back in her pocket. *Thank goodness Lexington is all right,* she thought. *If he wasn't, I couldn't have done anything about it from here. I must ask Jeremy who is training the horses at the reservation now that I'm gone. I guess no one.*

She glanced at Lily's easel and saw that her friend was drawing antelopes with charcoal, her hand making big loops. The antelopes seemed to be coming alive from her strokes and were leaping and running across the paper. Lily set down her charcoal with a flourish and looked over at Frances's easel. "Oh, Frances," she said.

"What's wrong? I want my vase to look like that," Frances insisted.

"With squiggly lines?" Lily asked. "With the bottom mud brown?"

"You don't understand. My vase is melting." Frances pointed

to the bottom of the paper. "Melting into the mud. It's a reservation vase."

"Lucky for Frances, we're not going to be painting still lifes much longer," Lily said to Isabel. "When we get our new art teacher this spring, she will be teaching us only native Indian arts."

"How nice," Isabel said. She didn't really think it would be, but she could see how excited Lily was.

Frances stuck her head behind Lily's back and rolled her eyes. *It won't work any better*, she mouthed.

"I know," Isabel said aloud.

"You know what?" Lily asked.

"That . . . we're going to enjoy our walk tonight into town with Miss Hayes, if the weather stays fine," Isabel said quickly. *Frances and I shouldn't be silly about art class when it's so important to Lily*, she thought, watching Lily's serious face as she added a bit of shading to her antelope drawing. *We wouldn't like it if Lily made fun of Frances's printing or my teaching ambitions.*

Frances shook her head, muttered something, then ripped the paper with the vase drawing off her easel.

But maybe Frances just can't be nicer about something as frustrating as art class, Isabel amended.

"Oh, yes, our walk," Lily said enthusiastically, finally looking up from her work. "That will be a treat."

"I can't go." Frances clipped a blank sheet of paper to her easel. "I have to work on the next issue of the newspaper in the print shop."

"Do you really?" Lily sounded distressed.

"I can always go for a walk." Frances shrugged. "But the paper has to get out on time."

"Well, we'll miss you," Lily said sweetly.

"Thanks." Frances stared at her blank sheet of paper. "I wish I could just write on it instead of trying to draw," she said. "Pictures are what we have photographers for."

"Photographers can't do what Lily can," Isabel said quickly.

"That's true," Frances said. "You're magical, Lily."

"Oh, you just think that because I can draw an antelope." Lily laughed.

"I take it back," Frances said. "You'd be magical if you could draw a buffalo."

"I never tried—" Lily began just as the teacher called, "Class dismissed!"

After lunch, Frances headed off in the direction of the print shop. Isabel lingered for a few moments talking with Lily before she and Lily split up for the afternoon, Lily to work at the hospital and Isabel at the dressmaking shop.

"Oh, I forgot to tell Frances about her dress," Isabel said. "Frances, you need to come over to the dressmaking shop so I can fit your dress!" she yelled.

Frances turned around and walked backward. Cupping her hand to her ear, she mimed, *What?*

Isabel and Lily made vigorous gestures at their blouses and skirts. Isabel pinched the shoulder of her sleeve in and out.

Oh, Frances mouthed. She pointed at the print shop. *In ten minutes!* she signaled with all her fingers raised.

"She'd better come over to the shop, or I won't be able to make her dress the right size—it will fit Miss Kingsley instead," Isabel said, referring to her stout mathematics teacher. Isabel had designed a high-waisted white blouse with puffy sleeves and a long, elegant dark brown skirt for Frances. Isabel had noticed first thing in the morning that the dress Frances had on today did not fit her well at all, although she didn't seem to care.

"Frances will probably forget all about it. I can't believe how much time she spends at the print shop." Lily touched a carnation she had pinned into her hair. "She's there all afternoon and some evenings too. And here she won't even go for a walk with us."

"Printing does look fun," Isabel said. "Arranging those letters and photos and cranking out the newspaper and other things."

"But printing is messy—ink flies everywhere." Lily wrinkled her nose.

"Miss Hayes said the teachers tried to talk Frances out of working there—not because it's messy, but just the usual reason: 'We don't know what you will do with that skill on the reservation,' Isabel said in a lofty tone, and Lily smiled. "Besides, it's almost all boys who work there, although I guess about half of them are Frances's cousins," Isabel added. "Frances says some of the boys who are learning printing don't plan to go back to the reservation. But Frances has always said she will."

"I know." Lily hid a smile behind her hand. "I heard that when the teachers told Frances to pick another activity—well, they practically ordered her to—she was very insistent about going into printing. So they let her have her way. Maybe she will somehow make a success of it."

"Let's stop by the print shop for just a second," Isabel said. She began to walk in that direction, carefully keeping to the path. A recent article in the *Arrow* had asked the students to please stay off the grass so that it would look nicer. "We'd better go get her."

"Or she will look unseemly all day." Lily laughed.

"We can't have that," Isabel agreed, quickening her pace as she passed the gazebo.

"But we're going to be late for work," Lily complained, running to catch up. "Isabel, why do you always have to walk so fast?"

"Our teachers won't mind if we're late to class because of Frances's dress," Isabel said, ignoring her roommate's comment about her fast walking. Lily liked to walk slowly, looking at the grass and flowers, but Isabel always wanted to get where she was going as quickly as possible. "Any teacher who knows Frances—and they all do—will understand how important this dress is. But you don't have to come."

"Oh, yes, I do." Lily grabbed Isabel's elbow. "I'm sure it will take at least two of us to persuade Frances to leave her beloved newspaper."

The print shop was behind the other school buildings. Isabel and Lily passed the staff quarters and approached it.

Isabel opened the door—and was almost blown backward by the roar of the printing machines. She saw Frances, wearing a long white apron, bent over a counter, arranging columns of lead type. Behind her, Albert and several of the older boys, some of them Frances's cousins, were feeding completed pages into large cylindrical presses, turned by wheels attached to pulleys coming from the ceiling.

Tugging on Isabel's arm, Lily mouthed something Isabel couldn't hear. The two girls walked over to Frances and stood behind her. Isabel waved her hand in front of Frances's nose.

"What are you two doing here?" Frances yelled.

Lily put her hands over her ears. "How can we even talk? Don't they ever turn off those machines?" she asked.

"That would stop the presses!" Frances pointed to the door, then guided them back outside. "So, do you want to hear the news or wait for this edition of the *Arrow* to be printed?" she asked.

"We just want to make sure you get your dress fitted," Lily reminded.

"Oh—I'd already forgotten about it." Frances glanced around as the door opened again. Albert, Frank, and Thomas and Frances's big cousins, Sam and Phillip, joined them. "Hello, girls," said Albert, bowing slightly to Isabel.

Isabel smiled. She liked the way Albert always took special notice of her. Standing this close to him, she could see that he was just a little taller than she was. *Maybe he's grown*, she thought.

"You boys get back to work," Frances ordered.

"We will when you do," Sam said, leaning against the side of the building. He was a tall, heavyset boy with short-clipped hair. His warm black eyes were deep set like Frances's.

"We're talking about something important," Lily said sweetly. "That's why we have to stay out here."

"You're going to get us all in trouble, Sam." Frances sighed. "As usual."

"What are you talking about that's so important?" Albert asked Isabel.

"Dresses," Isabel said immediately, then felt a bit foolish.

Phillip laughed. "Oh, sure, that sounds really important." Phillip was Frances's youngest cousin at the school. His hands and wrists stuck out from the too short sleeves of his shirt, and his pant legs were a couple of inches higher than his shoes. *He needs to have his clothes altered even more than Frances does*, Isabel thought.

"Isabel makes beautiful dresses," Lily said firmly.

"I'll say." Albert glanced at Isabel's dress, which was her finest creation yet: a blue-and-white-striped seersucker. The sleeves puffed softly at her shoulders, then tapered to her wrists, and the skirt was gathered trimly at the waist and fell almost to her ankles. The dress was a simple design, yet it looked elegant and modern.

What a very nice thing to say. Isabel smiled, and Albert smiled back.

"Come on, Frances," Lily said, taking her roommate's hand and tugging. "Time to get fashionable."

"If I must." Frances groaned. "Hold down the fort, boys. And don't change a single word in any of my articles while I'm gone."

That evening, Isabel, Lily, and several other girls, mostly from the Susan Longstreth Literary Society, joined Miss Hayes for a walk into the town of Carlisle. Isabel looked up, her gaze caught by the clear stripes of pink cloud stretching from one end to the other in the cold autumn sky. The clouds were ratcheted like feathers, as evenly spaced in their long rows as the columns of the Carlisle marching band. The hazy summer vagueness was gone from the autumn clouds, and a crescent moon carved a path between two cloud rows, marching in time to its own band.

"What a lovely evening," Miss Hayes said quietly. "I'm so glad you girls could join me."

Isabel looked at her favorite teacher and smiled. "It is pretty out. And not too cold."

"Soon enough it will be cold here in the North. But then we shall have ice skating on the river."

"I can't wait to try it," Isabel said eagerly. Frances had shown her pictures in the *Arrow* of Carlisle students ice skating last year. Each winter, the school dammed up the Conedogwinet River, and the students could skate on the enormous smooth pond that formed.

"I like ice skating," Lily said, catching up to Isabel and linking arms with her. "Last winter I skated almost every weekend. But I'm not very good at it."

"The boys always play crack the whip." Annabelle, the vice president of the literary society, spoke up from behind Isabel. "That's where the boys form a line, or whip, and crack the people on the end so they go flying."

"Sometimes almost into New Jersey," added Elizabeth, another member of the Susans. Like Isabel, she had recently joined the Susans. Elizabeth was one of the best speakers—when she presented her interpretation of a poem, the meeting room would go still as everyone listened closely to her impassioned argument.

The group approached the smooth, paved streets of the town of Carlisle. Tall wood houses, some with shops on the ground floor, clustered along the main street, and trees bare of leaves stretched between power and telephone lines. Isabel had been in the town once before, to go to one of the big churches for Sunday service, but she felt she was seeing it anew in the company of her friends and Miss Hayes.

A young couple passed the school group, and the man tipped his hat.

"The town is so quiet," Isabel said, then felt a bit silly—the town really wasn't quiet at all. Several horses and buggies clattered both ways down the street, and in the distance she could hear the rumble of a train. A number of people were walking along, chatting or looking at the sights, seeming to enjoy the evening as well. *Perhaps I meant that the town is quietly organized,* she thought.

Isabel glanced in the shop windows as they passed. She saw signs for a men's clothes store, a saddle maker, and a notions store. The owner of the notions store was just letting down the blinds in the front window, and she waved at the school group.

"I'd like to go in there," said Lily. "That store sells fancy soaps. They feel just like cream on your face, and they smell wonderful."

"The storekeepers are all closing up," Miss Hayes said. "We'll have to come back another time to shop."

A horse and buggy veered onto the street, and a couple of the girls jumped as it swung close to them.

"Reckless driver," muttered Annabelle, rubbing her arms.

Isabel shook her head. "I don't think he could control that horse. It seemed quite high-strung. I wonder what kind of horse it is—it's quite tall."

"I'm not sure," Miss Hayes replied. "You seem to have an interest in horses, Isabel."

"I sometimes rode at home," Isabel said, then caught her breath. *It's the first time I've told anyone I ride.* She remembered how it felt to be on a horse, the animal's light, deft movements beneath her responding to the slightest tug of the reins in her hands or pressure of her legs to surge ahead. The wind was stronger on the back of a horse, more like the wind that belonged to the clouds. *How I miss riding,* she thought. *But should I have told Miss Hayes? What if it somehow gets back to Father?*

"Excuse me," Miss Hayes called out to a middle-aged man passing the group. "Did you happen to notice what kind of horse that was?" She gestured down the street after the horse.

"It's a Standardbred," the man answered. "Sometimes they're used as racehorses—might be why that one was tearing down the street."

"Thank you," said Miss Hayes. She turned to Isabel. "So now we know."

"It was a beautiful golden color," Isabel said. "I wonder if all Standardbreds are that color."

"You can find a book on it in the library and look it up when we get back to the school," Miss Hayes replied.

"Here comes the train!" Annabelle said excitedly. "Right through the middle of the main street!"

"That is a rather odd arrangement." Miss Hayes gathered up her skirts. "Move to the far edge of the sidewalk, girls, so that you don't get covered in grime."

All the girls stepped close to the storefronts, then turned to watch as the big steam locomotive clattered into town, pulling a chain of passenger cars. "Are any more children aboard who are coming to the school?" asked Elizabeth.

"Not today," Miss Hayes replied. "But I hope more arrive soon. Now that our founder, Colonel Pratt, has left Carlisle, the school's direction isn't so certain. I hope it keeps going for many more years, but we haven't been getting as many new students while this is sorted out."

Miss Hayes is so poised and dignified, Isabel thought as the teacher delicately patted her face with a handkerchief. *She has even been to college to study history! I so want to be a teacher like her someday.*

Isabel was sure she felt eyes on her back. She turned.

Across the broad main street, she saw a girl about her age looking closely at the group of Carlisle students. The girl wore a flat white cap tilted to the side and had a plaid scarf around her neck. Even from this distance, Isabel could see that she had very bright blue eyes. Her medium brown hair was loose around her shoulders, which was a bit unusual, Isabel thought, since most girls their age wore their hair up. The girl was with an older woman in a long dark coat who was probably her mother.

She is rather rude to stare so. Isabel frowned.

The girl's mother poked her in the side, as if she thought so too. The girl jerked her head away and said something to her mother, then they both turned and walked toward a large black buggy parked at the side of the street. Two horses were in the harness, Isabel noticed. *They are the gold color of Standardbreds,* she thought.

"Isabel! We're heading back," Miss Hayes called from down the street.

"Run, Isabel," Lily said with a laugh.

They're headed home already! Isabel hurried to catch up. *I mean, not home—back to school. Strange,* she said to herself, slipping her arm through Lily's again. *That's the first time I've thought of the school as home.*

When Isabel walked into her dorm room, she saw Frances sitting at the little square table, glancing at a book, then scribbling on a piece of paper. With her other hand, Frances held a basketball on her lap. "Hi, Isabel," she said.

"Hi." Isabel hung up her coat and scarf on the peg behind the door. "What are you doing?"

"Working on an article for the newspaper." Frances stopped writing and sat back. "How was your walk?"

"Fun. A little cold, though. Winter must be coming."

"It gets *freezing* here in the winter." Frances tipped back in her chair, waggling her pen.

"Well, the mountains at home get pretty cold too." Isabel doubted any cold here would bother her after that, especially since she wasn't trying to live in a flimsy tent. She had written her father and brother, telling them to be sure to move into warmer shelter for the winter. *I'm afraid they'll tough it out in the tents since I'm not there,* she thought. *I just don't know if that's possible in the winter. How could they brave a snowstorm?* Isabel shook her head, trying not to worry too much. Surely Jeremy and her father were sensible enough not to freeze to death. "Lily's looking after a patient at the hospital," she said. "In case you were wondering if we'd lost her."

"I wasn't." Frances picked up her pen again. "Lily's always at the hospital or drawing somewhere. She's never lost."

Isabel stepped over to Frances and looked over her shoulder. "What is the article about this time?"

"I'm working on two—one that I want to write and the other the usual boring stuff we have to write." Frances raised one eyebrow.

"What usual stuff?" Isabel asked, leaning closer.

"It's called 'Boys Who Are Needed,'" Frances said, and glared at Isabel, tapping her pen on the page. "Yes, I know you're going to make fun of it."

Before Isabel could reply, the door opened and Lily walked into the room.

"There she is," Frances said. "See? She didn't get lost after all."

"Were you talking about me?" Lily asked, pulling off her coat and dropping down onto her bed. "I hope you were saying nice things."

"Actually, we were talking about an article Frances is writing about boys," Isabel said. "She was about to tell me who her sweetheart is."

"Ooh!" Lily clapped. "Do tell, Frances."

"This article is *not* about my sweetheart." Frances turned her chair around to face them.

"Did you hear that?" Isabel said to Lily. "Frances just admitted she has a sweetheart."

"That is not what I meant," Frances said loudly. "Major Mercer told me to write the article."

Isabel snatched up the piece of paper from the table. "'I don't know what we should do in this world without boys,' said one of the members of a large business house. 'There seem to be certain functions that only a boy can properly perform and if a boy— the right kind of a boy, I mean of course—is not forthcoming, one feels at a loss how to get these things done at all.'" Isabel laughed.

"Well, that's what the owner of the mercantile store in town told me," Frances said, taking the paper back. "Like it or not."

"I guess boys are useful," Lily said. "The right kind of boy, like that business owner said."

"What boy do you like best at school, Lily?" Isabel asked.

Lily blushed. "I don't want to say."

"Say," Frances commanded. "We want to hear this."

"Well, he's not really a boy." Lily blushed even more and looked away. "It's Mr. Carter."

Frances whooped. "The new basketball coach? The mystery of Lily's sudden interest in basketball is solved!" Frances tossed the basketball to Lily, who dropped it on her foot. The ball rolled under Isabel's bed.

"I play basketball because I want to be a tough girl like you," Lily said to Frances.

That did not sound in the least convincing, Isabel thought.

"No, you just like playing basketball now because of a certain someone." Frances laughed. "Funny how that works."

"I don't want to play at all—but all the girls have to play." Lily sounded desperate now. "I wouldn't say we're *forced* to, just strongly encouraged because it's part of keeping us physically fit. But I don't *like* it. Frances likes it, Isabel, if you can imagine such a thing."

"I can imagine a lot of things—such as Lily arm in arm with a certain basketball-playing young man." Frances wiggled her eyebrows.

Lily seemed about to die of embarrassment. She opened her mouth, then shut it without saying anything.

I'd better save her from Frances, Isabel decided. *She'll keep up this teasing all night!* "So what boy do you like, Frances?" she asked. Kneeling beside her bed, she fished out the basketball and threw it to Frances.

Frances caught it neatly with one hand. "I like a lot of the boys. My cousins, and some of the boys who are funny in class. But I don't want to *marry* any of them," she said pointedly to Lily. "What about you, Isabel? I hope you have a big surprise for us like Lily's basketball coach."

"He's not *my* basketball coach." Lily scowled.

"You only wish. So what about it, Isabel?" Frances asked. She folded her hands in her lap around the basketball and gave Isabel a big smile.

"I'm thinking." Isabel found she was actually quite interested in the question. *Like Frances, I do find many of the boys cute or nice,* she thought. "I don't want to marry anybody either," she said, and looked up at her roommates. They were both leaning forward, hanging on her words. Suddenly Isabel saw Albert in her mind, smiling at her and complimenting her on her dressmaking skills. "Maybe I kind of like Albert," she said, then regretted it completely. *They'll never let that one go if I live to be a hundred,* she thought.

"Albert is nice," Frances said in a neutral way, surprising Isabel. She felt a little surprised herself that she had admitted to liking Albert. *I guess Frances and I both like funny boys,* she thought.

"Albert always disrupts class!" Lily protested. "And isn't he shorter than you, Isabel?"

"I'm not in *love* with him," Isabel said, and Lily and Frances both hooted. "What did I say?" Isabel protested. "Albert's just kind of interesting. He's always up to something."

"At least we got our boyfriends all settled." Frances laughed. "So, Lily, what's your next move with the basketball coach? He is single."

"Stop teasing me! I'm not going to do anything about him," Lily said indignantly.

"You could fall under his feet the next time you miss the basketball," Frances said. "You miss it a lot."

"Did you notice that Frances hasn't said which boy she likes best?" Lily said to Isabel. "She's pretending she answered the question, but she's really avoiding answering it."

"I am not." Frances rolled the basketball over to Lily. "I just said I don't like anyone special."

"I don't believe it," Lily said. "No one is that principled."

"Is *principled* the right word?" Isabel wondered.

"Did Mr. Carter wink at you yesterday at basketball or did I just imagine it?" Frances demanded, shaking a finger at Lily.

Lily looked mortified. "Of *course* he didn't *wink* at me."

I can think of only one way to get relentless Frances talking about something else, Isabel thought. "What's the other article you're writing about, Frances?" she asked.

"The Russo-Japanese war," Frances replied, looking back at her work. "President Theodore Roosevelt just mediated the signing of a peace treaty last month between the Russian and Japanese empires."

"Tell me what that war was about again?" Lily yawned.

"I don't care much either," Frances said. "I mean, it happened all the way across the world. But it was the usual war—people were fighting over land, in this case Manchuria and Korea, and the Russians wanted a warm-water port."

"So who won?" Isabel asked. She found she was a little interested after all.

"I guess the Japanese. Russia lost most of its fleet, and the Russian workers are striking— you know, protesting. They're trying to get Russia's ruler, the czar, to treat them better. They want to work shorter hours, be able to vote, have freedom of speech."

"How do you know all that?" Lily asked.

"I read a bunch of newspapers," Frances said dismissively. "I mean, this stuff is interesting just because it's a battle—one side is going to win eventually, and I'm betting on the workers. But it's kind of like the Battle of the Greasy Grass—"

"Oh, Frances, everything isn't like the Battle of the Little Bighorn." Isabel sighed. "That was so long ago. When are you going to stop talking about it?"

"It wasn't long ago at all—the battle was in 1876, just twenty-nine years ago." Frances stared hard at Isabel.

"We weren't even *born* twenty-nine years ago. What good does it do to think about all that?" Isabel asked irritably. *Frances is just like Father, always living in the past,* she thought. *That's why he sat on the fence all that time and felt so bad.*

"You don't know what I mean," Frances said, with an air of trying to be patient. "The Sioux won the Battle of the Little Bighorn—everybody knows that. But they didn't really win, or win the whole war, because right after that, the army conquered them for good. So the Russo-Japanese war is something like that, only in reverse—the Russians lost the war, but I think they're going to lose the big war in their own country eventually."

The room fell silent. Lily gave Isabel a meaningful look.

Frances threw up her hands. "I know, I know—why do I worry about these things? Why aren't I learning to bake bread or something useful?"

"I wish I could bake bread," Isabel said, glad to change the topic.

"I'd like to bake bread and eat it," Lily added. "You have to admit, Frances, you can't eat your newspaper articles."

"What am I going to do with *printing*?" Frances gave a dramatic sigh. "You two sound like Major Mercer. And Isabel looks like him."

"I do not." Isabel jumped off her bed and pinched Frances's arm.

"All you need is a uniform and you'll look exactly like him." Frances elbowed Isabel back.

"Ladies!" Lily gently pulled Isabel away by the back of her skirt. "Maybe you and I both sound like Major Mercer, Isabel."

"*I* don't. Major Mercer sounds like he smokes cigars," Isabel said firmly. "But Frances isn't answering the question again—what *are* you going to do with printing?"

"It was my question," Frances pointed out.

"Answer it anyway," Lily said nicely.

"Maybe I'll start a newspaper at the reservation, like the one we have here. Except I'll write about Sioux history and what's happening at the reservation." Frances flopped back in her chair, seeming to dare them to object.

Isabel sighed. "Frances, how is that going to work?"

"What do you mean?" Frances stared at her again.

"Nobody wants to hear about all the . . . bad things that are happening at the reservation." Isabel could hear her voice rising, but she couldn't seem to keep it down. "And nobody wants to remember the old days either, except the old people! Talking about old times just makes it worse."

"Makes what worse? You don't know anything about old times—why should it bother you to talk about them?" Frances said vehemently.

"I'm tired of talking about the past and the dead!" Isabel realized she was almost shouting. "Talking won't bring them back. I'm tired of grief!"

"Stop it, both of you!" Lily plugged her ears with her fingers. "No more raised voices in our room. Come on, let's talk about something else. I don't like sad subjects either, Frances."

"You and Isabel are always ganging up on me," Frances said, sounding less angry. "Maybe we need one more girl in our room—then we could have teams of two. But she would have to agree with me about everything." Frances fluffed her curls.

"I'm sure we could ask for one," said Lily, smiling a little and taking her fingers out of her ears. "But you have to find such a girl, Frances—if you can."

Isabel drew in a deep breath. *I shouldn't get angry about the bad old days or the good old days,* she thought. *Frances is right—I don't really know anything about them. But for me, the good old days are all in my father's mind or . . . mine. Remembering them is what is bad. Frances can remember all she wants because she hasn't suffered as much as I have. Or is she just braver?* "I don't mind another roommate—as long as she has curly hair," Isabel said finally. She could still feel her heart beating fast, but at least her voice wasn't shaking with emotion. "I love your curls, Frances. If you just wouldn't talk . . ."

Frances tapped her pen on the table and looked at the other two girls. "So what do you think, Lily?"

"About what?" Lily sighed. "I think it's time to go to bed."

"About our little war here. About old times." Frances seemed to have calmed down completely and to really want to know what Lily thought.

"Isabel is right, Frances." Lily looked at Frances with an unusually grave expression. "Those times aren't going to come again." Lily got up and walked over to the mirror. "I know our parents still hope they will, but how can the buffalo or antelope come back?"

"That doesn't mean we should forget about them," Frances said.

9

Jennifer Schmidt sat in the window seat at her family's farmhouse, her arms wrapped around her knees, watching fat drops of rain slide down the panes and shower the green fields. *I wish I were in Philadelphia*, she thought. Just three days ago she had been, finishing a wonderful two-week trip to visit her aunt Elaine, her mother's younger sister. Closing her eyes, Jennifer could hear the clang of the streetcar bells, see the warm, bright electric lights in the dining room chandelier of her aunt's town house, and imagine the two of them emerging from the house to join the bustle and excitement of the big city, going shopping, to the theater, or the Free Library of Philadelphia, where Aunt Elaine worked now that she had graduated from Smith College.

My life here is certainly unlike that. Jennifer stretched out her legs, examining the thick, patched denim of her jeans. She had just come in the house from one of the farm's tall, red-painted barns, where she had milked the farm's twenty cows. Jeans and a heavy plaid flannel shirt were the right thing to wear when a bunch of cows were switching their tails and rubbing their grubby heads on your clothes and sometimes stepping on your boots. Jennifer sighed, remembering the silk dress, stockings, and pumps she had worn in Philadelphia, all purchased at the fashionable Wanamaker department store.

Jennifer pushed her brown bangs out of her eyes. The rain was now coming down harder, making little rivers on the window and splashing into the already soaked emerald green lawn around the house. *In three years, I'll be eighteen and can go to college like Aunt Elaine, but that's a very long time from now,* she thought. *And what if Mother and Father won't let me go? They're determined to see me married and settled on the farm.*

Seventy years ago, Jennifer's German grandfather had bought the farm when he emigrated from Munich, and her parents wanted it to stay in the family. Lately her parents had adopted a new line of argument with her—they needed her help around the farm, especially with the horses.

"Jen, come help me with dinner," her mother called from the kitchen. Jennifer sighed, looking through the living room toward the kitchen, where a towering pile of clothes waited to be mended. Outside, a cow mooed loudly, sounding wet and distressed. Jennifer touched her fingers to the cold glass.

In Philadelphia, I imagine my aunt is having dinner with a friend from . . . say, Boston, she thought. *Then tomorrow afternoon, after a refreshing sleep that does not involve the milking of cows at four in the morning, my aunt and her friend will attend a matinee at the theater. Then they will have tea with milk and scones—*

"I've been yelling at you for five minutes!" Benjamin, Jennifer's seventeen-year-old brother, shook her shoulder. "What are you waving your hand around for? Are you crazy?"

"What do you *want,* Benjamin?" Jennifer asked, pushing him away. "Or are you just bothering me?"

"Time for dinner," he said, shaking her shoulder again.

"Quit it!" Jennifer swatted Benjamin's hand. "I'm not four! Why couldn't I have a sister?" she muttered, hurrying past him into the kitchen to help her mother.

Mrs. Schmidt was lining up a row of colorful serving bowls filled with mashed potatoes, beets, and green beans from canned stores put up this summer. In front of the bowls was a china platter layered with sausage and slices of ham. Jennifer had to admit it all looked good, although not as fancy as city food.

"When are we going to town again?" she asked her mother.

"Jennifer, we were in town just two days ago." Mrs. Schmidt pushed a wisp of dark hair out of her eyes and handed Jennifer two of the serving bowls. She picked up the meat platter and a gravy boat. "But probably not for at least a week. Now stop asking. Let's get dinner on the table."

Jennifer managed not to sigh again and helped her mother finish bringing out dinner. She sat across from her brother at the table and served herself a spoonful of green beans.

"I finished plowing the field for the winter wheat crop," Jennifer's father announced, leaning forward. "That leaves just one more field to plow before winter." He was still in his work clothes—overalls and a flannel shirt nearly identical to Jennifer's—the way he was every day except Sunday. His tan, broad face was unlined and looked healthy despite his iron gray hair. Benjamin resembled their father except he still had a full head of brown hair. Benjamin was eating his way through a mountain of mashed potatoes, not looking up.

He can try to hide behind those potatoes all he wants, but yesterday's argument is sure to start again, Jennifer thought.

Mr. Schmidt set down his fork. "Jennifer, if the weather's better tomorrow—and it's supposed to be—please take out Celebrity and work on his canter," he said. "Then try to get in at least a brief work with the other three horses."

Jennifer made a face. "All right, I'll try. I mean, it's going to be muddy after all this rain. I'll have to go slow so the horses don't slip, and it'll take me longer."

"Maybe your brother can help you," Mr. Schmidt said loudly.

"I can't. I have to work at the shop all day tomorrow." Benjamin kept his eyes on his food, but he had stopped eating.

At least he has the decency to look guilty. Jennifer scowled at her brother's bent head. Two days before, Benjamin had dropped the bombshell that he planned to move to Carlisle and work for the town's first automobile repair shop. The shop still fixed saddles and harnesses because Carlisle had hardly any automobiles, but Benjamin was sure that was going to change. He was only going to live at the farm until next spring, when he would finish high school. Then he would move into a room in town, over the shop.

Thanks a lot, Benjamin. Jennifer glared harder at her brother, although he still wasn't looking up to see it. That left her with the farm and all the chores, including the horses to ride. The worst part was he had taken her by surprise, coming up with his idea to leave the farm before she could propose hers. Benjamin wasn't usually an idea person.

A heavy silence settled over the table, and everyone focused on eating. When they were finished, Jennifer cleared the dishes from the table and stacked them in the sink. She ran warm water and soap over them and picked up a sponge.

"I can't believe your brother is leaving home," Mrs. Schmidt said as Jennifer handed her a washed, clean plate to dry. "I didn't want to bring up the subject again at dinner because it upsets your father so, but it's very much on my mind."

"Well, Benjamin's determined to go, so I guess we'd better get used to it." Jennifer handed her mother one of the washed serving bowls, noticing again that she and her mother had the exact same shape and size hands—small palms, with slender fingers. Jennifer glanced at her mother's face. Mrs. Schmidt was still pretty, her dark hair hardly touched with gray, and she had kept her trim figure. Jennifer was glad she took after her petite mother and not her heavyset, square-faced father.

"I suppose Benjamin has made a commitment." Mrs. Schmidt

sighed. "But it's still a great disappointment." She managed a smile. "At least we have you around, with all your skills."

Jennifer didn't meet her mother's eyes. "Yes," she said. "That's right."

"Although I'm not sure you should ride those racehorses," her mother said. "The money we get from your work is welcome, but I don't want you to get hurt."

"I won't." Jennifer knew that accidents could always happen around horses, but in the two years that she had been training, she'd learned to understand the minds of the different horses and to tailor her ride accordingly. Often she saw accidents coming—a spook, a slip, a bolt—and was balanced in the saddle and prepared to handle them.

After the dishes were all washed and dried and the tile counters wiped down, Jennifer went to her room to get ready for bed. She changed into her soft cotton nightgown with the rows of flowers up and down it and brushed out her shoulder-length hair in her little bathroom, giving her hair a hundred strokes on each side and the back the way Aunt Elaine did.

Sometimes I hate riding. Jennifer leaned forward over the sink, silently addressing the girl in the mirror. *Well, I don't really, but it can be like milking the cows at four on Christmas morning— I'd rather do something else, like stay in bed and sleep or read. But of course I don't have any choice about milking or riding. I'm a farm girl!*

She set the hairbrush down rather hard on the light pink tile around the sink. Fetching her book from the top of the dresser, Jennifer curled up in bed, adjusting the wick of the kerosene lantern until her cozy bedroom was lit by its soft glow.

Fluffing her down pillows behind her head, Jennifer paged to her bookmark in E. M. Forster's novel *Where Angels Fear to Tread.* Aunt Elaine had given her the book, the novelist's latest work.

They were all at Charing Cross to see Lila off, she read. *Philip, Harriet, Irma, Mrs. Herriton herself. Even Mrs. Theobald, squired*

*by Mr. Kingcroft, had braved the journey from Yorkshire to bid her
only daughter good-bye.*

How exciting to be taking a trip to the Continent of Europe,
Jennifer thought, yawning hugely. *And Lila is traveling only with
her friend, Caroline Abbott. No parents!* She felt herself deliciously
drawn into the strange, romantic world of the novel. But after just
a few pages, she marked her place and set the novel on her bed
table. "That's the trouble with getting up at four every morning,"
she muttered. Aunt Elaine got up at the much more civilized
hour of six on weekdays and slept till eight on the weekends.
But here on the farm, the cows had to be milked, and they could
never wait till the sun rose.

"So how crazy are you?" Jennifer asked Celebrity the next morning, hefting the English saddle. The young horse was her father's
latest acquisition from a nearby Standardbred racing track. For
the past several years, her father had bought horses that were
retired from the tracks either because of old age or injury. Old
age on the track, for the Standardbreds, was about the age of five,
so the horses still had a long life ahead of them.

Jennifer had tied Celebrity to one of the vertical beams of
his stall in the ten-stall barn, and he twisted his head to look
inquiringly at her. Celebrity was quite good looking for a
Standardbred from the track, Jennifer thought. Not all of them
were—they were bred and built for speed, not beauty. Celebrity
was tall, about sixteen hands high, and dark, chocolately brown.
He had three white socks and a star and crooked blaze on his
forehead and muzzle.

The three other horses in the barn—Fancy, Cinnamon, and
Midsummer—poked their heads over the half doors of their
stalls to watch the other horse. Jennifer sighed. *That's a lot of
horses to ride*, she thought. *It's going to be a long day.*

"Celebrity has been ridden a bit, according to his jockey at
the track," Mr. Schmidt said as he walked up to her.

"So maybe I can get on him without getting killed," Jennifer said. The problem with retraining the retired Standardbreds—the first problem, Jennifer amended—was that they were harness racers and had only pulled a cart. Almost none of them were broken to saddle.

"I'd look out," her father cautioned. "The jockey didn't say what happened when he got on him. But Celebrity has a kind eye compared to some of them, don't you think?"

"I guess so." *He may be kind but still want to race with all his heart,* Jennifer thought. "How old is he?" she asked. Since the horse was a registered Standardbred, the horse's former owner would know its age.

"He's only three. He injured his back left hock, and that's why he was retired so young." Mr. Schmidt stepped up to the horse and bent to examine his leg. "I don't see any swelling now."

"Are you a pacer or a trotter?" Jennifer asked Celebrity. The horse tossed his head, then pulled back against the rope.

"I don't know," said Mr. Schmidt. "I didn't ask at the track."

I'd like to know. Jennifer frowned. After two years of riding the retired racehorses, she'd decided the pacers were the harder ones to retrain, even though they were gaited at the pace, meaning they moved their legs in parallel, which made for a very smooth ride. But the pacers were taught to move faster than the trotters.

"I wish I could help you, but I was never the rider you are anyway," her father said as she placed the saddle on Celebrity's back.

"It's okay." Jennifer watched Celebrity to see if he objected to the saddle. Her father had helped her with the horses until last year, when he broke his leg badly riding a rank gelding that had thrown him into a fence. His leg had healed, but not well enough to stand the strain of training young horses.

Celebrity flinched a little at the saddle, but then quieted. "He does seem saddle broke," Jennifer said.

"Good thing. I wouldn't even bother with any harness work with him," her father replied. "Pretty soon, people are only going to want horses to ride, not pull carts. I guess your brother is right—more and more people are going to buy those newfangled automobiles and use them to get places."

"Maybe they won't want horses at all." Jennifer tightened Celebrity's cinch with a quick tug. He looked surprised but continued to stand quietly.

"Oh, I think people will always want horses." Mr. Schmidt patted Celebrity's neck. "Roads don't go everywhere. But even if one day they do, a good saddle horse will always be in demand. Riding is enjoyable."

"Sure," Jennifer said. *I suppose I'd like riding more if I didn't have four horses to train!* she thought. She slipped a curb bit, a bit with a C-shaped bend in the middle, into Celebrity's mouth. A snaffle bit, which was two parts joined in the middle, was lighter on the horse's mouth, but Jennifer wanted to have more control with the bit since slowing down the former racehorse would almost certainly be difficult.

Mr. Schmidt led Celebrity out of the barn, and Jennifer swung quickly into the saddle before the horse could think to move.

"Be careful," Mr. Schmidt said, as he always did.

"I will." Jennifer tightened the reins and settled her tall English boots in the stirrups. "Off we go, Celebrity," she said, nudging the horse with her heels.

Celebrity stepped off, veering a little to the left. "No, we're not going around the track," Jennifer said, correcting him with the right rein. That was another problem with the Standardbreds—they were trained to go in a counterclockwise circle around the track, and so that was what they always wanted to do. "Let's go down that pretty lane in the woods instead." Jennifer squeezed Celebrity gently with her legs, careful not to startle him.

The horse obediently headed for the lane with a quick, light step. In yesterday's storm the first of the fall leaves had shaken from the maple trees that lined the lane, and Celebrity's hooves scattered a burst of red, yellow, and brown. Jennifer caught a brown-and-red-striped leaf in her hand, then tossed it, watching it swirl to the ground. *Riding isn't so bad*, she thought, smiling.

Celebrity snorted and jerked his head, startled by the sudden movement of his rider's hand. "I did that on purpose," Jennifer told him. "You've got to get used to different experiences. I'm not going to just sit here like a jockey moving my hands up and down your neck, and neither is anybody else."

Celebrity settled right back down. "Good boy," Jennifer praised. Celebrity was off to a good start—some of the high-strung racehorses got upset and then stayed that way for the entire ride. "Just keep it up," she added, "so I can get you trained fast and you don't wear me out first thing in the morning." Celebrity flicked his ears back a little, then kept them there. *He's paying attention*, Jennifer thought. *Another good sign*. She reached slowly forward to rub the horse's neck, then sat back.

The sky blazed clear and bright above them, washed by the storm, and the fall-colored oaks and maples looked like paper cutouts against the blue. The air smelled sweet from the leaves underfoot, and the rain had formed sparkling puddles in the ruts of the road. Jennifer relaxed, sitting the horse with the easy grace that came from riding her whole life. *This ride is going well*, she thought.

Sometimes she was surprised by just how responsive and forgiving the horses from the track were. Jennifer had been to the Standardbred track with her father once, and she had seen the severe, sometimes cruel treatment the jockeys, trainers, and owners subjected the horses to. One time she had seen a jockey beat a horse so hard across the head with his buggy whip for breaking gait she had thought the horse would surely not only keep galloping but go right off the track, toward any kind of freedom.

One of the puddles stretched almost across the lane. Celebrity walked up to it, touched it with his front hooves, and backed quickly away. He tried to spin to go back to the barn, but Jennifer straightened him out firmly with the reins.

"Uh-oh, that's a big old mean puddle." Jennifer let Celebrity look at it. The horse stretched out his neck, sniffed—and tried to wheel again. "No, that's not allowed," Jennifer scolded, turning him around again. She let him stand for another second or two, then urged him forward with her heels.

The puddle sparkled, sloshed a little in the wind, and changed colors from clear brown to green. *Funny, it even looks strange to me now,* Jennifer thought. *I wonder how deep it is?* Celebrity balked at the puddle's edge—then suddenly jumped right in the middle of it.

Jennifer very nearly fell off backward. When had a Standardbred ever jumped with her? Sitting forward, she grabbed Celebrity's mane. That was what horses' manes were for, right? Thankfully Celebrity stayed still, touching the puddle with his nose, while Jennifer regained her seat. The horse now seemed fascinated with the water. He began to splash with a front hoof. The water flew through the air, soaking Jennifer's legs and spattering her face.

"None of that!" Jennifer cried, pulling Celebrity's head up immediately. She hadn't forgotten the last time a horse splashed in a puddle while she was riding it—then lay down and rolled, almost squashing her, except Jennifer had barely managed to roll free.

Celebrity raised his head, then gamely tromped through the puddle, stomping his hooves to make a splash. "Oh, so you like water now," Jennifer said, wiping her face on her shirtsleeve. "Well, I hope you still like it on the way home."

She adjusted her reins, then looked down the lane. A short, level stretch, with no overhanging tree branches, was coming up. This was where she tried out the horses at faster gaits. Yet another problem with the retired racehorses was that although they would do what Jennifer called a ninety-mile-an-hour trot, they had been trained never to break that gait and canter, or they would have been disqualified from the races. Some of the horses felt very strongly about not cantering, Jennifer knew.

Others would take to it as a new form of racing and run away with her.

"Okay, Celebrity," she said. "First let's find out if you're a trotter or a pacer. But *try* to remember you're not at the races."

Celebrity pulled a little against the reins. He could probably feel a change in Jennifer's grip or posture and knew she was going to ask for a faster gait. Jennifer let him have a bit more rein, and Celebrity moved forward at a brisk walk. Abruptly he charged ahead.

Jennifer had been ready for that and kept her balance. "You're definitely a pacer." Celebrity sped up even more, then veered sharply to the left. "Slow down!" Jennifer cried, quickly straightening out the horse's head. "Not that you will," she muttered as Celebrity charged down the lane, going unbelievably fast but still pacing. Jennifer gradually eased him into a slower pace, marveling as she always did at how smooth and easy to sit the gait was, even at high speed.

Celebrity's long legs ate up several miles of the lane. Although he tended to ease back up into a faster pace, he did respond to Jennifer's tugs on the reins, asking him not to go at top speed. Finally Jennifer sat back and pulled him to a stop. "Not bad, Celebrity," she gasped. Celebrity, she noticed, was breathing easily and seemed scarcely winded. "Let's go over to the Whitmans' and get some lunch," she suggested.

Celebrity eyed her backward, as if he might have other plans, but he moved out at a walk in response to Jennifer's leg cues.

"I do want to try one more thing before we quit work for the day," Jennifer told the horse. "Let's see how you do with a canter."

Jennifer tightened her legs and, as always, wondered how this test would go. In her experience, many of the ex-racehorses didn't understand that cantering under saddle was even possible—when she tried to urge them past the pace into a canter, they just paced faster and faster until they were in a lather or bucked. Some of the horses seemed incapable of thinking, and those were the ones that might not work out as saddle horses.

The problem was, Jennifer wanted Celebrity to canter, but at a collected, slower rate than the pace, so she was asking the horse both to slow down and break gait. That was where whether the horse could think came in.

"Okay," Jennifer said. "Here we go."

Celebrity began to pace, and Jennifer urged him to go faster with her legs, at the same pulling up his head slightly. The horse shook his head, fighting the restraint.

Uh-oh, Jennifer thought as the trees skimmed past. *He's not getting it.*

Jennifer cued for a canter by increasing the pressure of her legs. "Canter, Celebrity," she called. Some horses could understand from her voice that she wanted a different gait.

Celebrity tossed his head, pulled against the reins and went faster, then suddenly broke into a canter.

"Good boy!" Jennifer cried. "Wonderful!"

Celebrity flicked back his ears. His canter was exaggeratedly rocking and jerky, but he kept doing it and didn't buck. As soon as Jennifer was sure he had gotten the hang of the canter, she pulled him to a stop. "That was nice," she said, patting his neck. "You're quite smart, aren't you?"

Celebrity bobbed his head and stretched his neck. He seemed very full of himself after his success, Jennifer thought. "Now that you've proved you're my saddle horse, let's go get lunch," she said. "Standing for an hour or so tied up will be another little bit of your training."

Celebrity's training is going very well, Jennifer thought as the horse picked his way across fallen branches. *Maybe he's the horse I should keep.* Her father had said that she could pick one of the horses to have as her own. Jennifer usually liked all the horses, and she missed them when they left the farm to go to new owners. But she hadn't found that special horse yet.

"We'll see if you're the one," she said, stroking Celebrity's neck. "But don't worry—if you aren't, we'll find you a kind new owner."

Glancing up, Jennifer saw the Whitmans' sprawling white house in a clearing at the end of the lane. The Whitmans' farm, similar in size to her own family's, produced mostly grain: wheat, barley, and oats. The Whitmans had only one cow. "I don't think they could take care of too many more living creatures," she said to Celebrity as she swung out of the saddle in the yard. "But one cow is definitely the right number for any family."

Adelia Whitman, who everybody called Dell, was Jennifer's lifelong best friend. She was out in her family's backyard, minding three of her sisters. Or maybe four, Jennifer amended as seven-year-old Susan swung to the ground out of a tree. Dell, who was fifteen like Jennifer, had five younger sisters and two younger brothers. *How does she manage?* Jennifer wondered, as she often did. *How can she hear herself think in such a household?*

Celebrity spooked a little as Susan hit the ground with a thud. He stepped forward, dropping his head to investigate.

"Hi, Jen!" Dell called. "New horse?"

"We just got him two days ago. Do you have a rope I can tie him with?" While Dell searched in the barn for the rope, Susan, Iris, Agnes, and Grace swarmed around the horse, petting him and talking to him. Jennifer kept a sharp eye on them to make sure nobody got under the horse's feet, but Celebrity seemed to enjoy the attention, even letting the children touch his head and legs without shivering or jumping away.

The other part of Celebrity's training, besides getting him broke to saddle, was getting him used to household and farm sights and sounds. At the track, he pretty much only knew his stall, the barn, and the racing oval. He had to learn there was more to life than that. *This,* thought Jennifer, *is the place to get him used to every possible distraction.*

Dell grabbed up baby Clarissa as she crawled toward Celebrity's front hooves, then handed Jennifer a rope. With her other hand Dell pushed strands of blond hair out of her eyes.

"Thanks." Jennifer tied Celebrity to a tree branch, then rubbed her hands on her jeans. Sometimes she wished she had a smart English riding habit to wear, but that went with having your own groom, not brushing dusty horses, and not having a best friend with too many little sisters and brothers, all with sticky hands. Jennifer sighed, looking down at Clarissa, who was now clinging to her leg.

"Children! In the house! Lunch." Plump Mrs. Whitman stood in the doorway to the house, beckoning vigorously. Jennifer noticed that she was not only as plump as usual but pregnant again.

"Do you want to try riding together this afternoon?" Dell asked as she and Jennifer walked toward the house together. Dell wasn't plump yet like her mother, but she was almost a head taller than Jennifer and much bigger boned. Luckily sheer strength was never what it took to train horses, or Dell would be a much better rider than Jennifer. Like most farm girls, Dell could ride a little, but she had never gotten serious about it. The Whitmans' two plow horses and one buggy horse couldn't keep up with the Standardbreds that Jennifer rode—and the farm horses' attitude seemed to be that they didn't care to try. On the other hand, Jennifer thought, Celebrity was doing well so far, and adjusting to being with another horse without trying to race would be another step in his training.

"Sure, let's try it," Jennifer agreed. "It'll be nice to have company. Maybe Celebrity will think so too."

"That's his name?" Dell laughed. "Is he a celebrity?"

"Not yet." Jennifer smiled back. "But he will be when I finish training him."

10

The winter clouds at home would be gray-white as they swirled over the mountains, which would be deep in snow by this time, the end of November, Isabel thought. She looked out from the porch of the girls' dorm over the big square of lawn, then to the gazebo and past it to the superintendent's quarters. *That's the boundary of the world for now*, she thought.

Here in the eastern winter the clouds were omnipresent for many days, making a thick fog that coated the sky and feathered down to the ground, sometimes bringing a flurry of snow. The air had a raw, cold tinge to it. Isabel shivered and buried her hands deeper in her blue wool muff.

"Where's Frances?" Lily asked, joining her on the porch. "She's never late for lunch."

"Oh, she's probably at the print shop, working away." Isabel stepped off the porch. "Let's go get her."

Lily swung the end of her red-and-green-plaid scarf over her shoulder. "If she is in the print shop, I guess we might stand out here forever, waiting."

"And it's so cold." Isabel could feel her teeth begin to chatter. She had experienced bitter cold at home, but this cold was both bitter and damp. She set off for the print shop at a jog.

"You don't get used to it either," Lily called after her. "Miss Hayes says it gets into your bones. By February and March we'll be very tired of it."

"I already am," Isabel muttered, pulling her blue knitted cap down more firmly on her head. "Hurry, Lily," she called over her shoulder.

"If I just keep thinking about hot soup for lunch, I'll be okay," Lily called back.

Puffing out deep breaths, the girls stopped in front of the print shop. A group of boys were clustered tightly together, waving their hands excitedly and talking. When they saw the girls, they shoved their hands into the pockets of their long dark coats and fell silent. *How very odd*, Isabel thought. *Why aren't they working? I don't have a good feeling about this at all.* She didn't see Albert, but Sam and Phillip, Frances's cousins, were among the group.

"Hi, Sam," Isabel said tentatively. "How are you?"

Sam only nodded. Lily and Isabel looked at each other with raised eyebrows, then went inside the print shop.

The shop was unusually quiet, with the presses standing idle and unattended. Mr. Bryson, the print-shop teacher, was standing behind his desk, talking to two other men. With alarm, Isabel realized one of them was Major Mercer. She and Lily hesitated in the doorway. In one corner of the room, more of the print-shop boys had gathered. They stood quietly. Isabel saw Frances among them.

Mr. Bryson looked up. "Boys, return to your work immediately," he ordered.

The boys glanced at each other, then slowly dispersed. They didn't start working, though—they kept looking back at the three men.

"What can possibly have happened?" Lily whispered.

Frances darted over to them. "Frank, Thomas, and Albert ran away last night!"

"What?" Isabel gasped.

"I can't talk anymore right now." Frances glanced at Major Mercer. "I'll tell you about it later in our room. Everybody who works in the print shop is going to eat lunch late because Major Mercer wants to talk to us."

Isabel and Lily exchanged a shocked look, but they left the print shop without another word. A spatter of icy snowflakes greeted them, and a thin blanket of snow shook down from the roof, stinging the girls' faces.

Isabel still could barely believe what she had heard. "They must hate the school to run away in a snowstorm," she said.

Lily rubbed the snow off her face with her scarf. Her eyes were wide. "This is terrible," she said. "What if they froze to death last night?"

"They're Indians." Isabel let out a deep breath. "They know how to travel across country." *They've just gone home*, she thought. *But their homes are a long way off in this cold.*

"I don't know if they really do know how to get home anymore." Lily shook her head, shivering. "The boys have been at the school for years, in warm rooms during the winter. And it was so cold and snowy last night."

"Well, worrying won't do any good," Isabel said, but all she could think was that Lily was probably right. *What if the boys are dead out there?* she thought. Isabel tried to control her chattering teeth.

"Yes, worrying will just make us feel worse." Lily sighed. "Boys have run away from the school before, and they are always caught and brought back, none the worse for it. But we know these boys well, so I guess that's the difference. Besides, a few years back . . ."

"What?" Isabel demanded.

"I probably shouldn't say this because we will just worry more, but several boys ran away from another Indian boarding school in the winter, right before a snowstorm." Lily kept her head ducked to avoid the snow. "People went after them, but the storm prevented their being found."

"So no one ever knew what happened to them?" Isabel asked.

"Oh, they were found, all right." Lily brushed snow off her coat sleeves with her gloved hands. "But not until spring. Maybe that was the worst part, waiting so long to find out what had happened."

"Where were they?" Isabel asked. *Perhaps those boys made it back to the reservation?* she wondered.

"When the snow melted, they were found together, dead at the base of a cliff. They had walked off the edge in the storm."

Isabel and Lily halted in front of the dining hall and stared at each other. "Let's go in and get warm," Lily said.

"Let's," Isabel agreed. "But I'm not very hungry."

Later that afternoon, Frances opened the door to the room so hard it banged into the wall behind it. Isabel and Lily, sitting at the small table, looked up from their homework. "No, they didn't find the boys," Frances said, seeing her roommates' expectant faces. "That's why Major Mercer was at the print shop—he was talking to Mr. Bryson and some of the boys to see if anybody knew where they might have gone or at least in what direction."

"Did anybody know?" Lily asked, setting down her pen.

"No." Frances sighed sharply and hung up her coat and scarf behind the door. "And the weather's awful. I mean, don't those boys have any sense?"

"The school authorities will go after them," Lily said. "They'll probably catch them."

"I hope so." Frances shook her head, making small ice particles fly from her curls.

"What will happen to the boys if they're caught?" Isabel asked. "Will they be sent back to the reservation? Maybe that's what they want—only by train."

"I don't think they want that," Frances muttered. "You wouldn't even imagine it if you knew what winters are like in South Dakota on the Rosebud reservation."

"They won't be sent home," Lily said. "They'll be locked in the guardhouse."

"The guardhouse!" Isabel stared at Lily. She remembered that Lily had told her the guardhouse was the worst punishment at Carlisle. It reminded Isabel of her father's stories of the soldiers' stockade in the old days at the Mescalero reservation. Prisoners had been put in irons, and once the entire Mescalero tribe had been shut in a horse corral and left to suffer and die in the mud.

"The boys won't be hurt in the guardhouse." Lily grabbed Isabel's hand reassuringly. "I think they'll only get bread and water, and it's cold and grim, but no one has ever been kept in there for more than a few days."

Frances sat down hard on her bed and ran her hands through her hair. "They're Sioux," she said without looking up. "That means they're strong—they'll survive."

Isabel and Lily exchanged glances. Frances didn't sound so sure.

Standing abruptly, Isabel gathered her copy of Tennyson's poems, a folder of notes, and a supply of pens for the Susan Longstreth Literary Society meeting that evening. "Do you girls want to come with me?" she asked. "I'm doing a presentation."

"I'd better keep working here." Frances got up and began to pace.

"We'll stay," Lily said quickly. "If we work hard, the time will fly. Good luck with your presentation, Isabel."

Isabel hurried down the stairs, glad she had something to do. *After so much talk about this escapade, I'm even more worried about the boys*, she thought. As she walked out the door into the cold, she realized that the weather was getting worse by the minute. The wind, carrying a burden of sleet and snowflakes, whistled in her ears, and the sky was turning black as the daylight faded.

Albert is so thin, he'll have gotten cold immediately. And when the boys stop moving for the night, he'll get even colder. Isabel had seen drunk and sick people freeze to death on the reservation, and she knew it was a very real possibility. *Why are the boys bringing that kind of death here, when they have a choice about it?* she wondered.

Isabel let herself into the warm front room of the teachers' quarters, where the literary society meeting would be held. She was proud that Miss Hayes had asked her to be a member her very first year at Carlisle. At the meeting last Wednesday, Isabel had talked a bit about Tennyson, and several girls had asked to hear more. "You are turning us all into Tennyson aficionados," Miss Hayes had said approvingly.

Isabel crossed the short entryway into Miss Hayes's sitting room, in which the teacher had set up two rows of chairs and a lecturer's podium for the literary society meeting. The walls all showed off framed student art, ranging from a beautiful piece of two horses' heads, white and palomino, to several very good still lifes of fruit. Isabel hung her coat, hat, and scarf on the rack at the doorway to the room.

She made her way to the front and sank into a chair next to Elizabeth, grateful for the warmth and comfort of her favorite teacher's home. "Hi, Isabel!" Annabelle called from behind her. Several of the other girls smiled, but Isabel could tell that everyone's mood was subdued. The missing boys were in the thoughts of all of them.

Miss Hayes stepped to the podium and clapped lightly. "Let's get started, girls. Margaret, will you announce tonight's program?"

Margaret Grant, the president of the Susans, took her place next to Miss Hayes up front. Looking out over the assembled girls, she said: "First on tonight's schedule is the singing of 'College Chum.' Next, we will hear an essay on the relative merits of Mr. Keats versus those of Mr. Wordsworth in regard to descriptions of nature, read by Elmira Walker . . ."

Isabel carefully examined the folds and hang of Margaret's dress, which she had made for the other girl in the dressmaking shop. The new kind of polished cotton she had used in the dress looked much like satin, although the material wasn't nearly as expensive. The deep blue color looked lovely against Margaret's dark hair. *Margaret is such a pretty girl that most if not all colors would look good on her,* Isabel thought. *I prefer red for myself, but it's been hard to find red material here at the school. If I had yards and yards of red and green material, I'd make all the Susans Christmas dresses—*

"And the debate for tonight will be, resolved: That the present system of football is a benefit to schools and colleges," Margaret finished.

Isabel started out of her daydream about clothes. *Oh dear,* she thought. *This school is very busy with football, so I guess we have to discuss it, but who of the girls here has the least interest in it? What side of the debate am I on? I think I wish that football didn't exist, but Frances and all the boys are very fond of it.*

After the song and Elmira's essay, Isabel took her place behind the podium and flipped to the bookmark in her copy of Tennyson's poems.

"Mr. Tennyson has not been as well received in these modern times as in the nineteenth century, when he lived," Miss Hayes said with a smile. "Isabel intends to rehabilitate him."

I don't know if I like Mr. Tennyson's work so much or if he was just the first poet I read, Isabel thought. *But certainly the poem I am reading tonight goes with this group's thoughts.*

She cleared her throat and looked out over the audience. The Susans were quiet and attentive, waiting for her to begin. "The poem is called 'Ode to Memory,'" Isabel said.

> *Thou who stealest fire,*
> *From the fountains of the past,*
> *To glorify the present, O, haste,*
> *Visit my low desire!*
> *Strengthen me, enlighten me!*

I faint in this obscurity,
Thou dewy dawn of memory.

She stopped reading and cleared her throat. *Go on,* she ordered herself. *Don't you dare let your voice shake.* Isabel moved her finger to the next verse on the page and continued.

In sweet dreams softer than unbroken rest
Thou leddest by the hand thine infant Hope.
The eddying of her garments caught from thee
The light of thy great presence; and the cloak
Of the half-attain'd futurity,
Tho' deep not fathomless,
Was cloven with the million stars which tremble
O'er the deep mind of dauntless infancy.
Small thought was there of life's distress;
For sure she deem'd no mist of earth could dull
Those spirit-thrilling eyes so keen and beautiful;
Sure she was nigher to heaven's spheres,
Listening to the lordly music flowing from
The illimitable years.
O, strengthen me, enlighten me!
I faint in this obscurity,
Thou dewy dawn of memory.

The room was utterly silent. Isabel lifted her eyes from the page and saw that Elizabeth and Annabelle were wiping their eyes with handkerchiefs. After a few moments Miss Hayes said, "That was a lovely reading, Isabel. Does anyone have comments or questions?"

No one said a word. Miss Hayes sighed. "Perhaps we all feel that we know what the poem means right now. Thank you, Isabel."

Isabel sat down again, trying not to cry herself. *It's good to be with my friends tonight, but I don't feel like reading or hearing any more poetry,* she decided.

"Let's go on to the debate," Miss Hayes said, taking Isabel's place at the podium. "Who wants to be against football in schools and colleges?"

Isabel felt a little smile creep across her face. Elizabeth, Rosetta Pierce, Ruth Shaw, and Mary Jane Gordon all had their hands raised. They were probably the most unathletic girls at Carlisle and firmly hated all sports.

"I can see where this debate is going," Miss Hayes said, smiling herself. "I shall take the pro side of football."

Isabel leaned back in her chair, ready to enjoy the debate. *Miss Hayes will certainly win, no matter what side she's on,* she thought. *She is so very clever.*

"Football is hateful to play and boring to watch," began Mary Jane. Isabel almost laughed. None of the other anti-football girls had much to add to that.

"We would not want the boys to be unhappy without football," Miss Hayes concluded after several minutes of argument. "If we assume allowing them their sport shows us women to be of a kind and generous nature, we can expect like treatment from them, such as gallantry and patience."

"Let's vote on the question of the debate," Margaret said. "Is the present system of football a benefit to schools and colleges?"

Isabel raised her hand along with all the other girls. Miss Hayes had won again. *Imagine—all of us are happy to support football now,* Isabel marveled. *Miss Hayes wins by looking for the good in any subject and then defending it.*

"That concludes our meeting," Miss Hayes said. "Good night, girls."

Isabel joined the other girls at the coatrack, settling her long, gray wool coat around her shoulders. *I haven't worried about the boys for an hour,* she realized. *That felt good.*

A blast of frigid air hit Isabel's face when she stepped outside but no ice or snow. Overhead, a pale half-moon wavered in the cold air. "The storm is over," Elizabeth remarked, tying her hat strings under her chin.

"Yes." Isabel tried to stop shivering now that she was out of Miss Hayes's cozy heated rooms. "Now the real cold will come since the sky has cleared," she added. Several girls around her nodded.

Here come thoughts of the boys again, Isabel realized as she trudged across the lawn and to her room. She dreaded the night of worry she knew was ahead of her. *What will we find out tomorrow?* she wondered. *Could it be even worse to know what happened to them?*

The next morning Frances was unusually slow in getting ready for breakfast. "We're going to be late," Isabel said as Frances lingered in front of the mirror. "Why are you just standing there?"

"I think we're going to find out what happened to the boys—Major Mercer will probably announce it at breakfast." Frances continued to gaze into the mirror and tugged on her curls. "I'm just trying to brace myself. I—I don't want to lose any more friends."

"Well, we have to get it over with," Lily said sympathetically. "We might as well go down."

Frances nodded, but she looked very unhappy.

In the dining hall, Isabel saw several teachers huddled together in a corner, talking. *Frances is right—we're going to hear news of the boys,* Isabel thought. *At least we won't have to wait until spring, especially if it's terrible news.*

Miss Kingsley, the math teacher, rapped a pointer on the nearest table. "Students!" she called. "Quiet, please."

The loud chatter in the room stopped instantly as the hundreds of students in the room turned to look at the teacher, anticipation on their faces. Isabel, Lily, and Frances lingered by the door, waiting in silence with the rest of the students.

"I know you have all been worried about the boys who were missing," the teacher continued.

Frances turned immediately on her heel. "*Were* missing," she said. "I'm going to see them."

Isabel and Lily cast worried looks at Miss Kingsley, and Lily laid her hand on Frances's arm. "Frances, don't get in trouble," she said. "We're supposed to eat breakfast, then go to class."

"I won't get in trouble. I'm going." Frances was already striding out of the dining hall.

Isabel and Lily shared a look of concern, then hurried after Frances. "Miss Kingsley didn't even say if the boys are alive or not," Lily whispered to Isabel.

"I think she would have looked much unhappier if they were dead. Where are we going?" Isabel called after Frances, running to catch up.

Frances pointed at the superintendent's quarters. "Right there. If they just found the boys, they'll be in there with Major Mercer, getting a dressing-down."

"We can't go in!" Lily puffed, trying to keep up with her roommates as they darted across the lawn to the imposing tall white building.

Frances yanked open the door. Right in front of them were Major Mercer and two of the runaway boys—Frank and Albert. Major Mercer had his index finger in the air and appeared to be in the middle of a lecture. Frank was looking at his feet, but Albert was staring straight at Major Mercer. All of them ignored the girls, despite the blast of cold air that had just swirled through the door when they entered.

"You're so stuck on your old school!" Albert said furiously. "I just wanted to show you I don't have to stay here if I don't want to!"

Major Mercer looked weary and dropped his hand. "Albert, I am not so very stuck on my old school myself right now. But we both have a duty to be here. So let's get you boys to the kitchen to warm up and find something for you to eat."

"How stupid are you two?" Frances demanded.

"Now, Frances," Major Mercer began. "The boys have already apologized—"

"VERY STUPID!" Albert shouted back at her. "Okay?"

"It's not at all okay," Frances snapped. "People care about

you, Albert. People here at the school and people at home. You had no right to run away in a snowstorm and practically freeze to death and cause all those people grief."

Albert stared angrily at her. Then he dropped his gaze to his shoes and drew a shaky breath. After a few moments he said, "I know. And I'm truly sorry, not just sorry to the teachers."

"You should be," said Frances. She didn't seem much less angry.

"Where's Thomas?" Lily asked softly.

"He has severe frostbite on his hands and feet." Major Mercer looked sternly at the girls. "The doctor at the hospital is right now attempting to save his fingers and toes."

"I'll go see him," Frances said immediately.

"He might appreciate that." Major Mercer's tone softened. "Unfortunately, he is in quite a bad way."

"So don't yell at him, Frances," Lily whispered.

Major Mercer heard and smiled slightly. "Thank you for stopping by, girls," he said.

The three girls backed out the door. "Major Mercer isn't so bad," Frances said abruptly once they were outside. "He really does care."

In the dining hall that night, Isabel hurried to join her roommates at their usual table. Lily had been allowed to see Thomas because she worked at the hospital, and Frances had told the on-duty nurse that she was Thomas's sister and so gotten to visit him, but Isabel had been told to leave. She hadn't wanted to go into that awful place anyway. "How is Thomas?" she asked, pulling her stool up to the table.

Lily looked sad. "Major Mercer was right—he's badly off. He lost six toes. They were totally black and dead, and the doctor amputated them immediately. We'll have to wait and see about his fingers. The three middle fingers on his left hand are severely affected."

"Oh, my." Isabel shook her head. *How will he practice a trade if he loses three fingers?* she wondered. *This stunt has had even worse consequences than we feared.*

Frances stuck her fork upright in her sweet potato, looking frustrated. "How were they caught?" Isabel asked.

"The old-fashioned way." Frances scowled. "One of the maintenance men is part Indian, and he's a tracker. With all the wind blowing the snow around, he had a hard job following the tracks, but he managed to figure out in what direction they'd gone. North—can you believe it? I guess they wanted to get even colder than they already were in the blizzard."

"Thomas said they planned to stop at a farm where Frank worked last summer," Lily interjected. "Then the boys had no idea what they were going to do. Wait for the storm to stop and decide, I guess."

"Why on earth did they take off in a storm?" Isabel asked. She had been served a delicious plate of food, including a piece of roast beef, but for once she wasn't very hungry.

"Those idiots thought it wouldn't get that bad—they weren't too worried about a storm in the East since they were used to such awful storms in South Dakota." Frances lifted her shoulders slightly.

"So they were just having an adventure," Lily said.

"That's right," Frances agreed. "Just a very, very stupid adventure."

"Will they be punished?" Isabel asked, looking over toward the boys' side of the dining hall. "I don't see any of them here."

"Oh, they'll be punished, all right," Frances said grimly, starting to eat her food at last. "They'll be put in the guardhouse forever."

"Not forever, Frances," Lily chided. "And they aren't there now because it's too cold—they're confined to their rooms; I overheard Major Mercer telling Miss Robertson, the head nurse, outside the hospital. Besides, they deserve to be punished. What if their families knew? I don't care if they're Sioux—they could have died out there."

"Yes, they could have." Frances sighed. "I almost wonder . . . if that's what they wanted."

"Frances!" Lily stared at her in surprise. "Do you mean they were homesick? Why not wait at least long enough to take the train home?"

"They weren't homesick, not exactly." Frances looked down at her food.

Isabel thought of her father and brother, facing the long, dark winter in Mescalero. Although Jeremy's last letter had been cheerful, she worried that they were cold and uncomfortable. Jeremy had said nothing was going on but the usual logging work when the snow wasn't too deep, and one of his friends had gotten married. Their father was anxious for news from Isabel. *I must write them tonight*, she thought.

"When are you next going home, Frances?" Lily asked, changing the subject. Isabel sighed with relief.

"This summer. I think. I want to see my little brothers and my mother and father. But summer is so long from now." Frances's expression was troubled.

"I had some thought of working here full-time for a while to make money," Lily said. "But I decided to go home in May and see my grandfather. After all, he isn't getting any younger. What about you, Isabel?"

"My father has arranged for me to go home at the beginning of June for a long visit." Isabel looked at her barely touched dinner and determinedly picked up a roll. "My family would be glad to see me at any time, especially my father. But if I ran away from school, he would also be disappointed that I had failed here. When those boys' families find out what they have done—"

"And Major Mercer will surely tell them," Lily interjected.

"Their families will be concerned and sad," Isabel finished.

"Frank, Thomas, and Albert just didn't think," Frances said. "Boys never do."

Later that evening, long after her roommates were asleep, Isabel sat at the table in their room, a candle lighting the small square of blank paper in front of her. She wanted to write a letter to her family, but she didn't know what to say.

If I tell them about the runaway boys, which is what is most important to me now, they'll worry that all the students are unhappy at Carlisle, including me, or that I am somehow at risk in a place where such dangerous things happen, she thought. *But I haven't written my monthly letter home—I have to put down something.*

Isabel nibbled the end of her pen and looked at her sleeping roommates. Frances turned onto her back, her curls fanning out around her head, and snored softly. Lily lay on her side, her hands folded under her head. She was smiling slightly, as if she were having sweet dreams. *I can always write more about Frances and Lily,* Isabel told herself. *Father will be pleased to hear about my good friends' accomplishments and that we are all doing well. He doesn't need to hear about the runaway boys.*

The candle flickered. Isabel rested her head in her hand and imagined her father's worn face, then her brother's laughing, cheerful one. But according to Jeremy's last letter, their father had kept his word and stayed off the fence; he was working hard. He still often talked to himself—their father said he was addressing the gods or their mother—but Jeremy had said that he didn't look too gloomy when he was doing it.

By now, the snow must be deep in the mountains in Mescalero, Isabel thought. *Even if Father and Jeremy don't have to work, they'll have to go through the snowdrifts, searching for firewood.*

Picking up her pen, she wrote:

Dear Father and Jeremy,
I hope this letter finds you well. I am doing fine, continuing my studies in languages, art, history, and mathematics. My drawing is even better because my roommate Lily has worked with me so much, and I can now draw an acceptable horse and antelope. On Wednesday evenings, I go to a literary society

meeting where we discuss the meaning of books. When the weather is fine, I and the other girls take a walk with one of our teachers. Sometimes we go into town or simply circle the school grounds and enjoy the trees and birds and other aspects of nature.

Isabel sat back hard in her chair. *This letter doesn't say anything about what I'm really feeling and thinking,* she thought. *But even if I did try to explain the fright we have had about the runaway boys, Father and Jeremy couldn't understand it properly because they don't live here and don't have all the facts. Heaven knows their lives are hard enough without them worrying about me.*

She started to write again anyway.

> *This evening we had quite a debate about the merits of football—you know how to play that game, Jeremy, and can explain it to Father. Although we girls are by and large not fond of football, which is a rough and dirty sport, our English teacher, Miss Hayes, is such a good debater, we ended up agreeing that football must be played! Miss Hayes is a wonderful teacher and friend, and I model my behavior on hers.*

After a moment, she finished:

> *I must get to bed now, for I have breakfast and classes early. I miss you both.*
> *Love,*
> *Isabel*

She changed out of her school dress into her cotton nightgown. Outside the window, a sharp gust broke icicles off the roof. They shattered with cold tinkles on the walkway below. Isabel got into bed, pulling the blankets up under her chin, and rested her head on the plump soft pillow. She thought of her father and Jeremy sleeping in their tent, but just as she began to fall asleep, she imagined them as perfectly comfortable as she was. "Good night," she whispered. "Sleep well."

11

"At last, at last—we're in town again!" Jennifer cried, throwing her arms wide as she stood on the narrow sidewalk next to Carlisle's Main Street. She turned her face up to the winter sun, bright if chilly in a clear sky. "But I'll never get all my shopping done in just one trip. And it's only three weeks till Christmas!"

"All right, calm down!" Her mother laughed, stopping beside her on the sidewalk. "Why are you such a city girl? And who are all these people you have to buy presents for?"

"Just our family and Aunt Elaine. But I want to allow plenty of time to mail Aunt Elaine's package to Philadelphia. Mother, when can I visit her again?" Jennifer asked eagerly, tugging on her white beret. She had gotten it while visiting her aunt—like everything else stylish she owned, Jennifer thought.

Mrs. Schmidt frowned. "Not for a while, Jennifer. You know that we need you at home more than ever now that Benjamin is in town so much. Your father's leg still hurts him . . ."

Jennifer sighed loudly, and her shoulders drooped. *In other words, I'll never see Philadelphia again*, she thought.

"Jennifer, please don't argue so much about what can't be changed," her mother pleaded. "If you want, someday you can leave for a city or town, like Carlisle—"

"It won't be Carlisle," Jennifer interrupted.

Mrs. Schmidt opened her mouth, then hesitated. She shook her head and walked on down the street.

"What?" Jennifer asked, hurrying to catch up.

Her mother stopped, then turned to face her. "Our farm has been in the family for several generations," she said. "What will happen to it when your father is too old to work? With Benjamin gone and you wanting to leave so badly, your father thinks he'll just have to sell it someday."

Jennifer could feel her Christmas spirit plummeting with guilt. "Maybe I can stay at the farm for a while once I'm grown," she said. "Or you and Father could lease it out, and I'll come back someday after I live in the city."

Her mother didn't respond but just continued to walk down the street. "Why do you always want me to run the farm?" Jennifer asked from behind her. "You never yelled at Benjamin about it."

"We did yell at Benjamin, but it didn't do any good," her mother replied, turning her head. "He was never going to be a farmer, whereas you have a way with animals and a real feeling for the farm, although you may not know it yet. Besides, Jennifer, your father and I aren't being purely selfish about this. The farm life is a good one: stable, safe, and enjoyable."

Mother will never understand my point of view because she sees no attraction in city life whatsoever, Jennifer thought. *So . . . why argue?* She caught up to her mother. "It's just—not that enjoyable for me to work on the farm, Mother," she said at last. "I don't really like taking care of all the animals, especially the cows. And girls have other opportunities these days besides growing up to be wives and mothers."

"Well, don't close your mind to the possibility of staying on the farm. That's all your father and I ask." Mrs. Schmidt smiled a little. "We bother you about it because we think there's hope you'll stay. You need to think about all of your life, not just the part where you're a dashing young woman in Philadelphia with an apartment and a career. You might think quite differently when you're a mother, trying to raise children who play on the city streets."

"Maybe," Jennifer said doubtfully. For any children she might have, playing stickball on the streets of Philadelphia for boys and the huge, welcoming libraries of the city for girls sounded like much more fun than the endless chores on the farm. Besides, Aunt Elaine wasn't stuck in the city, looking at streets lined with gray buildings or walking the concrete sidewalks every minute. She often took the train out of town to enjoy a nature walk. *Mother doesn't know the first thing about cities, and so the farm looks wonderful to her,* Jennifer decided.

"Let's shop!" Her mother clapped and pointed to the novelties store next to them. "No more serious subjects!"

"You don't have to convince me," Jennifer said, smiling as she followed her mother through the doorway.

Inside the store, shelves covered the walls from top to bottom, heavily laden with every possible kind of goods for presents. *Nothing's in the least useful in here, hence its attraction,* Jennifer thought, her eyes greedily hovering on a long row of fat, deliciously scented candles in Christmas colors but also pink, blue, and purple. While she and her mother shopped, Jennifer's father was at the saddle repair shop, picking up buckles for the horses' harnesses. *I much prefer this store,* Jennifer thought. *Doesn't that mean I don't want to be a farmer?*

She turned slowly in a full circle, savoring the choices. *I intend to search every item in here for the perfect presents for Mother and Aunt Elaine,* she told herself, hardly knowing where to start. *But should I get them perfume, stationery, or one of those nice scented candles? Mother never treats herself to perfume or any of those things, so she needs them all.*

Jennifer felt in her dress pocket for the carefully folded

bills she had put there, earnings from her training work on the Standardbreds. She had given most of the money to her parents, but she still had enough left to feel rich.

Prowling the aisles, she carefully selected a tall, evergreen-scented candle in the shape of a Christmas tree for her mother and stationery with a wildflower design at the top for Aunt Elaine. She'd shop later for her father and brother, when they met her father later at the harness shop. Jennifer and her mother had discussed buying Mr. Schmidt a brand-new harness to replace the one that he kept getting fixed.

I'll just get Benjamin a car part or something, Jennifer thought, carrying her selections to the register. *Probably Father knows where to find that.*

The shopkeeper, Mrs. Rickey, was happy to help Jennifer keep the secret of her purchases, hiding them under the counter with her plump hands when Mrs. Schmidt passed by, then quickly wrapping them in green-and-red-striped paper when Jennifer's mother became absorbed in her own shopping. Mrs. Rickey finished the packages with gold braid tied in a big bow and put them in a shopping bag.

"I want to see them," Mrs. Schmidt said, leaning over to peer into the bag.

"Not until Christmas!" Jennifer snatched the bag away.

Laughing together, she and her mother left the store.

"Let's watch the ice skaters for a bit and eat the sandwiches we brought." Mrs. Schmidt put her arm around Jennifer's shoulders.

"Sounds good," Jennifer agreed. "I wish I'd brought my skates, but then I'd have had to lug them all around town."

"You can come another time," her mother said. "Maybe when you're off from school for Christmas."

As they walked to the ice-skating pond, they saw a few people they knew from church and nodded and smiled in greeting. Jennifer didn't see any of their farm neighbors, but she hadn't expected to: they seldom went to town to shop. *Farm people have more cows than money*, she thought. *But I wish Dell was here.* Jennifer hadn't invited her along because her friend didn't have money to spend; she would have to give all the members of her big family homemade Christmas gifts. Last year Dell had knitted eleven scarves for her family. She'd had to start practically the Christmas before to get them all finished. *I'm very lucky that I can train the horses to earn money*, Jennifer thought. *And it's fun to be with Mother when we have nothing else to do but talk and shop.*

Jennifer and her mother walked to the edge of town, then cut through an alleyway that led onto a footpath to the Conedogwinet River. The skating area on the river was just behind the Carlisle school. Jennifer caught a glimpse of the school buildings through the big trees. She had never been on the grounds, but she knew that hundreds of Indian children went to school there.

On a small bridge with a railing, Jennifer's mother stopped. She dug in her carryall for their lunch. Jennifer leaned over the railing.

"What a strange sight, all those Indian children skating," she said to her mother. "They have a huge place to skate. It's funny that they get almost all of the ice and the townspeople have to stay on a tiny part on the other side of the bridge."

"I don't know how that was decided, but I'm sure the Indian children deserve the treat of a fine skating area," her mother said firmly, handing Jennifer a cheese sandwich.

Jennifer bit into the sandwich, tangy with mustard, and sipped milk from a bottle. *Some of those skaters are pretty good*, she thought as a laughing, jostling crowd of skaters glided by her. One girl, by herself in the middle of the pond, was especially talented. She wore a bright blue cap and had her hands in a matching blue muff. She skated with long energetic strides, her straight black hair flying out behind her.

"Why, that's the same Indian girl I saw in town last fall," Jennifer said to her mother in surprise. "She was walking with that group of girls."

"I'm not surprised you remember her—she's very pretty," Mrs. Schmidt said. "I think she must be a little sad right now since she and all the other children at the school are so very far from home at Christmastime."

"She doesn't look sad," Jennifer muttered. "Do Indians even know about Christmas?" she said in a louder voice.

"Of course they do." Mrs. Schmidt sounded exasperated. "Jennifer, those children are in school, just like you."

"Well, we don't hear much news out on the farm, so I don't know much about the Carlisle school," Jennifer said pointedly. "Mother, can I spend next Christmas with Aunt Elaine in Philadelphia?" She suddenly imagined the holidays in the big city: stores thronged with elegantly dressed, wealthy people, selecting exotic goods from around the world as presents, then dashing across streets full of honking automobiles to dine in restaurants while snow piled high outside on the tall buildings.

"You belong at home on Christmas," her mother said firmly, turning away from the skaters. "Just be glad you have one to go to."

Isabel pulled her arms toward her body, spinning clumsily at first on the blades of her skates, then faster and faster until her arms were pressed tight against her chest and the low-hanging streamers of clouds spun too against the pale gray sky. The air was bitter cold and hurt a little to breathe. The cold had lasted for weeks already, and every day was short and dark. The skeleton trees, bare of leaves, bent over the edge of the skating area, seeming to watch the laughing, gliding, slipping students.

"All right, I've had enough," Lily complained as Isabel pulled her back upright off the ice for the fourth time. Lily brushed snow off the back of her skirt with her glove. "I'm going back to our room and warm up."

"I think I'll skate just a little more." Isabel glanced up at the sky. Its gray had darkened as the afternoon waned, and she could feel the icy cold of the coming night beginning to creep up her fingertips. "I'll come in soon—I'm almost frozen too."

"I'll see you for dinner." Lily skated slowly to the riverbank, wobbling a little.

Isabel pushed off on her skates. Pumping her arms, she skated quickly, digging her blades into the ice, which was crunchy with last night's dusting of new snow. Her feet soon warmed from the activity, but the private cold wind she had made with her swift flight across the ice stung her cheeks. *I haven't had so much fun in ages*, she thought as she sped by the shore, piled with uneven, high drifts of snow. A few other skaters, thickset rectangles in their heavy sweaters and coats, and the skinny trees on the bank with their hats of snow passed in a blur. Isabel raised her arms for balance, admiring the sleeves of her pretty dark blue wool sweater. Emma had knitted it for her in the dressmaking shop.

Digging the sides of her skate blades into the ice, Isabel stopped abruptly, sending up a shower of snow. As she caught her breath, she glanced over at the bank. Lily waved from a bare patch of ground, where she sat taking off her skates. Isabel waved back, then dropped her hand suddenly.

Oh, no, she thought. Albert sat not far away from Lily, leaning against a tree. He still had his skates on and was looking directly at Isabel.

Isabel quickly turned her head. Pushing her toe picks frantically into the ice, she skated rapidly toward the middle of the pond. *Slow down—it's very obvious that he's having an effect on you*, she scolded herself. She hadn't spoken to Albert once since he had run away more than a week ago. At a school as large as Carlisle, avoiding him hadn't been difficult—since the boys ate their meals separately from the girls, all she had to do was not run into him in the doorway of the dining hall and not turn around in math class, where Albert sat in the back with his friends as always.

I'm not the only one who doesn't want to talk to those boys, Isabel thought as she skated slowly in a big circle. No one was actually mean to the runaways, but Isabel had seen other students walk away when they saw them, and hardly anyone spoke to them.

Isabel kept skating, working on balancing on the side edges of her blades as she turned both ways and finally even managing a small jump while she waited for Albert to leave. But after half an hour, she was cold and tired, and Albert was still there under the tree, watching her. *I give up*, she thought. *Apparently he is determined to talk to me. I might as well get this conversation over with.* Isabel skated to the bank and stopped sharply with a flourish of shaved ice from her blades, then walked in her skates to a bare spot under her own tree, a little distance from Albert.

"You're a good skater," Albert called.

Isabel didn't reply, although she knew she was being rude. She bent over her skate laces.

Albert got up and walked over to her. He stood there a moment, then sat beside her. Isabel kept her head down, although her heart began to beat fast.

"You're still angry with the boys who ran away," he said with a sigh, clasping his hands around his knees.

Isabel jerked her head up. "Why wouldn't I be?" she snapped. "I guess I am—especially with you." Isabel could feel her face flushing with anger and embarrassment. She looked quickly over at him to see his reaction, but Albert was staring at the skaters.

"I don't know why we ran away," he said at last. "We weren't going home. But we've been in awful trouble ever since, especially with our parents."

"The school told them?" Isabel looked at her fingers.

"Yes." Albert sighed again and didn't go on until the last wisp of his frozen breath had faded into the air. "Major Mercer said he had to tell our parents because we put our health in jeopardy. They telegraphed back immediately—all of them were very angry and disappointed. They were also worried about the effect the school was having on us since we had done something so foolish." Albert shook his head. "We did almost freeze to death. I guess we finally realized that we were really in trouble when it started to get dark and cold, and we'd missed the farm where we were going to stay the night."

"So how did you survive?" Isabel asked, stretching out her legs and staring at the tips of her skates.

"We were very lucky to find an animal shed at the edge of the woods. By that time it was so dark, we couldn't see if a farm was nearby. So we stayed in the shed, but we got awfully cold. At some time in the night, Thomas said he couldn't feel his feet, but we thought if he took off his shoes and tried to rub them, they'd just get colder. That's when we knew that we might not make it," Albert finished quietly.

Isabel turned and looked right at him. "Why did you run off into the woods in a blizzard?"

Albert shrugged. "We were just so tired of all the rules, like we told Major Mercer. Getting up too early every day at the same time, sitting in class all morning and working all day. But I still don't see . . . Why are the other students so angry with us?"

Isabel rubbed her gloved hands together slowly and gazed at the sky while she considered Albert's question. The clouds were clearing, revealing a pale, violet dome as evening fell. The last skaters were walking back to the school, leaving the ice empty. Soon she and Albert would have to go in for dinner. "I can't speak for everyone," she said finally. "But if I had to guess, I'd say that we are all sometimes tired of school and our responsibilities here. The rest of us don't just run off, though. We have obligations to the teachers and to our families. I mean, we all signed contracts agreeing to stay at the school; don't you remember? But I thought—"

"What?" Albert asked quietly. He had dropped his head, and Isabel could see the straight part in his neatly combed black hair.

"That you only ran away because you hated the school very much and cared nothing for your classmates," Isabel said in a rush. "Do you wonder that everyone is angry with you?"

"Well, I hope I've convinced you that wasn't why we ran." Albert frowned, then looked directly into Isabel's eyes. "I do care about my classmates."

Albert leaned slowly toward her. Isabel felt her shoulders relaxing as her anger melted away. *I believe him*, she thought. Albert's soft lips lightly touched hers, and Isabel closed her eyes, giving herself to the kiss.

When Albert finally drew back, it was so dark, Isabel could only see his eyes shining and the silhouette of his face. But she could hear the smile in his voice as he said, "Frank plays the trumpet every morning to get everyone out of bed. Did you notice that it was gone for a couple of days?"

Isabel laughed and jumped to her feet. *I'm not one bit cold*, she realized. "Are you saying we should thank you for running away?" she asked.

12

John rode Sun That Rises at a quick walk, letting the mare pick her way along the overgrown old deer path on this frosty Christmas morning. Long icicles hung from the trees, glistening in the cold, bright sunny light. Sun That Rises tossed her head, then bent her neck to watch the deep drifts of snow that buried the ground in front of her. The horse's hooves crunched on the thin coating of ice covering the snow, and then she sank up to her knees. But the little horse seemed to be enjoying herself. She gathered her legs under her and hopped out of the drift. Shaking her mane, she pulled on the reins, trying to charge ahead.

"You must behave yourself," John told the mare. Mostly she did, now that he had ridden her so much. Getting away from work at the reservation was hard, but he had usually managed to ride Sun That Rises once a week since he found her. That meant riding in the rain and wind at times and now snow, but he and the horse understood each other fairly well.

He still hadn't gotten her completely predictable, and that was what he needed Isabel's horse to be. *How can I make Sun*

That Rises safe? John wondered again. The palomino would walk, trot, and canter when she was told, but sometimes she expressed her opinions with bucks and dashes across meadows and woods. "I know when you are going to do it," he warned the mare. After that first escape across the meadow, he had learned to watch for the slight tightening of the mare's shoulder muscles and rolling of her eye as she looked back at him—as if she was checking to see if he was awake in the saddle. He knew then to tighten the reins and his legs. These days, she usually only got away with one good leap forward before he pulled her up.

Sun That Rises huffed out a quick steamy breath and shook her ears, where a patch of snow had fallen from one of the coated trees. John smiled and reached forward to pat her neck. He had succeeded in one part of her training—she could not be a more loving animal. Isabel would surely like how Sun That Rises nosed him for apples and other treats and stretched her head toward him looking for endless petting. Constantly fussing over a horse was not John's usual way to treat animals, but this was not his horse, he reminded himself, and the fact that the horse was lovable seemed to be one way to become partners with her. That was the real goal—to be one with the horse, achieving either great enjoyment or successful work, like raiding ranches. Since Isabel would be unlikely to raid these days, she would want a horse of spirit but kindness.

One good part of the raids was the feeling of freedom that came with riding so fast, he remembered. *Isabel can have that, even if she cannot have the feeling of cleverness and winning that came with a successful raid.*

"So I am back to how to give Isabel an enjoyable horse." John sighed. "Sun That Rises, you could make this work of training easier for me if you were not so willful. I think that you will prefer Isabel as a rider, but I do not know why I think that, and I cannot count on it. You must be a good horse for me to ride as well, or I will not trust you with Isabel."

Sun That Rises flicked back an ear, but she suddenly walked

faster. Up ahead was a clearing, where John had once let her run to stretch her legs.

"You don't forget," he said to the horse. "That is good, because I cannot teach well. You were the good teacher," he continued, addressing Maria. "I have trouble remembering that Isabel is only a beginner around horses. I must be very careful she doesn't get hurt—and I also want her to love this horse. She will not love a horse that takes her for wild and frightening rides."

She seems to like school very much, he thought wistfully, remembering Isabel's last letter. *She is not at all homesick. That is good, of course. But I must make very sure she has a fine horse when she comes back so that she does not miss school.*

"I wish I had Jeremy to talk to instead of people who are not here," he said aloud, pulling up Sun That Rises at the edge of the clearing. Jeremy had not come with him to work with the horse today because he had said the weather was too cold to stand around. Also, he wanted to be one of the first to arrive at the Christmas party the agent's wife planned to have that night for the Indians. She had gotten some special food, including cakes, and Jeremy wanted to be sure he got some of the treats before they were gobbled up by hungry people.

Sun That Rises twisted her head around to look at him. Then she stretched her neck, tugging at the reins, and looked back at him again. John laughed. "You can almost talk," he said. "I know what you want, so it is the same thing. We will run across this open space, but you must be good and not give me what Jeremy calls a wild ride."

He gave the mare a bit of rein, and Sun That Rises responded instantly, plunging into a quick, smooth gallop. Certainly she was sensitive to his signals, John thought, settling himself deep into the saddle to follow her movements. Now he had to hope she would be sensitive to the signal to stop. Also, that she would not slip and fall. The clearing was almost free of snow, but icy spots might be hidden in the shadows of the trees that stood around the edges.

The palomino mare's strides were steady and strong, pounding crisply against the hard, frozen ground. The sun burned away the air's cold, bringing a delicious warmth to John's face. He closed his eyes briefly, enjoying the strong bond he felt with the horse and the quick power she gave him as she carried him so easily across the field. *If I thought no one would hear, I would give an Apache yell*, he thought.

Sun That Rises kept her pace steady, not throwing in a spirited buck even though John had not ridden her for a week. She slowed with no asking from the reins as they approached the woods and finally settled into an easy walk.

"That was a good ride," John told the horse. He guided her to the sturdy shelter he had made out of brush and boards so that Sun That Rises wouldn't forget it was there. He had hidden the shelter far back in the woods so that the wranglers who sometimes rode out looking for horses to capture and sell wouldn't find her. It had taken him all fall to build since he had to take time off from work and carry the boards off from an abandoned barracks when no one was looking, but at last it was finished enough to keep off most of the winter's wind and snow.

John sighed. That was the other big problem besides training this horse to be calm—how to keep her from getting stolen. "I have gotten very fond of you," he said, reaching forward to pat the horse's golden neck. "That will just make losing you more painful if it happens. I lost another horse long ago, Moon That Flies. Although I owned his heart, I did not own him as property, the way white people own horses and houses and wagons. So I do not think I can bring you back to the reservation, because I am not your owner in the right way. I must find out how to become that."

He swung out of the saddle, landing with a stifled sigh. Sun That Rises glanced back at him, then suddenly her gaze was riveted on the black shadow of a tree, sharply outlined on the snow. She jumped away, her shoulder colliding with John.

"None of that." John pushed her firmly away. It was hardly

necessary—she had not bumped him very hard. "I don't think you were really afraid," he said. "You were just making life more interesting by pretending. And I don't think you meant to hurt me. I think you are so smart, you were careful about that.

"So maybe I only have one problem," he went on, pulling off the mare's saddle and setting it in a corner of the shed. He didn't like leaving the saddle there, because even an old saddle like this one could be traded for whiskey if someone found it, but he couldn't leave it outside in the snow. "I need to buy this horse, then get a piece of paper saying that I have done so. Once I have the money, Robert will help me with the paperwork. So now the question is just of money."

Sun That Rises watched him, her ears relaxed. She was a good listener, like most horses. John smiled. *So I will go to the tree where my silver is hidden*, he thought. *Then I will have plenty of money.*

The horse's ears shot forward. John grabbed her bridle. He had a sudden clear vision of the little palomino racing off, still bridled, then stomping on the reins and breaking them just before he managed to catch her again.

"Why do I think you would find that funny?" he asked. "I know horses do not have such feelings."

On Christmas Day, Isabel walked into the dining room and stopped short in amazement. Frances and Lily, who were behind her, collided with Isabel and then each other.

"Watch out!" Frances gave Isabel a little extra push as Lily said, "What's the matter?"

"Look!" Isabel couldn't believe what she saw. "It's—it's our Christmas dinner!"

"My goodness," Lily said, peering around Isabel.

"It's a party!" Frances declared.

The girls walked slowly into the gaily decorated room. The walls were festooned with evergreen wreaths, a long line of red-and-green bunting, and tall banners proclaiming *Happy New*

Year and *Merry Christmas.* The long tables were thickly covered with white bowls, plates, and cups, waiting to be filled with Christmas foods.

"I wonder what we're having!" Lily said gleefully. "That's even more dishes than at Thanksgiving."

"I've never seen such a Christmas," Frances said slowly.

"Let's sit!" Isabel glanced behind her, where other students were crowding by them into the dining room.

"I'm ready to get started." Frances strode toward the girls' usual table.

Once all the students were seated, the teachers and other school employees emerged from the kitchen, bearing huge platters of turkey, lapping over the edges, serving bowls of sweet potatoes piled into orange mountains, and sloshing gravy boats. The hot food filled the air with savory scents. "Merry Christmas!" said Mr. Carter, the young basketball coach, from behind the girls.

"Lily's Mr. Carter!" Isabel couldn't help whispering to Frances. He set a platter of turkey on the table.

"Ooh, he put the food closest to Lily!" Frances whispered back. "Oh, Merry Christmas, Mr. Carter," she said in a louder voice.

He is cute, Isabel thought. Mr. Carter was tall and muscular, with green eyes and a good-natured smile. *Lily has good taste, I guess . . . except he's so old! Twenty-five, at least.*

"Merry Christmas, Mr. Carter." Lily flushed, but she looked bravely up at the teacher and returned his smile.

Frances dug her elbow into Isabel's side. "Stop that!" Isabel cried. Mr. Carter had moved a safe distance down the table and was serving other students, so she added, "He's Lily's Mr. Carter—elbow her!"

"Look, an orange!" Frances exclaimed, grabbing the little globe by her plate and ignoring Isabel. "All the students got one. How yummy!" She immediately began to peel hers.

"I'm saving mine for dessert," Isabel said, running her fingers over the precious orange's nobby, beautiful skin. She felt a bit amazed that the orange was actually in her hand. She had heard of oranges since she'd been at Carlisle, but she'd never had one of her own to eat.

"And I'm going to take mine back to our room." Lily held her orange up to her nose, closed her eyes, and inhaled deeply. "Nobody else better eat my orange, *Frances*."

Frances held up her hands in surrender. "Just don't blame me if a *mouse* eats it if it sits around too long," she said. "I mean longer than a day."

Isabel reached under her plate and drew out three chocolates in ridged white paper cups. "Look what else we got!" Sometimes the Susans got a chocolate at meetings, but here she had three to eat all at once.

"Now I have to decide how to eat these, too," Lily said, practically shouting over the excited bustle of voices in the room.

Frances walked two fingers toward Lily's hand. "I'll help you."

Lily smacked her roommate's hand. "Thanks, but no thanks."

The girls devoured the wonderful food, course after course, barely speaking as they relished the meal. *This is giving thanks*, Isabel thought. She sighed and sat back. *Of course I wish that Father and Jeremy could enjoy Christmas in this way too.*

Lily had also stopped eating. She and Isabel exchanged glances, and Isabel could tell that her roommate was thinking about home as well.

I wish I didn't feel guilty so often when I enjoy what the school gives me. Isabel took a gulp of creamy milk and set down her glass. *But I can't help thinking about Father and Jeremy's cold, hard Christmas at the reservation. They won't have a beautiful Christmas tree and a sumptuous dinner.*

At the end of the meal the servers took away the empty plates and dishes and brought out dessert platters. "Bananas and mince pie!" Frances clapped.

"Frances, you're practically wailing," Lily said, laughing.

"These desserts are worth wailing about," Frances replied. "The whole meal deserves at least a scream. Who cares if I get put in the guardhouse for bad manners?"

Lily looked so alarmed that Isabel began to laugh. "She's joking, Lily." A server had put an enormous piece of the mince pie in front of her. Isabel put a bite of the sweet, tangy pie in her mouth and closed her eyes in bliss.

After the three girls had downed dessert to the last crumb, Lily reached under her stool. "I have something for both of my room-mates," she said, smiling. She handed Frances and Isabel each a flat package. Isabel's was wrapped in red tissue paper and Frances's in green, and a jaunty matching bow adorned each package.

"I have something for both of you too," Isabel said, reaching under her own stool. She almost laughed at how clever she and Lily had been, sneaking the presents into the dining room under their coats and hiding them under the stools. *Wait till the girls see what I got them*, she thought happily. Several weeks ago, Isabel's father had sent her money to buy herself something nice for Christmas. She had been a bit surprised but touched since despite her father's stories of how rich he was, he always seemed so very poor. Isabel had used part of the money to buy material downtown in Carlisle. Then, after she finished her work at the dressmaking shop each afternoon, she had cut out and sewn each of her roommates a brand-new blouse and skirt. Lily's skirt was of brushed maroon cotton, and Frances's was russet corduroy. Isabel had trimmed each of the white cotton blouses with lace.

Lily's eyes widened with delight when Isabel handed her the thick package, wrapped in crackly green tissue paper. She care-fully slipped the ribbon off the package so as not to tear the paper. "Oh, Isabel!" she squealed, holding up the skirt and blouse. "I love these! They're the most beautiful clothes I've ever seen. Thank you so much!" She pressed the blouse against herself.

Frances hesitated, holding her package in both hands, then she set it on her lap. "I'm sorry . . . I don't have any presents to give you two," she said quietly. "I wasn't expecting anything—we never exchanged presents at home."

How could I be so thoughtless? Isabel scolded herself. *Lily and I have more means than Frances, and so of course she couldn't return our presents.* Lily sold paintings and drawings through the school to townspeople. Even if Isabel's father hadn't sent her Christmas money, she knew she could have earned some by doing clothes alterations for the school employees or people in town. *Frances isn't so fortunate at turning her trade into money,* Isabel reminded herself.

Looking at Lily's face, Isabel could tell that she was concerned as well. Lily took Frances's hand. "Please don't worry about it, Frances," she said. "Just enjoy our presents to you—it's better to give than to receive."

"All right." Frances sighed, lifted her shoulders, and smiled. "Thank you both." She picked up Isabel's package and began to untie it.

Isabel opened her package from Lily. Inside was the most exquisite drawing she had ever seen of horses by a lily pond. The horses were in a realistic style and were looking at each other and off into the distance, as if they had just heard a sound. But they weren't frightened. *Perhaps their owner is simply calling them into the barn,* Isabel thought. "This is just lovely, Lily," she said. "Thank you! I'll put it on the wall in our room for now, then take it home this summer. It will remind me of you."

"Perfect!" Lily clapped. "That's exactly what I had in mind."

Frances held up her new skirt and blouse. "You've really gotten skilled at sewing, Isabel. Even I'll look pretty in these."

"Russet is a very good color for you." Isabel studied Frances, taking in her friend's laughing dark brown eyes, perfect complexion, and curly hair framing her face. "And you don't have to worry about being pretty, no matter what you wear," she added.

Frances smiled and squeezed Isabel's hand. "Thanks," she said. "It's nice every now and then to think I have brains *and* beauty—even if I don't believe it myself."

The teachers appeared by the doorways, and the students rose from their seats. Miss Hayes beckoned to Isabel, who walked over to her. "Please join me and the other Susans in my rooms for a quick Christmas celebration," Miss Hayes said.

Isabel hesitated and looked back. Frances and Lily were still over by their table. Frances was holding up her new blouse and skirt, and Lily was laughing at what Frances was saying. *I don't want my friends to feel left out*, Isabel thought.

Miss Hayes, seeing her expression, quickly added, "Don't worry, all the other students will be going to celebrations of their own, with other teachers and clubs."

Isabel smiled in relief. "I'd love to come," she said.

She walked out into the cold Christmas night with Miss Hayes. The moment they left the shoveled porch of the dining hall, Isabel felt her low boots sinking into several inches of freezing snow. Looking up, she saw the dark sky sprinkled with pale eastern stars that winked with their small arms, as if the stars were both watching the Christmas below and a part of it.

In Miss Hayes's softly lit rooms, Isabel sank into a plush armchair. A fire crackled in the grate, adding to the good cheer of the atmosphere.

"You are the first to arrive," Miss Hayes said, setting a log on the fire, then replacing the grate. She reached up on the mantel, then handed Isabel a package wrapped in plain brown paper with a silky white bow on top.

"*Another* present?" Isabel said in astonishment.

"Open it," Miss Hayes urged. "It's something you need very much."

Isabel undid the big cloth bow and slowly removed a small book from the wrapping.

"It's a journal—you can write down your thoughts and share them with your family when you get home," Miss Hayes said.

Isabel tentatively ran her fingers over the soft, buttery leather cover of the journal. *I have never owned anything so beautiful*, she thought. *This is just the most wonderful Christmas!* "Thank you so much, Miss Hayes," she said.

"You're very welcome." Miss Hayes looked at Isabel thoughtfully. "I hope you do fulfill your dream of someday becoming a teacher. You are one of my best and most promising students."

Isabel blushed and smiled. *That is the nicest compliment I have ever had*, she thought.

A knock at the door signaled the other Susans' arrival, and soon the rooms were full of talking, festive students.

"Isabel!" Emma cried, throwing her arms wide for a hug. "Merry Christmas!"

"And happy new year," Isabel replied, laughing.

The girls sat in a circle to enjoy eggnog, cookies, and conversation. After about an hour of fun, Isabel slipped away to her room. She sat on her bed, the new journal in her hands. Lily and Frances were still at their Christmas parties, so Isabel was alone. That, she realized, was unusual at Carlisle. Being alone was much more like her life had been on the reservation.

Isabel opened the journal to the first page. The white, blank paper was endless with possibilities.

Every day I will first put what the clouds did, she decided. She wrote:

Thin white clouds crisscrossed the sky today, like breath on a cold morning. The low winter sun barely rose above them, even in the afternoon, then sank with relief into them, turning them fiery at sunset. I now realize we have had several days of such clouds, and we may have many more. Winters are said to be long here. Already I am anxious for spring and its colorful flowers and warm temperatures.

Isabel set down her pen and rested her head in her hand. Lily had strung a streamer of shiny paper above the door, saying *Merry Christmas!* in green, silver, and red. It was a shorter version of the colors and styles of the decorations in the dining hall, and Isabel realized then that her roommate had been the mastermind behind those too.

She let her thoughts drift away from the school and her busy life, far across the wide country to the reservation, where she imagined a sole light twinkling. That was in the cabin where she'd lived with her mother. Her mother was waiting with a warm smile. She—Isabel broke off the thought.

Now she saw a cold, tattered tent on the hard ground, the whistling wind lifting its flaps and what was left of her family huddled, trying to stay warm.

Father and Jeremy, she thought wistfully. *I wonder how they spent Christmas?*

John trudged toward the reservation town as the short day ended and Christmas night approached. *The town does not look so bad from the mountain*, he thought. The snow was thick over the dirt roads and paths, and a layer of snow on the roofs of the buildings disguised their awkward shapes.

As he reached the edge of the town, he saw Earl Green, the worst of the reservation drunks, lurching across the main road. Earl tripped over a rut and almost fell but caught his balance and staggered on. Earl clutched an army canteen in one hand.

John knew better than to try to persuade him to go inside, despite the rapidly dropping temperature. *I thank the gods that I have never had to drink to forget my pain, either from old injuries or my sad thoughts. But I do understand it.* Although Earl's face was wrinkled and drooping, he was about the same age as John. Earl limped to an alley between two buildings and disappeared. John frowned. Probably Earl would lie down back there and pass out.

Jeremy had helped cut and bring down a Christmas tree, and John could see it through the window of one of the agency buildings, alight with candles and decorated with ornaments and silver streamers. Next to the tree, Jeremy stood with a cup in his hand, talking to several other young men and women. Jeremy laughed, then leaned forward and said something to his friend Harry, a boy about his age.

John smiled. *I am very glad that Jeremy is having a good time,* he thought. *Where does he get his happiness with life? Not from me.* Then he remembered that Maria had always been happy, even though their life outside the family was often hard and not good.

John hesitated. He still could not make himself go into that overheated, stuffy room, with all those illnesses lurking in the air and floorboards. But he also could not make himself return to his thin, freezing tent to spend the night alone while his bones ached from cold and loneliness. *Of course it is my fault that I have to stay alone*, he thought, feeling guilty. Jeremy was staying in town that winter with the Johnson family.

Snow began to fall, first in small spits, then in gusts. John looked up, suddenly very weary. *Don't get tired now*, he chided himself. Going to ride the horse today, on top of the trip he now had planned for tonight, had almost certainly been a mistake. John dropped his head and closed his eyes. He had a vision, not for the first time, of lying down on Maria's grave and falling asleep until he became part of the earth as she was. But he could not leave his children to deal with this difficult life themselves, especially since he had done it in the past. Maria would be very disappointed if he did it again.

John stood in the doorway of the agency building and beckoned to Jeremy. At last he got his attention. Jeremy came over, holding a cup of punch. He was still smiling from his last conversation. "I need to go get some money," John said.

"Where?" Jeremy asked, bending down to hear better over the conversations behind them. Suddenly he was much taller than his father. "It's Christmas—nobody's working."

"I'm going to the woods to get it." John gestured behind him.

"You're going now?" Jeremy asked. "In this?" He pointed to the sky, where thick snowflakes were slowly falling.

"I will be fine," John assured him.

"When will you be back?" Jeremy wrinkled his forehead.

"In a couple of days."

"But why?" Jeremy looked completely perplexed.

"I must pay for the horse." John tapped his foot. He knew

that he sounded not right in the head again, and he was trying to make Jeremy understand, but at the same time he could feel an almost physical pull from outside, urging him to go.

"Oh. You're going to—"

"Shhh!" John looked nervously around. But the laughing, talking people in the crowded room weren't paying them any attention until skinny Joan Lambert, a distant relative of theirs, called, "Shut the door!"

"You should not try this," Jeremy said, frowning as he closed the door. "You must know the storm is going to get worse."

"I have to go." John looked at his son's concerned face, but the need to go on this journey was too strong for him to resist. "Jeremy—" John lightly touched his son's shoulder. "One more thing. Please gather some of your friends and lift Earl out of the alley next door."

Jeremy nodded. As John left, he was gratified to see that Jeremy was already walking toward two of his stockier friends. They would rescue Earl right away.

John walked back down the snow-dusted main road of the reservation. He glanced up at the sky, which was almost completely black now and spilling snowflakes in thick gusts of wind. The cold was increasing as night fell and had a sharp edge. John breathed deeply, feeling the winter air scald his lungs. *I have been in worse weather*, he consoled himself.

At the edge of the reservation land, he headed southwest. The storm winds were coming almost straight from the west and helped him find the way. He settled into a steady pace of walking, careful that the wind did not blow him off course. The snow was not deep, and although he occasionally slipped on the layer of ice, the hardness of the ground made for better walking. He began to feel good, as he always did when he was taking action.

I will get this silver, then I will do more good with it than buy the horse, he told himself. *I need to put my children in a warm house with me. I will get enough silver to do that, although not too much, so that people aren't suspicious.*

John shivered. How could he have made Jeremy and Isabel live in ragged tents? That should have nothing to do with his grief over his wife's death. "I know that I have done wrong, Maria," he said. "But I will make it right—I will get us back in a house before Isabel returns."

The wind rattled the trees and seemed to rattle even his bones. Accusing spirits took shape in the whirlwinds of snow that spun out of the dark sky. *Perhaps Christmas is causing them,* John thought. *Certainly the missionaries have told all the Apaches often enough that Christmas is a time of spirits.*

The spirits and cold were making him sleepy. John shook his head, hard. He needed not to listen so much to spirits. "Even you, Maria, although you will always be with me, belong in the ground—I cannot live in a dream," he said, addressing the black sky. "The dreams keep me from working and acting as I should. I need to change my ways so that Isabel will be happy here."

The wind whipped his face brutally, stinging it with snow. John undid his headband and tried to wrap it around his face without stopping.

Jeremy was right—I should not have tried this, he thought, bowing his head as he fought through the storm. John's legs were tiring, and the sleepiness kept returning. *It is too cold, and I am an old man. Now I have said it to myself—I cannot walk for days in the snow and cold the way I did when I was young. I must begin to accept the truth. Once I do that, I can live right again. I must not die from old truths and leave my children alone.*

"Things are not simple, though," he said aloud, with difficulty moving his numb lips and keeping his mind thinking. "I am not acting completely recklessly. I am too old to be getting money in a snowstorm, but it is necessary to have money to own a horse or a house, and the only money I have is out here."

He had been Jeremy's age when he had hidden the silver under a tree, his last act before the soldiers had bound him in chains and taken him to the reservation. Although half of the silver was Robert's, Robert had not used much of it over the years because he was afraid the agent would find out he had been an outlaw. Besides, he was a very successful businessman and had no need to dig under trees for silver to make ends meet.

John's toes dragged through the snow, and he realized he was barely moving. *I am not going to make it to the silver*, he thought, with more annoyance than fear. He could feel his knees sinking into the snow. *Truly my life is over. So simply, as if I had been shot through the heart in battle. But because I have no pain, perhaps my death is that of an old man, sliding into a final sleep.*

He fell, his hands outstretched. They touched the rough bark of a tree and slipped down it to an opening. The bottom of the tree was hollow. John dragged himself in and with difficulty undid the blanket roll on his back. Slowly he wrapped himself in the blanket, dropping his head onto his arms. Oddly, he seemed to feel not only the tree around him. He had come to such a place, marked by a protecting tree, the last time he had ridden Moon That Flies, the last time he had touched his special horse. He felt he was touching Moon That Flies now—not just the horse's spirit but in some way his warm, very real self. *I do not think death could ever touch you, my horse*, he thought.

John jerked up his head. He did not want to fall into some fantasy of the cold, imagining that his beloved horse was near him again. But although he shook his head again and again, the presence stayed.

All right, he thought, moving closer to his horse until his soft breath was nearly upon him. *You really are here, in whatever way this is.* John smiled. *Isabel and Jeremy would never believe me, and so I will never tell them this story of how my old horse came to me and saved me this night. But I can give Isabel a horse that will be just as magical for her.*

John curled up to sleep, letting his eyes close. *The miracles in my life are not yet over*, he thought.

13

The clouds are most unsatisfactory at Carlisle, Isabel wrote in her journal.

> *They coat the entire sky, and I can't make sense out of them that way. Spring approaches, but even so, today's clouds are white and featureless, hiding the blue that must be underneath. Here in Pennsylvania it's blue sky that is a mystery, since the sky is seldom clearly seen. That is very unlike Mescalero, where the clouds pile on each other in just one part of the sky and are discreet. There they make towering, dramatic thunderheads. Carlisle can so often be a world of fog, covered ground to sky with a soft wool coat of gray.*

Isabel glanced up. She had carried her study chair from her room to the porch on her floor of the dormitory, hoping that as she wrote her cloud log, she would catch an early spring breeze, tinged with the scent of melting snow and damp earth. The days were getting longer, and so she had a bit of time in the daylight between getting off work at the dressmaking shop and dinner. The big grassy rectangle before her, between the school buildings, was mostly empty since the other students were in their rooms, getting ready to go to dinner. Isabel could see the gleam of new grass striping last year's brown with the life of this spring.

But I must not forget that the rain is kind here, she went on.

It comes down gently, sinking into the ground as if it wants to help the earth create new, shining green plants. The many buildings on the school grounds and in town turn slick and gleam after their wash in the rain. On the reservation, the great rains come only in the summer and are torrents of water blown in sheets by the wind. Those rains flatten the fields of corn and break branches off the cottonwood trees. So much water has nowhere to sink and carves new arroyos in the flat land and shoots across the ground. The rain makes little arroyos by the tents and other homes, sometimes flooding them with muddy cold water.

The door to the porch opened and Lily looked out, an eager expression on her face. "Miss De Cora has invited all the students in her art class to walk with her," she said excitedly. "Can you come, Isabel?"

"Of course." Isabel smiled at her roommate and got up. "It's a lovely afternoon for a walk. Just let me put my chair back in the room."

"I'll meet you downstairs." Lily disappeared from the doorway.

Isabel set her chair back in the girls' room and hurried down the stairs. *I hope Miss De Cora doesn't single out my bad artwork on this walk*, she thought. Isabel had barely spoken to Miss De Cora, the new art teacher, in class because she hadn't wanted to draw the teacher's attention to her still faulty artwork. *Lily tries to help me, but to be honest, the vases and fruit in my still lifes are always lumpy and off center, and my animals are strange creatures that look as if I got them out of a nightmare*, Isabel remembered. She hoped Miss De Cora wasn't the kind of teacher who criticized even outside the classroom.

On the lawn, Lily and five other girls were waiting with Miss De Cora. "Hello, Isabel," the teacher greeted. "Let's walk around the school grounds, girls. Probably that is all we have time for before dinner."

"Hello, Miss De Cora," Isabel said politely. She looked curiously at the young teacher as they started their walk. Miss De Cora, who was college educated, had announced to the class that she wanted to teach the Carlisle students Indian styles of artwork. "They don't learn the native skills at home anymore," Isabel had overheard her say to one of the other teachers in the doorway to the classroom. "Although, of course, Lily did." Miss De Cora had smiled at her prize pupil as Lily took her seat that day. Most of the students had struggled with the new styles of artwork, but Lily had immediately taken to them and could already weave a passable wool rug with a bold native pattern.

Across the lawn, Isabel saw Thomas, limping badly on his left foot, where he was missing most of his toes. Albert walked slowly beside him. Both boys waved, and the group of girls waved back. Isabel felt a soft glow just at the sight of Albert. *Stop that*, she told herself. *I hope I'm not blushing.* Albert had thanked her for getting the other students to stop snubbing him—once they saw Isabel talking to Albert again, they had followed suit. *Really, everyone is just forgetting about the runaway episode*, Isabel thought, smiling at Albert. *People don't like to stay angry here— they have better things to think about.*

"There's Frances!" Lily cheered, pointing to their roommate. Frances walked toward them but slowly, so finally Isabel and Lily stopped to wait for her.

"Come on, Frances!" Lily called. "We want to stroll with our other roommate."

"I'm just going up to the room. I needed a break from all that commotion in the print shop," Frances said, rubbing her forehead.

Lily and Isabel looked at her in surprise. "Since when?" Isabel asked.

"That's a first," Lily chimed in. "Are you well?"

"Sure." Frances shook her head, her curls flying. "I just have a bit of a headache."

"Maybe you do need some fresh air," Lily suggested. "Come on our walk, Frances."

"Well . . . okay." Frances sighed. "This is good for me, right? We're taking a constitutional."

"Right," Lily said firmly.

"Welcome, Frances," Miss De Cora greeted. Isabel couldn't help thinking that if Miss De Cora chose to criticize one of her art students, Frances was the only student worse at art than Isabel was and so would bear the brunt of the teacher's wrath. But Miss De Cora only smiled warmly at Frances and walked on, continuing her conversation with Ivy, one of the younger girls in their art class.

Isabel looked around for Frances to tell her they should probably try not to draw attention to themselves. To her surprise, she saw that the other girl was lagging behind again. *Perhaps Frances had the same idea*, Isabel thought, dropping back to join her.

"Hurry up, Frances," Lily chided, also slowing to walk with them. "What are you doing?"

Frances stopped and drew a deep breath. "I'm just looking at the crocuses coming up," she replied.

"But they aren't coming up yet." Lily looked at Frances quizzically.

"Well, I thought they might be." Frances rubbed her forehead again. "Major Mercer says we must plant flowers when we are back at the reservations to beautify them."

"Right, in the mud that's everywhere at home." Isabel sighed. "I'll keep it in mind."

"I'll plant flowers when I go home this summer," Lily said

seriously. "I'll make a special flowerbed, with a rock border. My grandfather will help me tend it and will take care of it when I return to school in the fall."

"I don't think any flowers I planted would live long," Isabel said shortly. She had a sudden vision of Earl, the sad old drunk who was always coming around their tents because her father was kind to him. *Earl would stomp my pretty flowers right into the ground*, she knew. *Besides, the heavy summer rains would wash a garden away unless I put it on high ground. But the only high ground nearby is the cemetery.* Isabel had no intention of going near *that* place.

"Will you plant flowers this summer, Frances?" Lily asked.

"I might." Frances touched her sleeve to her face. "This walk is getting me overheated. I guess I should spend less time in the print shop and more time getting fit, playing basketball."

Isabel waited for Frances to make a joke about Mr. Carter, Lily's basketball coach, but Frances remained uncharacteristically silent. Glancing at her, Isabel thought that Frances did look a little pale, despite the bloom of fresh color in the other girls' cheeks. *We must definitely get her out more often*, Isabel vowed.

After their walk, Isabel went to dinner, then back to her room to do homework. She had a big paper to finish in two weeks, comparing the images of travel in William Wordsworth's poetry with those in Tennyson. Isabel opened her Tennyson book, settled the pages with her notes next to the book, and picked up her pen.

A rattling sound startled her. Isabel half rose out of her chair, then saw that the window was ajar and had caught a blast of wind. She crossed the room to the window and pulled it shut, fastening the latch. The moon had set, hiding the lawn in heavy darkness. *Where are Frances and Lily?* she wondered uneasily. *It's quite late.*

Isabel sat back down at the table. Despite the bright electric light, the room seemed full of shadows all over the walls and the ceiling. *Maybe Frances is working late or playing basketball or something*, she thought, resting her chin in her cupped hands. *But that doesn't account for Lily.* Isabel continued with her work, but she found herself glancing at the clock every few minutes.

Finally, at nearly eleven, Lily walked into the room.

"There you are!" Isabel said with relief. "Where have you been?"

Lily slowly took off her scarf and coat and hung them on the peg behind the door. Then she dropped down on her bed and burst into tears.

"What's wrong?" Isabel asked, alarmed.

Lily shook her head and finally looked up. Her eyes were red rimmed, and tears flowed down her pretty face. "It's Frances," she said. "She's in the hospital."

"The hospital?" Isabel repeated, dumbfounded. Frances was never sick. "How . . . what happened? Did she get hurt?"

"No, she's very ill—she has rheumatic fever." Lily buried her face in her hands.

Isabel rose slowly from her chair, gripping the table's edge. She saw Frances's laughing, lively face, then what she imagined the hospital looked like, with very sick people lying torpid in beds. *How can Frances be in that place of illness and death?* she thought. The conversation didn't seem possible to her, although she could tell from the tone of Lily's voice that it was very real.

Isabel sat next to Lily on the bed and looked at her. "How bad is Frances?" she made herself ask.

"Very bad. Many people are sick and in the hospital with rheumatic fever right now, but except for one of the teachers' children, Frances is the worst off." Lily rubbed her eyes, blinked, and rubbed them again. "I'm going back over to the hospital as soon as I change into my uniform. I'll probably spend the night there."

"Don't get sick yourself!" Isabel said. *Frances can't be so very sick*, she thought. *The Carlisle school isn't a place where people die— that's what happens on the reservation.*

"I won't get sick." Lily managed a wan smile. "I'm a trained nurse, remember?"

"Good. I'm sure Frances will be fine." Isabel could hear how flat her voice was.

"I don't know. Oh, Isabel, I'm so worried." Lily wrung her hands, then stood. "I'll let you know what I find out," she said, sounding determined.

"Frances is lucky to have you," Isabel said, and at least that sounded like her real voice.

She watched Lily dash out of the room. *Lily is so kind,* Isabel thought, tears pressing at the backs of her eyes. She closed her eyes, willing the tears away. *Lily didn't even ask me to come along because she knows I can't bear hospitals. But Frances is so strong, she'll be all right.* Isabel sank slowly down onto the floor, her back against her bed, and clutched her hair in her hands.

The next day a new storm was moving in. Isabel stopped in the middle of the lawn, looked straight up, and checked the clouds. She opened her journal to a fresh page and wrote:

> *The clouds are gray this morning and completely cover the sky except to the west. There a faint, pale blue stripe tries to break through. But because this is Pennsylvania, the black-bottomed clouds to the south are moving toward me, and I think they will win the battle of the weather. In moments, the clouds will burst with rain. So that is all I will write for now—I must get inside before my journal gets wet and loses all its memories when the ink runs.*

Lily hadn't come back last night, and Isabel had barely slept, praying the door to the room would open. *But Lily said many patients are very ill right now,* Isabel argued with herself. *No doubt she's taking care of those people.*

To Isabel's left, the students were walking through the academic building for their second class of the day. Automatically, Isabel turned to follow them. *Frances,* she thought suddenly. *I need to go see her now.* The voice was so clear in her head, it was as if someone had spoken.

Isabel hesitated. She would have to cut English class to see

Frances, and she had never cut a single class before. *It will be all right*, she decided. *I'll explain to Miss Hayes.*

Isabel walked quickly in the direction of the hospital, then began to run. *Why do I feel that I have to do this now?* she wondered. *Maybe I just know Frances needs a little encouragement.*

Isabel stopped abruptly in front of the hospital building. It looked quite ordinary, like a smaller version of the girls' dorm, with a porch along the entire second story and a long window for each room. Trees, still without their spring leaves, grew close to the front of the building. A few of the nurses and a patient wearing a long gown stood on the second-story porch.

Isabel shook her head. "I just can't go in there," she murmured. "Everyone is sick or dying behind that door."

What if Frances needs me? the voice in her head asked. Isabel walked slowly to the door and opened it. No matter what awaited her, she had to see her friend.

Inside, the hospital smelled clean and of medicine. Isabel remembered that Lily had said she worked in the women's ward on the second floor and climbed the stairs, trying to be very quiet.

The beds in the women's ward were in a long row. Isabel walked past each bed, looking for Frances. Four other girls and a woman were in the ward, and none of them looked very sick. They were reading books or talking in low voices to friends sitting in chairs beside their beds.

In the last bed in the row Isabel found Frances. *Oh, dear God*, she thought, almost sinking to her knees. Frances had only been in the hospital for two days, but she already seemed thin under the white blanket, and her curls were stuck to her sweaty forehead. Lily was asleep in a chair beside her. Black circles ringed her eyes.

Frances was awake and waggled her fingers. "Sit," she said softly, motioning to the sleeping Lily. "It's good to see you, Isabel. But you're not supposed to be here—you might get sick too. The rheumatic fever patients are quarantined."

"I'm more worried about cutting class than getting a fever." Isabel sat gingerly on the bed, trying not to jog Frances and taking time to arrange her skirt—and her expression, she hoped. "How are you?" she asked.

"Very hot," Frances answered. She seemed to be having trouble breathing. "I'm . . . glad you came. I know you don't like hospitals."

"Well, I just thought I would see how you were doing." Isabel tried to sound cheerful. She doubted that she did—she didn't have Lily's perfect nurse personality. "Can I bring you anything? I have chocolates in our room. I've been saving them since Christmas for a special occasion, and I'm sure they're still good."

Frances tried to smile, but it faded almost immediately. "I'm not hungry," she said. "Do you believe it? For once."

Isabel felt a quick rush of panic but covered it by speaking quickly. "That's all right. We'll eat the chocolates when you get back to the room. I'm sure that will be soon—maybe even tomorrow."

Frances shook her head. "Isabel . . ." she began. "You are my dearest friend."

Isabel swallowed hard and blinked. "Thanks, but—"

Frances held up a hand. "I don't want to talk about this either, but I need to ask you . . . Will you write to my parents?"

Isabel knew the thin layer of false cheer on her face was breaking into a million pieces. She touched her forehead to Frances's hand so that her roommate wouldn't see her expression. "Don't be foolish. I can't write Sioux—and I don't have the least reason to write to your parents anyway."

"Write in English," Frances whispered. "We both know why you must write." Frances stopped to cough. Isabel covered Frances's hot, damp hand with both of her own and waited until Frances could speak again. "Say in the letter that I worked hard at school and never forgot my parents and brothers. And say . . ." For the first time, Isabel saw the shine of tears in the other girl's eyes. "Say that I died among my good and trusted friends who I loved so."

Isabel could barely hold back her own tears. She squeezed Frances's hand tight, and her dear friend squeezed back. *Don't let go and leave me,* Isabel thought desperately. *Not for that awful place of darkness and cold.* Clinging to Frances's hand, Isabel prayed she could somehow hold the life in it.

"Don't worry, Isabel." Frances's grip was failing, but she managed to press Isabel's hand gently once more. "You always worry too much." Frances sighed and turned her head slightly toward the wall. She didn't speak again.

So many people, Isabel thought. The crowd stood close in front of her at Frances's funeral two days later. Isabel stood at the very back, where she couldn't see the freshly dug earth and the smooth silver coffin that had passed her on its way to the cemetery from the church in town. Mr. Bryson from the print shop, the three runaway boys Frank, Albert, and Thomas, and Frances's cousins Sam and Phillip had carried it to the cemetery after a hearse had brought the coffin back to the school. *I think all the students must be here,* Isabel thought. *We're supposed to be here to show respect, but I know we would all have come anyway. Frances was much admired.*

One speaker after another stepped behind the coffin and took a turn remembering Frances. Isabel learned that her roommate had always done a kindness for her fellow students whenever she could. One boy said that Frances had worked two jobs at the print shop so that he could be sure to keep his job when he had to take an extended leave to care for a sick parent on the reservation. Mrs. Dawson, the French teacher, told how Frances had volunteered at a church in town helping the unfortunate. The story that surprised Isabel the most was Charlotte Steton's. Charlotte was fourteen, a year younger than Isabel. Frances had counseled Charlotte when a boy had broken her heart and she threatened to kill herself. Charlotte wept openly as she described Frances's sympathy and wise words.

The references to Frances in the past tense and the nearby dreadful burying ground made Isabel's knees shake. Isabel tried to compose herself because she knew that in a moment, she must speak for Frances. Mr. Bryson had put her on the list of speakers, and anyway, Frances would have wanted her to talk for her. *She never did keep anything to herself,* Isabel thought, smiling wanly. *I'm very sorry she couldn't read the splendid tribute to her in the* Arrow. *She would have enjoyed it immensely.*

Isabel bent her head back and looked at the sky. *This is no day for a funeral,* she thought sadly. The storm that had blown sheets of rain on the day of Frances's death had swept through, and this soft, gentle spring morning shed its grace over the funeral. Isabel blinked at the clear, sweet call of a bird. *How can Frances miss that lovely sound?* she wondered. *She also missed apple pie at dinner last night, her very favorite dessert. Will I begrudge any goodness and beauty for the rest of my life because Frances isn't here to see it?*

"Isabel, would you like to speak?" Major Mercer looked up from the list of names.

Isabel simply couldn't make herself step forward. *This is the weight of sorrow,* she thought. *It's not so much a physical weight as the weight of trying to find a reason to move.*

She caught Albert's gaze. He stood next to the coffin with the other pallbearers. Albert nodded firmly, and Isabel managed to make her way through the mourners to his side. She didn't look at the waiting grave or the coffin in front of her but out at the circle of faces. "I shall read a poem for Frances," she said, and cleared her throat. "It's called 'I Wander in Darkness and Sorrow,' by Alfred, Lord Tennyson."

> *I heed not the blasts that sweep o'er me,*
> *I blame not the tempests of night;*
> *They are not the foes who have banish'd*
> *The visions of youthful delight:*
> *I hail the wild sound of their raving,*
> *Their merciless presence I greet;*
> *Though the roar of the wind be around me,*
> *The leaves of the year at my feet.*

In this waste of existence, for solace,
On whom shall my lone spirit call?
Shall I fly to the friends of my bosom?
My God! I have buried them all!
They are dead, they are gone, they are cold,
My embraces no longer they meet;
Let the roar of the wind be around me,
The leaves of the year at my feet!

Several of the students sobbed into handkerchiefs. "Thank you, Isabel," Major Mercer said softly. He looked gray, sad, and tired. The thought crept into Isabel's numb brain that he felt very bad indeed. She knew that the headmaster regarded all the students as his children and responsibility. His letter to Frances's family would be as difficult for him to write as hers.

Isabel stood very still as the other mourners began to leave the cemetery. *This is my first time in one of these places,* she thought. Vaguely she registered that the other people were dispersing in all different directions, as if they were setting out on trips into the wide world and were never coming back. Isabel wanted to leave the cemetery too, but her feet and thoughts seemed stuck in the mud surrounding Frances's grave.

"I miss her already."

Isabel jerked her head in the direction of the voice and saw Albert still standing next to her. "I do too," she said after a moment. *That really says it all, doesn't it?* she thought.

"She always talked about starting a newspaper back home," Albert said.

"I know." Isabel could hear her voice going flat again.

"Maybe I'll start her newspaper." Albert kicked the soft ground near the grave with his boot, and clods of dirt went flying. "Maybe. I mean, I guess I've known her longer than anyone else here. Maybe I'm supposed to start that newspaper for her."

"You knew Frances on the reservation?" Isabel was surprised. "Why didn't either of you ever mention it?"

Albert shrugged. "I didn't know her very well. I'm an orphan, and I lived by myself. I was the reservation teacher's servant, so I helped him all the time."

"Well . . . if you started a newspaper on the reservation, that would please Frances more than anything," Isabel said. "I'm quite sure of that."

"I think so too. But I'm not so steady as Frances was," Albert said quietly. "That's one reason I didn't know her well back home. She was much the same there as she was here, kind and serious. I was often in trouble—not terrible trouble, but I didn't obey the rules. So I don't know if I can really start a newspaper."

"Maybe you'll become steadier when you get home," Isabel said. She knew Frances would have said she sounded like Major Mercer, and at any other time the thought would have made her laugh, but Isabel meant what she said.

Albert touched her shoulder. Walking close together, they headed toward the classrooms. *I suppose it's better to think about mathematics than death*, Isabel thought. *Now I just have to try to do it.*

That night, Isabel reached for the library book on horses she had put on the top shelf in her room.

"What are you doing?" Lily asked. Her voice trembled.

Isabel looked over at her roommate, who sat at their table, the usual homework papers and books spread out around her. "I'm looking up the colors of Standardbreds," she said. "I've been meaning to do that for a while."

Lily was silent. Without wanting to look at Frances's empty bed, Isabel felt her eyes drawn there. Mrs. Jordan, the history teacher, had told them it would be taken away tomorrow. Next fall it would be given to a new girl. *At least we aren't getting a new roommate right away*, Isabel thought. *I don't think we would be able to treat her very well. But I guess the school authorities know that.*

Lily's face was so sad that Isabel could hardly stand to look at her either. "You know, it's very selfish of me, but I'm glad Frances is buried here at school," Lily said. "She would have wanted to be buried at home, but now we can visit her—it's like she won't ever really leave us."

Isabel nodded because she was sure Lily needed her to agree and not be inconsolable. *But I don't feel that way at all,* she thought. *When someone dies, it's as if a light is turned off and the switch is smashed with a rock. That person is gone, and nothing is left but a dreadful grave surrounded by other dreadful graves. I don't know how people can consider cemeteries places of peace.*

"Don't you want to write Frances's parents that letter tonight?" Lily asked. "Then they will receive it along with the letter from the school—Major Mercer will certainly mail his tomorrow."

Isabel sat down at the table across from Lily. She reached for her journal and carefully ripped out the last sheet.

"I have some fine art paper," Lily said.

"No, I want to use this." Isabel picked up her pen. Lily nodded, and her lips quivered.

For a moment Isabel's hand hovered over the page. Then she wrote:

> *Dear Mr. and Mrs. Twiss,*
> *I was a friend and roommate of your daughter, Frances, and so was Lily Monroe. I only want to say how sorry we are about Frances. She was always brave and cheerful, and she missed you very much. We were with her all along, and her last thoughts were of you. She inspired many people at this school, and Lily and I are glad we knew her as long as we did. We will never forget her.*
> *We loved her.*
>
> *Sincerely,*
> *Isabel Chavez*

Lily looked over Isabel's shoulder. "I will draw some horses on the letter," she said softly.

Isabel pushed back her chair and picked up the letter. She handed it to Lily, splashed with a solitary tear.

"Yes," she said. "Draw some horses for Frances."

Go to sleep, Isabel ordered herself later that night, pulling her blanket more tightly around herself. *If you don't, you won't be able to stay awake tomorrow in class and at work.* She turned onto her back and stared at the dark ceiling, trying to shut off her mind. *They buried Frances in the skirt and blouse I made her for Christmas.* Isabel sat abruptly upright. She knew sleep would be impossible tonight.

Isabel pushed off the covers and walked to the window. A tilting half-moon traveled across the darkness. Isabel pressed her palm to the glass, feeling the damp chill seep through it, and wondered if Frances was cold. "Of course not," she whispered.

"Frances has gone to a better place," the pastor had said at the service this morning. Isabel sighed. *How does he know?* she wondered. *People always say that when someone dies, so maybe it's true.* But it didn't feel true. Frances didn't seem to have gone anywhere. She was just gone.

The tears Isabel was trying so hard to hold back hurt her head. *What if Frances is cold? What if my mother is cold too?* she thought desperately. *But I can't do anything about it. I may feel like screaming or sobbing or throwing something, but that won't change the fact that Mother and Frances are dead. How am I supposed to believe that they're waiting for me in heaven or traveling the world as ghosts? But how can so much goodness be only a cold stone on a pile of earth?*

Isabel reached into the wardrobe for a dress and rapidly buttoned it, then slipped on her shoes. *I'm going to go see Frances*, she told herself. *She can't really be gone. If she's anywhere, it's in that cemetery.*

Lily slept, the moonlight showing the shadows under her eyes. *Poor Lily is so tired—I can't wake her to visit Frances*, Isabel decided. *Besides, I don't think Lily needs to come with me. She has said goodbye.*

Isabel made sure to put on her coat and wrap her scarf snugly around her neck before heading outside. "I shouldn't act too crazy," she whispered. "There's no point in running to the grave not properly dressed and getting sick too."

Stepping through the door into the night, Isabel looked around. No one else was outside. "Just the moon and Frances," she murmured, and shivered. *The moon takes the place of the sun when it's gone at night.* "But who takes the place of the dead?" she asked aloud.

The damp grass soaked her shoes as she walked across the lawn toward the cemetery, but Isabel was beyond caring if it made her sick. She forced herself not to break into a run. *What will I find out here?* she wondered. *Frances or utter emptiness?* In Isabel's mind, her roommate's animated face lit up with joy as she shared a joke, and her mother's sweet eyes shone with that gentle, special love they always did when she looked at her daughter, comforting and encouraging her. "Where are you?" Isabel whispered.

Just ahead, she could see the tombstones sticking up in the cemetery, gleaming white and gray in the dim light. Frances's grave stood out, the raw dirt piled high. Isabel stopped walking, filled with utter dread. "I'm so afraid, Mother." She could barely form the words.

Although her mother didn't reply, Isabel forced herself to go on. She hesitated again at the edge of the cemetery. *I'll have to step over dead people to be with Frances!* she thought. *But . . . are they the same as her? Stop it! Just do this!*

Trying to take as few steps as possible, Isabel crossed three rows of graves and stood before the mound that was Frances. Since this morning, someone had placed a headstone. Even in the moonlight, Isabel could easily read the big words on it:

〰

FRANCES TWISS

1891–1906

Friend and Good Printer

〰

How did the boys in the print shop find such silly, true words to put on the headstone? And those words are finally breaking my heart. Isabel fell to her knees beside her friend's grave. "Oh, Frances," she murmured.

The soft ground sank under her knees, as if it would pull her down. Isabel touched the chilled, disturbed earth with a shaking hand. "Are you there, Frances?" she whispered. "Can you hear me? Please, please don't leave me."

The grave remained silent. "You get to rest in peace, but I can't live that way," Isabel sobbed. "Frances, come back!"

Isabel threw herself across the grave, grasping fistfuls of dirt. "Stay with me," she begged, resting her cheek on the ground. "But it's too late, isn't it?" Tears streamed down her face. She knew she would never stop crying for Frances and her mother and most of all for herself—she had loved them but been left behind with no answers.

Maybe hours had gone by or only minutes before Isabel felt a hand on her shoulder. "Come, Isabel," Miss Hayes said gently. "The ground and air are damp. You must not stay out here."

"I had to see Frances," Isabel whispered, sitting back on her heels. "She's all alone . . ."

"Frances is all right," Miss Hayes said firmly. "She does not feel this."

"But that's so wrong too . . . she used to feel everything." Isabel wiped her eyes, trying to stop crying.

Holding out her hand, Miss Hayes leaned over the grave. Isabel reached up and took the teacher's blessedly warm fingers. "We cannot believe Frances is truly gone," Miss Hayes said quietly. "We will see her as the flowers bloom in the spring and the sun sets in a glorious blaze and the skaters laugh at the pond. Now she will watch over you."

The teacher pulled Isabel tightly to her, and Isabel hugged her back. "And we will watch over each other," Miss Hayes said.

PART III

"THE SUPREME AMERICANIZER":
THE OUTING SYSTEM AT CARLISLE,
SPRING 1906

14

Today we are to get a Carlisle girl, Jennifer wrote in her diary. *I know that all of us who live near the Indian School are expected to treat the Carlisle students kindly, but that is different from having one live in your bedroom. I am sorry, Mother, but that is the last thing I need.*

Jennifer sat up straight on her bed and looked out the rain-battered window. Spring seemed to be coming early this year. It was only Valentine's Day, but a chilly, not quite freezing wind was blowing across the farm, bringing the first thaw. The icicles hanging from the barn eaves dripped steadily into flashing rows of puddles, mirroring the sun.

Jennifer looked back down at her diary entry. *Maybe I shouldn't have written that,* she thought. *Now the Indian girl's arrival seems more real than ever.* With a sigh, she remembered her mother's unwelcome announcement last night at supper.

"A little Indian girl will be coming to stay with us for a month or so," Mrs. Schmidt had said, right when Jennifer was starting to eat a delicious, creamy piece of cheesecake for dessert. "Her name is Isabel Chavez."

"Why is she coming here?" Jennifer had asked, too shocked to put the fork in her mouth.

"To work," her mother replied. "The Carlisle school sometimes sends Indian children to people's homes to work and to learn our ways."

"You'll get the sister that you always wanted." Benjamin smirked.

"I never wanted a sister." Jennifer scowled at her brother. "Please, Mother, this isn't a good idea."

"Why not?" her mother asked. "You're always complaining about having too many chores to do. This girl will help you."

"She might even be able to help with the horses," her father interjected. "Don't Indians ride Indian ponies?"

"I have no idea." Jennifer stared at her father in dismay. "I'm quite sure they don't ride Standardbreds."

"She'll learn," Mr. Schmidt said comfortably, taking a big bite of cheesecake. He appeared to have no idea what a disaster this was.

"Where is she going to sleep?" Jennifer asked, her voice rising. She had a horrible feeling she already knew the answer.

"On the extra bed in your room," her mother had said. "Jennifer, please don't be so difficult."

At that point Jennifer had retreated to her room—the last night it would be hers!—and read Jane Austin's novel *Sense and Sensibility* until almost three in the morning. She had gotten up scarcely an hour later to milk the cows, but then she had returned to her bedroom. She realized her mother had not told her when the Indian girl would arrive today.

Well, I'm not going to hang around here waiting for her, Jennifer told herself, hopping up from her desk. *I'm going to be stuck with her quite enough, thank you. I'll saddle up Celebrity and go see what Dell thinks of all this.*

She grabbed her coat from the rack in the hall, mercifully not running into any of her family, and forced herself not to slam the front door behind herself.

Celebrity had not yet been sold, although Jennifer thought he was going better than any horse she had ever trained. *I'd like to keep him*, she thought as she walked to the horse barn. *I'm kind of tired of selling every horse just when I've got them trained. But even if I do sell him, Celebrity needs work in the rain first.* Celebrity, she had discovered, was not only afraid of puddles but of thunder, lightning, and even the approach of a storm, which he could sense extremely well.

As she entered the barn, Celebrity popped his head out over the stall half door. "Hi, boy," Jennifer said. "Want to go for a ride?"

The big horse eagerly reached for her with his nose as she haltered him. Jennifer gave him a slice of apple, then led him out of the stall and put him in crossties.

"I really don't want to sell you because you're so pretty," Jennifer said, smiling as she ran a finishing brush over Celebrity's glossy dark coat. "Plus you're fun to ride, if there's no storm or puddles, and you actually listen to me. Who else around here does?"

Jennifer rested the light English saddle and pad on Celebrity's back and tightened the girth. Celebrity looked around at her. "Can you believe what's happening?" Jennifer asked. "I'm going to be stuck with that girl day and night."

Celebrity nodded—but probably not because he agreed with her, Jennifer thought. He just wanted to get going. "You're right," she said. "Let's think about other things."

The trees were still bare, and the pale yellow sun shone strongly through their branches as Jennifer rode Celebrity out to the lane to Dell's house. The wind had died to a cool whisper, as if the spring sun had subdued it. "Nice day," Jennifer commented to her horse.

Celebrity tossed his head and broke into a slow trot, arching his neck and collecting well, with good contact on the bit. Although Jennifer hadn't asked for a trot, she let him keep going. "You can have opinions on what we do with our ride," she told him, leaning forward slightly to stroke his warm neck. She easily sat the faster gait, imagining what a handsome pair they made. People often commented on Jennifer's perfect seat on a horse.

As Jennifer rode up to Dell's house, she saw her friend out in the front yard with her mother and Susan, her oldest younger sister. Mrs. Whitman and Susan were pulling weeds from one of the gardens, and Dell was turning over dirt with a shovel.

"Hi, Jennifer!" Mrs. Whitman called, wiping her hands on her apron and waving.

Dell stuck her shovel in the soft ground and came over to Jennifer and Celebrity, with Susan following. "Hi," she said. "How about we go for a ride once I finish turning over one more row?"

"That sounds good." Jennifer swung out of the saddle.

"Can I go?" Susan asked, patting Celebrity's nose. "I could ride Barton."

"He's a plow horse, but I guess he's broke to ride." Dell looked at her little sister dubiously. "Barton's seventeen hands high, but he's gentle, I think. Since when do you like horses, Susan?"

Since always, Jennifer thought. Susan never missed a chance to be around the horses Jennifer rode to the Whitmans'.

Susan shrugged and kept rubbing Celebrity's nose. The horse bent his neck so that the little girl could reach his ears.

"We can't take you today," Dell said. "Jennifer and I need to talk."

Susan looked so disappointed, Jennifer added, "But we'll take you with us sometime. Or I will."

Susan beamed. "Really? Tomorrow?"

"Next week, or as soon as I can," Jennifer promised. "I'm going to be busy this week because I have to show the new Indian girl staying with us how to do chores."

"Okay!" Susan skipped back to the garden.

"Is that girl from the school coming today?" Dell asked, wrinkling her nose. "I know your mother's been saying it's a possibility."

"Yes." Jennifer sighed for what felt like the thousandth time this week. "You may not see me for a while. She's going to be a lot of work."

"I can't believe you're going to be stuck with her." Dell shook her head. "I mean, isn't she just some kind of charity case?"

"The worst kind. I don't think she can do anything—except whatever Indians do, and that won't help me on the farm," Jennifer said in exasperation. "I'm going to have to do all the chores while she stands around, and I'll have to feel sorry for her to boot. At least my mother is saying the girl will *only* be with us for a month."

"Well, that's something." Dell sighed too.

"Dell, finish up over here!" Mrs. Whitman called from the garden. "I can't do all this myself!"

"When is the baby due?" Jennifer whispered.

"Lord knows." Dell shrugged. "Pretty soon. Let's get out of here as soon as possible."

"I heard that." Mrs. Whitman tossed a handful of weeds into a big pile next to the garden. "Honey, I'm sorry, but I really need your help today. I don't think you can get away for a ride."

"Oh, wonderful," Dell grumbled. More softly, she said, "And when she has the baby, I'll have to help with that since I'm the oldest. Maybe you should ride with Susan."

Jennifer patted her friend's shoulder. "I really have to get back home. Don't worry, I won't be having fun either."

"Good luck." Dell rolled her eyes. "Hurry home," she added. "Looks like rain." She strode back to her garden work.

Swinging into Celebrity's saddle, Jennifer gathered the reins and trotted the horse onto the lane home. She caught herself starting to slump in the saddle in dismay at the thought of what she was facing there. "I'm going to be in so much trouble if I miss that girl's arrival," she muttered, forcing herself to sit up straight. "But for now, I need to keep my balance and stay on this horse. And if it rains—"

Jennifer glanced up at a rumble of thunder and felt Celebrity shiver under her. "Uh-oh," she said. "You're not going to like—"

The next second Celebrity spooked, lunging at the air with his front hooves. Jennifer was thrown backward until she was almost lying across Celebrity's rump. She hadn't lost her grip on the horse's sides with her legs, but she struggled to sit back up because Celebrity had burst into an uneven, wild gallop and was racing for the barn to escape the terrifying thunder. Jennifer finally jerked herself upright again in the saddle and pulled hard on the reins, yelling, "Whoa!"

Celebrity slowed a little, but just then a streak of lightning cracked the sky, and he tried to bolt again. Jennifer eased the reins back, pulling steadily, until she had him stopped. She could feel the horse violently trembling.

"Goodness, what was that all about?" she asked, loosening her grip on one rein to stroke Celebrity's tense neck. "You're so sensitive to electrical storms. I think all horses are, but you act as if the electricity shoots right through you. What a performance. Well, at least we're almost home, but this isn't how I wanted to get there."

Jennifer let Celebrity trot again, keeping a tight grip on him. He danced a bit sideways at the next thunder crack, but she was able to hang on to him.

As she rode her horse out of the woods, Jennifer saw a tall, slim girl, holding a travel valise, standing at the drive to the house. The buggy that had brought her was just returning to the main road.

Oh, no, Jennifer thought. *She's here.* She turned Celebrity around, then took him through the trees and into the horse barn the back way.

So this is the farm where I will do my outing, Isabel thought, setting down her valise on the gravel drive. *What a pretty place!* The drive went in front of a tall, white two-story farmhouse with green shutters. To the left was a huge red barn with a peaked roof, and behind it were acres of deep brown freshly plowed fields. A smaller, newer-looking red barn was to the right, close to the house. Isabel smiled, feeling much better than she had last night about the outing. *Miss Hayes did say that the farm was nice, but it's positively grand.*

Taking a deep breath, Isabel tried to prepare herself to meet her host family. Socializing was still difficult. Frances had been dead only a week, and Isabel had been unable to fill the emptiness in her heart. She had managed to be of good cheer outwardly, and so had Lily. But Miss Hayes hadn't been deceived, and Isabel knew the teacher was watching her closely. Two days ago, after English class, Miss Hayes had stopped Isabel to tell her that the Schmidt family wanted to host a student at their farm as part of the outing program at Carlisle. Most students participated in the program, where they lived with families in the surrounding area and learned housework or a trade.

Miss Hayes had already suggested Isabel to the Schmidts. Then she tried to talk Isabel into going. "I can't possibly," Isabel had said right away.

"Isabel, I really think a change of scene would be best for you," Miss Hayes said gently. "And because you will be returning to a rural community when you go home, you can learn much that is useful about farming and animals on this outing."

Isabel knew her favorite teacher was right; she just didn't think she had the strength to leave familiar people and surroundings right now, especially Lily. But Lily had been sure she should go too.

She and Lily had hugged tightly just before Isabel got in the buggy that would take her to the farm. "Take care of yourself," Lily whispered. "I'll see you when you get back."

"Yes, you will," Isabel said firmly, and because she could tell that she and Lily were about to cry, she turned immediately to Albert, who was also there to see her off.

"I may be gone when you get back," Albert said, running a hand through his short hair. "I have to go home to help plant the crops. But I'll be here again next fall."

Isabel was silent. *That is so very long*, she thought. *But of course he must help at home.* "Do you promise you'll be back?" she asked finally.

"I promise," Albert had said. He took both of her hands in his and squeezed them. His lips brushed hers, and then he stepped back to let her go.

Isabel startled as the door of the farmhouse opened, pulling her out of her thoughts. A pretty woman in her forties with her brown hair pulled back in a bun walked quickly toward her, smiling. "Isabel!" she said. "Hello, my dear."

Mrs. Schmidt smelled faintly of cinnamon and apples, and her clear gray eyes greeted Isabel as sweetly. Isabel found herself smiling back. "Hello," she said. "I'm very glad to be here." She made sure to be quick to talk. At the reservation, the agent and the missionaries expected Indians to speak up and not be shy. If they didn't, they were thought to be sullen or about to steal something.

Across the yard, Isabel saw a girl about her age leave one of the barns and walk toward them. Isabel had just seen the girl lead a horse into the back of the barn. She had an energetic, athletic stride that was a bit like an Apache's, Isabel thought. She was wearing trousers made of heavy blue denim and a work shirt.

"Jennifer, meet our new guest," Mrs. Schmidt said. "Isabel has just arrived from Carlisle."

The girl stepped forward. She had medium brown, shoulder-length hair and bangs, and her eyes were very light blue. "Hi, Isabel," she said. She smiled, but the smile dropped quickly from her face.

"I'm pleased to meet you," Isabel said formally. She wasn't deceived at all by Jennifer's false smile. *Why isn't this girl glad to see me?* she wondered. *I'm going to be her servant.* Then she realized she had seen Jennifer before. *She's that rude girl who stared at me so in the streets of Carlisle.*

"Jennifer will show you to your room," said Mrs. Schmidt. "Then come out to the kitchen, Isabel, so we can get acquainted. I have to start dinner—it's almost time to eat," she said with an annoyed look at her daughter that Isabel assumed had to do with an earlier quarrel. Mrs. Schmidt touched Isabel's shoulder and smiled again. "Come inside, Isabel," she said.

"Thank you. Your house is lovely," Isabel replied, and she meant it. Carlisle was neat and clean, but it looked like the public place that it was—almost like a military fort, with barracks and administration buildings. Isabel had never seen a big, beautiful, gracious home like this one. She could hardly wait to see the inside.

"How nice of you to say so." Mrs. Schmidt looked pleased.

Isabel picked up her valise and followed Mrs. Schmidt to the front door. *My outing is going to be quite pleasant,* she told herself. She could feel herself relaxing—until she turned to say this to Jennifer and caught the scowl on Jennifer's face. Her first impression of Jennifer had been correct. *She doesn't like me one bit,* Isabel realized.

Jennifer kept the stiff smile on her face as Isabel helped Mrs. Schmidt in the kitchen with dinner, even though Jennifer thought Isabel talked too much. Isabel didn't seem to know anything about cooking and asked many questions—but instead of being annoyed at the interruptions, Jennifer's mother found it charming. Jennifer felt her smile slipping again. *Starting tomorrow, I'm going to have to show that girl how to do all the chores—like I don't have enough to do as it is,* she grumbled inwardly. *I'm sure she'll be useless at chores too.*

Her mother frowned slightly every time she looked at Jennifer, then switched back to a smile for Isabel. Jennifer almost laughed at her mother's struggle to get the right expression on her face, but really, she didn't find the situation funny. She knew her mother was upset with her for not being here to greet their guest and for being barely polite, and Jennifer was sure to hear about it later. Also, she was just sitting on the kitchen stool and watching the other two prepare dinner. Although Isabel didn't know what was needed or where anything was in the kitchen, her eagerness to help meant Jennifer had nothing to do.

"Are you going to school, Isabel?" Jennifer asked finally. She didn't want her mother to be *too* mad at her, so she supposed she'd better make conversation. "I've only got a few months left before vacation."

"Isabel doesn't need to go to school with you if she doesn't want to," said Mrs. Schmidt fondly. "She'll just stay here with me."

"I prefer to stay here." Isabel glanced at Jennifer with her bright black eyes, then looked back at Mrs. Schmidt. Jennifer couldn't tell at all what the other girl was thinking through her mask of politeness. "I can learn how to do the chores while you are at school," Isabel went on.

Does she really mean that? Jennifer studied Isabel. She had an air of quiet sadness about her that seemed to fall over her face every time she stopped speaking. *But maybe all Indians are sad,* Jennifer thought. *I don't see why Isabel should be now, though. She'll have an easy time here—Mother will make sure of that. Besides, she's really very pretty.* Isabel wore her sleek black hair back in two tortoiseshell barrettes, and her perfect eyebrows and black lashes strikingly set off her black eyes.

"I only have school three days a week because a lot of the students have to help on the farms this time of year," Jennifer said. "So I can show you around tomorrow."

"I'd like that," Isabel replied. Her words were so light and carefully spoken, Jennifer couldn't tell if she meant them or not. *Probably not,* she thought.

"I work with our horses in the morning," Jennifer said, reaching for a slice of pickle from the plate her mother had just set out on the counter.

Isabel had her back to Jennifer, but Jennifer saw the other girl's shoulders stiffen. Isabel turned. "How very nice," she said. "Do you have many horses?"

"Only three right now. We have our buggy horse, Tulip, I'm finishing training Celebrity, and now we've got Touch of Dandy. He just came to us from the Standardbred track yesterday. I train former racehorses, then we sell them." Isabel was still looking at her intently, so Jennifer asked, "Do you ride?"

Isabel shrugged. "I don't know if my form is good. I've never ridden with other people."

"Oh." *That doesn't really answer my question,* Jennifer thought. *I guess I'll just find out how well she rides tomorrow.*

"Who have we here?" Mr. Schmidt walked into the kitchen, followed by Benjamin. "I'm Mr. Schmidt," he introduced himself. "And this is my son, Benjamin."

"I'm pleased to meet you." Isabel stepped forward, smiling.

Isabel almost curtsied, Jennifer thought. *Where did she get manners like that? They're just perfect.* Her father and brother, of course, were smiling back at Isabel and seemed to be enjoying meeting her just as much as her mother had.

Jennifer silently picked up the gravy boat and the serving platter with slices of roast pork and carried them to the dining room table. The rest of her family and Isabel followed, bringing in other bowls of food. "You sit beside me, Isabel," Mr. Schmidt said. "I'd like to hear about the Carlisle school."

"Of course," Isabel said, sitting down gracefully next to him. "I know our neighbors in the town and countryside are very interested in the school."

"Is it just like regular school?" Benjamin leaned forward on his elbows from across the table. "I mean, do boys and girls go together to class?"

"We actually have many different classes and teachers," Isabel explained. "I'm with students about my age, and we learn many different subjects, such as English literature, mathematics, and French. I especially like my English class and the teacher, Miss Hayes."

"How was your trip here?" Mr. Schmidt asked. Jennifer noticed that her family was barely eating, they were so interested in what Isabel was saying. That was highly unusual, especially for her brother and father.

"I enjoyed the buggy ride and seeing the countryside," Isabel said. "I had wondered while I was at school what lay beyond the school grounds, past the woods, and since I arrived at Carlisle from the reservation in the night, I really had no idea . . ."

I guess no one is going to ask me about my day, Jennifer thought, disappointed, as Isabel talked on and on. Jennifer started to say something about the riding paths in the woods, but her mother took over the conversation with a remark about planting the flower garden. "What kind of flowers do you have in your garden?" Isabel asked, and the talk about that went on for another ten minutes.

Jennifer sat back in her chair, picked up her knife, and cut off a bite of pork. "This is very good," she said to her mother, interrupting Benjamin, who was describing his auto shop job to Isabel in detail.

Mrs. Schmidt smiled. "I'm glad you like it, sweetie."

"Most automobiles are brand new, but they break down all the time," Benjamin went on, not even noticing the interruption. "I've learned how to fix almost any problem."

Isabel nodded, seeming to struggle for once to come up with something to say. Jennifer felt a sudden flash of sympathy. *Isabel's not at liberty to tell Benjamin what a bore he is,* she thought.

"My older brother, Jeremy, would love to have an automobile," Isabel said finally. "He's also a very hard worker, and so perhaps he will have the money to buy one someday."

"Tell us about your family, Isabel." Mr. Schmidt set down his stein of beer. "Have they come to visit you at the school?"

Jennifer kept waiting for her family to run out of questions and Isabel to run out of things to say, but it didn't happen. Long after the family's usual bedtime, Isabel was still talking about her brother and father and an uncle who was some kind of important man in the tribe. The tribe! Jennifer kicked the table leg with her heel, shaking the table. She knew she was being childish, but really, *someone* could include her in the conversation.

"Oh, I forgot all about dessert." Mrs. Schmidt jumped up, probably stirred by the rattling dishes. She hurried to the kitchen and returned with a tall German chocolate cake, buried in a thick layer of whip cream and coated with chocolate sprinkles.

"My favorite!" Jennifer said, reaching for the cake cutter.

"Give Isabel the first piece," Mrs. Schmidt said. She patted Isabel's hand, then sat down again. "Did you ever have German chocolate cake, Isabel?"

"No, but it looks delicious," Isabel replied. She suddenly looked directly at Jennifer. "I think it will be my favorite too."

Poor Isabel. Jennifer again felt a bit of sympathy for the other girl. After all, Isabel did have to try to make everyone here like her right away or she would be sent back to school or the reservation, both of which, despite her family's enthusiasm, sounded awful to Jennifer. *There's a lot Isabel isn't saying,* Jennifer noticed. *She hasn't said a word about her friends at school or her mother. I suppose at bottom, she must be dreadfully unhappy or hardened by her experiences. I wonder why no one else sees that about her? We've actually met before—she's the girl from Main Street in Carlisle and the skating pond. But Isabel doesn't seem to recognize me.*

Jennifer's family listened, completely rapt, as Isabel talked about the school newspaper. *Why on earth is some newspaper called the* Arrow *so very interesting to everyone?* Jennifer wondered. *It's as if Isabel is from the big city and has exciting news while I have done nothing worth mentioning. Is every meal going to be like this, with Isabel monopolizing the conversation? She's only staying a month, but that's starting to seem like forever.*

"At school, all of the students have jobs in the afternoon,"

Isabel went on. "But I have never worked on a farm. I think I will learn much that is useful here."

"We have to get up at four tomorrow morning, and we don't have breakfast until after we milk the cows," Jennifer interrupted, then hoped she didn't appear completely mean.

Her mother raised her eyebrows at her in warning. Jennifer pushed her chair back from the table. "So I'd better get to bed," she added.

"It's all right if we get up early," Isabel said, sounding completely polite. "I'm usually awake before sunrise."

"Well, I'm not," Jennifer muttered, heading for her bedroom. *If only the plan were for me to show Isabel how to milk the cows, then for her to do it while I sleep in,* she thought. She heard the other girl saying her good-nights. When Isabel came into the room, she hesitated a moment in the doorway, then walked in and sat on her bed.

"Thank you for sharing your room," Isabel said. "I know it can be difficult to adjust to a new roommate."

Jennifer turned from her closet, her nightgown in her hand. *You're absolutely right,* she felt like saying, but then she met her roommate's eyes. Under her Indian look of perfect cool and politeness, Isabel's dark eyes did seem very sad and withdrawn. "What is your room like at school?" Jennifer asked.

Isabel looked around. "Much like this," she said. "My roommate, Lily, and I also have a lot of books on shelves and photographs. Lily is a very good artist, and so we have many paintings and drawings on the walls."

"I thought my mother said you had two roommates," Jennifer said.

Isabel gazed down at her hands. "No, just one. But . . . I'm glad I have her. I think it would be hard to be alone."

What is she talking about? Jennifer wondered. *Being alone is splendid—especially in your own bedroom.* "We'd better get to sleep—it's already ten," she said.

"I'll see you in the morning. Good night," Isabel replied, back to polite again.

Jennifer turned down the wick on the kerosene lamp on her nightstand. She could hear Isabel rooting around in her valise, then getting into bed. Isabel seemed to fall immediately asleep, or at least she lay very still.

"Thank goodness she doesn't snore," Jennifer muttered into her pillow.

The next morning, long before dawn, Isabel woke and quickly dressed. She had set out her clothes on a chair by her bed the night before so that she could find them easily in the dark. *I don't want to keep Jennifer waiting to milk the cows*, she thought. *She seems like a rather difficult person.*

Isabel stepped to the fogged-up window of her new bedroom and tried to see outside. The night was very black, much darker than at Carlisle. *So many trees must block the moonlight and stars*, she thought.

Turning from the window, she wondered if Jennifer would get up soon. Isabel would have liked to explore the house, which was full of hand-crafted furniture and rugs in an odd new style that Mrs. Schmidt had described as Bavarian. Isabel hadn't had a chance to really look at the house last night, what with all the conversation. *I hope I remember all the details and facts my hosts told me at dinner*, she thought. The only person who hadn't really said much was Jennifer.

At that moment Jennifer sat up in bed and lit the kerosene lamp. She seemed surprised to see Isabel already up. Or maybe she had just forgotten she had a roommate.

"Good morning," Isabel said politely, rather expecting Jennifer to groan at the early hour and the company.

But Jennifer just nodded. "That's a very pretty dress you're wearing, but it's really too nice to milk cows in," she said, jumping out of bed. "We're going to be covered in muck by the time we're done."

"Thank you for the compliment." Isabel looked down at her dress. "But this is my oldest dress—I have nothing else to wear."

"You can borrow something of mine. We're about the same size." Jennifer yanked open a drawer in her dresser and started digging through stacks of clothes.

Isabel's eyes widened. *I have never seen so many clothes in my life*, she thought. *They would outfit ten girls. And Jennifer has more in her closet!*

"Where did you get that dress?" Jennifer asked over her shoulder, tossing shirts onto her bed. "It doesn't look old at all."

"I made it. Dressmaking is my job at the school." Isabel stepped to Jennifer's side and took the pile of clothes the other girl handed her.

"Oh, really." Jennifer began stuffing the extra clothes back into the drawer.

I said something wrong again, but what? Isabel wondered. "We wear trousers?" she asked, holding them up.

"They're called jeans. I wear them most days instead of a skirt since I do so much work outside around here." Jennifer tossed her lace-trimmed pink nightgown on her bed and began buttoning a flannel shirt.

That nightgown is very fashionable, Isabel thought. *Quite the opposite style from jeans!* "Where did you get your nightgown?" she asked. "It's lovely."

"I got it on a visit to my aunt in Philadelphia. That's where I'd like to live instead of down on the farm." Jennifer stepped over to the mirror above her dresser and carelessly fluffed up her straight brown hair.

Frances used to do that every morning, Isabel thought, suddenly terribly sad. Jennifer pulled her hair back with a clip, and then she was just a stranger again. Isabel sighed. *It's so hard getting used to this new place—it's even hard to remember who I'm with.*

She shook her head slightly and what Jennifer had said about living in Philadelphia registered. *Why on earth would Jennifer want to leave her family's beautiful farm?* she wondered.

Isabel changed into the jeans and a flannel shirt, then ran her hand over the thick jean material. "Jeans seem a very good choice to wear for chores or riding horses," she said. "But they're cut for men. I could alter them so that they fit us better."

"Good luck finding time to sew," Jennifer grumbled. "We're pretty busy around here."

"Please show me what to do first." Isabel followed Jennifer out of the bedroom.

"The cows are always first." Jennifer handed Isabel a heavy padded jacket from a hook beside the front door and took down a lantern. "And you're right about the clothes—all of them are men's size small, from the Sears catalog. That shirt you're wearing is an old one of Benjamin's. Do you wear your brother's clothes when he outgrows them?"

"No," Isabel replied. "He wears them out too quickly." *That's putting it politely*, she thought. Jeremy's clothes were made of cheap cloth, and he wore them into rags.

Jennifer's bobbing lantern led the way across the yard to the big barn to the left of the house. Isabel tried to pick up her feet, but the grass still wet them, and the thick, foggy air formed tiny droplets in her hair. The cows heard them coming and began to moo.

With several hard yanks, Jennifer pulled open the tall sliding barn door. "Hi, ladies."

Isabel couldn't help smiling when she saw the cows. They were milling around the barn, trying to get close to the girls. *They're so sleek and fat and healthy*, she thought. She patted the coarse, shiny coat of the nearest cow and got a strange, almost puzzled look from it. *"Mooo,"* the cow said loudly.

"She's surprised—I don't have time to pet them," Jennifer explained. "We've got twenty cows to milk, morning and evening, so I don't socialize with them much. They do all have names, though. That one's Katie." Jennifer had collected several halters and large tin buckets as she talked. "Take some of these," she said. "We tie the cows in the chutes to milk them."

"You do all this by yourself every morning and evening?" Isabel asked. "My goodness."

"Well, my father and Benjamin used to help, but my father hurt his leg, and Benjamin stays in town most of the time since he got that job with the automobiles. I guess you're the help for now. Don't forget we have to milk in the evening too."

"That's all right," Isabel said, patting the pink nose of another cow. She secured it with a halter, then led it to a chute. Sitting on a handy stool, she admired the cow's heavy, pink-and-black-spotted milk bag. *It's just bursting with milk*, she thought, running her hand over the cow's flank. Isabel had never been around cows before, much less enormous, friendly cows like these. At the reservation, the Apaches had sometimes kept a few goats, but all the animals seemed to sicken and die, or maybe they weren't fed enough, like the people. Except for the agent's and soldiers' horses, no animals lived for long there.

Isabel wrapped her fingers around the cow's teats and pulled. A strong splash of foaming white milk hit the pail.

Jennifer looked over from the adjoining chute. "Good work." She seemed surprised. "I guess the cows like you—or they know you like them, because they don't let their milk down for everybody that easily. That cow's Annie."

"I do like them." Isabel carefully continued to milk the cow, trying to work as fast as possible. Annie occasionally swung her head around to regard Isabel with big, gentle brown eyes.

After Isabel thought she'd gotten all the milk out of the first cow, she stood, unclenching her stiff fingers. *My fingers are tired after just one cow, and Jennifer milks twenty twice a day—she has many chores. No wonder she's so grumpy.* Isabel glanced at Jennifer with new respect.

"Now we let the cows out into their pasture," Jennifer said when at last the girls were done with the milking. "All we have to do is open the back door and they'll wander out by themselves— they love to go out and eat grass. Breakfast will be ready for us now too."

Jennifer pulled open the back sliding door of the barn. The cows were already crowded around her, and they quickly trotted out into the pasture. Dropping their heads, they began to munch on the thick green grass. Over the treetops, the sky was turning gray-pink. *There's no real sunrise in the country,* Isabel noticed. *The sun comes up behind the trees, already born.*

"I always like it when it finally gets light," Jennifer said, turning and walking backward. "That means it's time for breakfast, and the day gets better from here. We ride the horses next."

That sounds very enjoyable. Isabel smiled.

"So you like horses," Jennifer said, shooting her a curious, slightly suspicious look.

"Even more than cows," Isabel replied.

Jennifer laughed. "Well, I guess in your case, that's saying something."

Mrs. Schmidt opened the front door for them. "How did your first milking go, Isabel?" she asked.

"She actually *liked* it," Jennifer answered for her. "Wonders will never cease."

"Well, the cows are sweet, although I know they're not your favorite animal, horse girl. Come and eat, you two. Benjamin left early this morning, but Mr. Schmidt has already gotten started with breakfast. He's planning to seed the back ninety acres today."

"Sit next to me again, Isabel," Mr. Schmidt greeted from the dining room table. "That's your regular place now."

"Thank you." *How many different kinds of food are on this table—fifteen?* Isabel wondered as she sat in her chair from last night. Mr. and Mrs. Schmidt handed her and Jennifer platters of crisp bacon and sausage lined up in rows, eggs over easy, and slices of whole wheat toast. Glass pitchers held apple juice and milk, and a silver coffeepot dominated the center of the table.

Don't be greedy, Isabel warned herself as she forked bacon onto her plate. But bacon and coffee were definitely her favorite food and drink, and she seldom had them. Bacon was expensive, and so the Carlisle school didn't serve it for breakfast, and coffee was thought to be bad for children, so the students didn't get that either. Isabel stopped herself at four slices of bacon. She almost forgot where she was in the pleasure of pouring real cream and ladling two full spoonfuls of sugar into her coffee. "This is a delicious meal," she remembered to say.

Mr. Schmidt handed her the platter of bacon again. "Why don't you have some more?" he asked with a smile.

I thought we had a lot of food for each meal at school, Isabel thought, gratefully accepting the bacon. *But the food here would form a small mountain if I piled it up.*

"How are you liking life on the farm, Isabel?" Mr. Schmidt asked.

"So far, the day has been wonderful," Isabel said sincerely, drawing another big smile from Mrs. Schmidt and a disbelieving look from Jennifer.

"Just try milking cows on Christmas morning if you think you like farmwork so much," Jennifer said tartly.

"Now, Jennifer, don't be cross." Mrs. Schmidt dropped a kiss on her daughter's head.

"I'm ready to get back to work." Isabel hastily got up from the table and reached to gather her dishes.

"Don't let Jennifer rush you," Mrs. Schmidt insisted. "Please, have a piece of coffee cake, Isabel. Or, if you don't have room now, come in for a snack after you ride. Don't worry about the dishes."

"Thank you so much." Isabel hurried out of the room after Jennifer. She was quite sure the other girl had given her what she could only describe as the evil eye before leaving the table.

Outside, the spring birds sang and fluttered in the trees. *I wonder what kind they are?* Isabel thought, trying to see them better through the branches.

"So can you really ride?" Jennifer asked, stopping in front

of the horse barn. She sounded skeptical. "I mean, I don't know what you were talking about last night at dinner when you said you rode the agent's horses."

"Yes, I can ride," Isabel said simply.

"I guess I'll have to let you ride Celebrity while I risk getting killed on the new horse, Dandy," Jennifer grumbled. "You never know how the first ride will go with one of these horses from the track. But if you ride Celebrity along with us, Dandy should go better."

"Of course." Isabel nodded. *I wish Jennifer would let me make her work easier,* she thought. *She's so contentious.*

Jennifer looked at her sharply. "Celebrity's not easy to ride either, but I've ridden him for months now, and we've gotten used to each other. Remember, he was a racehorse—he's got a lot of get-up-and-go even when he is behaving. Do you really think you can handle him?"

Suddenly Isabel saw in her mind the horses she had ridden at home. Spirited, half-crazy Lexington had probably been the best of them. The worst horses had almost certainly been the soldiers' horses, beaten down and afraid, desperate to get her off their back. One of the first horses she'd trained had been for a soldier, and it had tried to roll on her; she'd barely had time to throw herself off before being crushed. Isabel had gotten that horse to go fairly well at last, but she'd never quite trusted him—his fear of people was so deep, she'd always known it might appear again.

I still haven't found out who is riding the difficult horses on the reservation now, she remembered. Perhaps Daniel Tyndall, the missionaries' son, unless his parents had moved on to another reservation, which often happened with missionaries. Isabel had realized that Jeremy couldn't say anything in his letters about who had taken over training the reservation horses, if anyone had, because their father was helping him put the letters together.

Isabel started to tell Jennifer that she was quite sure no horse, even from the racetrack, could be more of a challenge than the wild, frightened horses she had ridden at home, but she stopped.

If I tell Jennifer about my past experience with horses, she will surely mention it to her parents. They might tell Father in a letter or Miss Hayes at the school, and she will tell Father. Then he will find out that I haven't been telling him the truth for a very long time about what I have been doing.

If her father found out that she had not only ridden dangerous horses at home but was continuing to do so here, he might fear so much for his daughter's safety that he would order her to come home from Carlisle. Then, once she was there, he would forbid her to ride. All of that was too awful to contemplate, but Isabel could see how it could easily happen. She hoped that if her father did find out she was riding at the farm, he would assume the horses were very tame.

Jennifer was standing in the doorway to the barn with her arms folded. "Well?" she said.

"I will give you the short answer," Isabel replied, keeping her face calm to hide her thoughts. "I think I can ride almost any horse."

"Okay, let's get out Celebrity and Dandy." Jennifer shook her head and went into the barn. "Why was that such a big secret?" Isabel heard her mutter.

Isabel stepped into the barn and smiled broadly as she saw the heads of the three horses bobbing over the half doors of their stalls, all looking eagerly for treats and attention. "This is Celebrity, I can tell," she said, walking to the first horse's stall.

"How do you know?" Jennifer asked from behind her.

"He looks like a Celebrity." Isabel held out her hand for Celebrity to sniff. The big, dark brown horse arched his neck and took a deep breath, taking in her scent. Then he lightly kicked the stall door with a front hoof, but it wasn't a mean kick. More a *let's go!* kick, Isabel thought.

"I'll hurry, Celebrity." Isabel took down a halter from a nail beside his stall. She wasn't worried about Celebrity's liveliness. The only horses she had ever found to be a problem were frightened or mean ones. Celebrity seemed bold and sweet enough.

"Take Celebrity around the yard before we go out on the trail and see how he does," Jennifer said when Isabel had tacked him up. Jennifer was holding the reins of a gray horse that was even taller than Celebrity. The horse trembled slightly, then shook himself hard, rattling the stirrups.

He looks very nervous, Isabel thought, but Jennifer didn't seem alarmed. "That's a pretty horse," she commented as she led Celebrity out of the barn.

"I only buy the nice-looking ones," Jennifer said. "Even if I like the way a horse is moving when I see it at the track sale, if it isn't pretty, I don't buy it. I know people just don't want an ugly ex-racehorse pulling their buggy or as a riding horse. I learned that a long time ago."

"So you have been retraining the racehorses for a while?" Isabel asked.

"A couple of years," Jennifer replied.

Isabel put her foot in the stirrup and quickly mounted Celebrity, shortening the dangerous seconds when she was off balance while getting on and didn't have control of the horse. Celebrity stood perfectly still, his neck arched. The tight muscles in his neck showed that he was eager to go, but Isabel could almost see him remembering his training to stay put while his rider mounted. That was a good sign that he was obedient and good-natured.

Isabel took Celebrity around at a walk in front of the barn. He quickly stepped out but responded nicely to cues from the reins and Isabel's legs when she asked for a trot, a couple of turns, then a halt. *I'm going to enjoy this ride!* she thought. *All of the horses I have ever trained, I lost back to their owners way before they went this well.* "He has perfect manners," she called to Jennifer.

"He's usually a gentleman." Jennifer gathered Dandy's reins in her left hand and prepared to mount. "But watch him when we get out on the trail. Celebrity—and all these ex-racehorses, really—sometimes will get to the start of a lane and take off, as if they're running a race. I just about went off the back end of a horse once when he heard in his head the bugle to start the race."

Isabel laughed. "I'll be careful about that," she said. "Thank you for the warning."

"I'm just trying to prepare you." Jennifer adjusted one of her stirrups, moving with Dandy as he danced away. "I'm going to be busy with him—I won't be able to help you once we get started."

"All right," Isabel said. "Let me know if I can help you in any way."

Jennifer mounted Dandy in a single swift movement. The horse immediately lifted both front hooves and lunged, but Jennifer was already balanced in the saddle and pulled him up hard.

"And we're off," she said, wiggling her feet to adjusting the stirrups.

The girls rode the horses to the lane at a walk, with Celebrity leading the way. The sun had moved above the trees, and new, yellow spring light shone on the lane, warming the gray branches. The old leaves from last fall, dried and curled, crunched under the horses' hooves. Isabel tipped back her head, letting the cool air lightly sting her face. The call of a bird rang out from a large tree.

Jennifer moved Dandy up beside Isabel and Celebrity. Dandy leapt forward again, but Jennifer promptly pulled him back down to a walk. "What kind of tree is that?" Isabel asked, pointing when Jennifer had Dandy settled. "And what kind of bird is singing?"

"An oak and a robin—the robins are back early this year." Jennifer patted Dandy's neck, and the high-strung horse snorted and pranced in place, rolling an eye back to look at her. "It's good training for Dandy to go out with another horse—he has to get used to normal trail riding. He still thinks every time he comes up on another horse, he has to race past him to beat him to the finish line." Jennifer suddenly laughed. "Oh, yes, one other thing about these Standardbreds. They race at the trot or pace. So if

Dandy takes off, he'll start trotting or pacing full speed ahead, not galloping."

"I did know that—I read about it in a library book," Isabel said.

"Why?" Jennifer sounded surprised, but she kept her eyes firmly fixed on the lane ahead.

"I saw a Standardbred in the street in Carlisle, and I was curious about the breed." Isabel felt confident enough about Celebrity's trustworthiness to lean back and pat the big horse's rump. "I think I like Standardbreds very much. Thank you for giving me this pleasant ride—you have put a lot of work into Celebrity's training."

Jennifer glanced over. "You're welcome, but I think he's giving you a good ride because you're asking him for one. You ride him about as well as I do."

Isabel looked quickly over at Jennifer, but the other girl had her eyes on her horse. *She sounds annoyed with me again*, Isabel thought. *But I don't really blame her. I'm having fun on a horse she trained while she does all the work with the new one.* "Celebrity goes very well without my doing anything," she said "I'm sure you're an excellent trainer."

"He should do pretty well—I've ridden him a lot these past months," Jennifer replied. "Father says I can keep him as my own pleasure horse if I want. I'm thinking about it."

How lucky can a girl be? Isabel sighed. *Jennifer does have to work hard with the horses, but at the end of the training she gets a reward—she can have this beautiful horse or any other horse from the track for her very own.*

"The horses are behaving so nicely, let's try them at a trot." Jennifer shifted in the saddle and tightened her reins. "This is the first big test for Dandy—I have to see if I can get it through his head that you don't always *race* when you trot. I don't know if these racehorses ever completely forget that, so you might always have to watch them, even Celebrity. You go first."

Isabel squeezed gently with her legs and gave Celebrity a bit more rein. The big horse instantly moved into a faster gait, but it wasn't a trot, where the horse hit the ground at the same time with the front and back legs diagonal to each other. Celebrity was swinging his legs in parallel, one side moving together. *This must be a pace! How wonderfully smooth*, Isabel thought in amazement.

She remembered that Jennifer had asked only for a trot. Isabel eased back on Celebrity's reins until she could feel the horse slow into the trot. Isabel kept her attention close on Celebrity, remembering Jennifer's warning about former racehorses running away, but he kept up a controlled trot. Isabel glanced over to see if Dandy was behaving. The other horse was trying to plunge ahead of Celebrity, but Jennifer kept firmly checking him with the reins, and he finally trotted alongside Celebrity without pulling too much. Celebrity continued to mind his manners and go at the steady gait.

"Very good—Dandy's getting the idea," Jennifer said, sounding slightly out of breath. "And I wondered how Celebrity would do when another ex-racehorse came up on him from behind. So now we know." Jennifer eased one hand off the reins and patted Dandy. "Good boy!"

The tall horse flicked back his ears, and his taut neck relaxed a bit. "All the horses like to be talked to and petted." Jennifer sat back slightly in the saddle. "Even though these racehorses never were before."

"That's a very important part of training," Isabel said without thinking. "The horse trusts you and soon feels affection. Then it will do anything for you."

Jennifer glanced at her sideways. "Maybe someday you'll tell me how you learned to ride."

"Yes, someday," Isabel said, biting her lip. *If you swear never to tell my father*, she thought. *But you can't know how important your silence would be.*

That night, Isabel plumped up the white down pillows on her bed, leaned back, and opened her journal to a new page. She nibbled the end of her pen. *I feel like the queen of England,* she thought. *Here I sit, writing down my thoughts, while Jennifer and her parents discuss farm business. I am truly grateful to all of the Schmidts for making this wonderful outing possible.*

Isabel tapped her pen on the page. *I'll turn part of my writing into a letter home,* she decided. *Father and Jeremy will enjoy hearing how well my outing is going.* She wrote:

> *The Schmidt farm has no horizon—or the horizon is the trees. The clouds fly right out of the treetops and seem to come from there. Sometimes the trees catch the clouds, which then drift down to the ground to become fog. But mostly the clouds whip across the sky, white, bulging, blurring into one another and not stopping, as if they carry the seeds of spring and must hurry along. No rain here at the farm so far—although Jennifer says we must expect some soon. I don't know quite what to think of Jennifer (although I hesitate to write my thoughts down completely—what if she finds this journal!). I do have high regard for her after watching her ride; really, after watching her work so very hard all day. Maybe if we continue to ride together, she will like me as well.*

15

John found Robert sitting on the steps of his front porch, enjoying the early spring sunshine. Robert's head was tipped back, and his eyes were closed. John could tell, though, from the slight stiffening of his old friend's shoulders, that Robert was awake. As John got closer, he also saw that Robert's eyes weren't completely closed. *That is an old habit of his*, John thought. He held out a letter that had just come from Isabel. "What does this say?" he asked.

"Are you ever going to learn to read?" Robert sat up straight and took the letter. "I thought you saw a long time ago that reading can be useful."

"Someday I'll learn," John said. "Just read the letter, please."

While Robert put on his reading glasses, John sat beside his friend on the steps and looked out over the reservation. Robert and his wife, Trudy, had built their new house at the edge of the town, away from the mud and clatter of horses' hooves. From the house John could see no sign of the poor people of the reservation. He watched the bushes and low trees of the desert, turning green in the sun, and the sprouts in Robert's gardens, which Trudy tended. Today's air was clear and cool, smelling of damp ground from the melting snow clumped in the shadows.

"'Dear Father and Jeremy,'" Robert began, and John immediately turned his full attention to the piece of paper.

I have been sent to a very large farm twenty miles from Carlisle. The farmer has many sleek cows and fat chickens. I have learned to milk the cows and what chickens eat. I also bake in the kitchen with Mrs. Schmidt, the farmer's wife, and we talk about the farm and our day. She is very nice.

"I wonder if they have horses," John interrupted. "They must, because it is a farm. But Isabel doesn't speak of them. She may not like horses."

Robert looked at John over the top of his glasses. "Isabel doesn't say she doesn't like horses." He continued:

I share a room with Jennifer, who is my age. She doesn't like the farm so much, but I do. It's quiet, and everyone is very friendly. Jennifer says nothing has happened on the farm for a century, but I think that is a good thing. The farm is lovely the way it is.

"Isabel seems happy." John sighed heavily.

"Doesn't that make you happy?" Robert asked. "She is having just the experience at school we hoped she would—she is learning much, has good friends and teachers, and is in a healthy place, free from the sadness and sickness here."

John nodded. The reason he and Robert weren't working today was that they had just returned from burying old Earl the drunk. Along with the agency missionary and two hired hands with shovels, they were the only ones in attendance. Earl's ex-wife was still too angry at him for spending his scanty wages and agency handouts on drink to even come to his funeral. "I still worry about Isabel," John said. "Perhaps I am a wretched and selfish old man, but I do not want her to like the Carlisle school so much that she doesn't want to come home."

"That's a real worry," Robert replied. "As I said before Isabel left, some of the children who go to fancy boarding schools in the East don't come back. And of those who do, some don't want to have anything to do with their families. They think they're better than people on the reservation."

"My Isabel learning so much has to be a good thing," John declared, although his heart hurt at the thought of Isabel not caring about him anymore.

"I don't think it's good if the children don't return," Robert said. "Not good for us here and not good for them to leave their families forever. We do have to face the truth that some will. But," he added, "Isabel ends her letter—'Please write soon. I miss you and Jeremy very much.'"

John got up from the steps with determination. *I will find Jeremy, and we will work with Sun That Rises. When Isabel comes home this summer, I must be ready.*

"Here is your money for the silver," Robert said from behind him.

John turned, his face brightening. He looked around first to see if anyone was watching, but he saw no one even in the distance. He held out his hand. Robert reached into his coat pocket and took out a fat wad of bills.

Staring down at the money in his fist, John wondered how a handful of paper to pay for a horse could be the difference between his daughter remaining at home and being gone forever.

"Jeremy told me how you got the silver," Robert added. "Four days out in a snowstorm at Christmas? You never learn not to take awful risks, either. How did you survive?"

"I dressed warmly." John frowned. *You will never learn not to lecture me,* he thought, but he did not say it out loud, or he and Robert might argue for days.

Robert shook his head. "That was most unwise," he said unnecessarily.

"Jeremy should not have told you about it." John sighed again. Pacing a slow path up and down in front of Robert's house, he wondered how many times in the past Robert had told him he was unwise.

"Jeremy thought I should know what you are up to." Robert shielded his eyes from the sun with his hand and looked over at him.

"Well," said John, "this is what I am up to. I am making a good home for Isabel to come back to and for Jeremy to live in." He wondered if now was the time to tell his old friend about Sun That Rises. The problem was, he did not know how. He had not yet told Robert how he found Moon That Flies, his magical pinto horse, all those years ago in the mountains. Robert would never understand that Moon That Flies was a gift from the Mountain Gods because even when he and Robert were young, Robert did not believe in them.

Perhaps the simple explanation is best, John thought. *I found another horse in the mountains, and it is just as important as the last horse.* He wanted to tell Robert about the new horse because he needed his help yet again. John was more convinced than ever that he must properly own this horse or he would lose it just like the last one. Getting the necessary paperwork in order might take some time, like everything else on the reservation that had to do with the agent, and so he wanted to ask Robert to start work on it.

"How are you making a good home for your children?" Robert asked.

John was glad that the other man did not sound accusatory. "I have found another horse," he said.

"You have?" Robert did not sound surprised. "Where?"

"In the mountains," John replied. "I must find a way to keep this one."

"Where is the horse?" Robert asked. "And how will that help

to make a home for your children?" He hesitated. "Now, in these times."

John was sure he had been right to skip the story about magical horses from the gods. "The horse stays in the mountains," he said nonchalantly. *Just as before*, he added to himself.

Robert stared at him, a gleam in his eyes. But he only said, "So it is a fine horse."

"Yes, truly. A beautiful little golden mare." John smiled just thinking about her.

"And you do not know who the horse belongs to."

"No. I am sure it is another stray," John said cautiously, because for once he did not want to get into the story of Sun That Rises but to move along in solving this latest problem with owning a horse. "I think I would know if the horse had an owner on the reservation. But others may want her. Can I own this horse?"

Robert thought for a second. "Yes, you can," he said. "I will draw up one paper saying that you purchased the horse from a rancher in another part of the country. Then I will draw up another paper saying that he transferred ownership of the horse to you. That way we have what is called a paper trail."

"This is just what I need." John smiled broadly.

Robert pulled a small notebook and a pencil out of his vest pocket and flipped open the notebook. He looked at John. "What is the horse's name?" he asked. "I will need it for the ownership papers."

John sat down on the steps again. "Sun That Rises," he said.

Robert wrote down the name. John watched as Robert's hand made the strange but now familiar pencil strokes that were writing. *Writing makes life simple in many ways*, he thought. *To own a horse in these times, I do not have to fight bravely in battle. Robert's knowledge is enough. That is a good thing.*

"So when do you go to see this horse?" Robert asked, continuing to write in his notebook. John knew that Robert was thinking hard about how he could best make this horse deal work for him. For a moment, looking down at the top of his friend's head, with its still thick black hair, John remembered the old times so many years before, when Robert had been Yuu-his-kishn, thinking hard as they rode their horses to a raid or sat around a campfire, just like now, to help him make life good.

How many times has my dear old friend helped me, even though I am not wise? John thought affectionately. He stood, then stretched out his hand with the money to Robert. The other man would need the money to buy those papers. "I am going to see the horse now," he said. "Thank you, Robert. As always."

"You're welcome." Robert looked up from his notebook and waved away the money with his hand. "Do you know that you speak half in English these days?"

The scanty forest was scented with juniper and growing flowers pushing up from the earth. John felt the usual quick relief when he saw the palomino waiting under a ponderosa pine. "Hello, girl," he said. "I am glad you are here—but you are coming too close to the reservation these days. You have learned again that people are good and mean food and petting." John walked up to Sun That Rises and gave her an apple.

The little mare quickly lipped up the apple and crunched, then bumped his arm, looking for more.

"No more just yet," John told her, rubbing the palomino's ears, her favorite petting spot. "We must work first."

"She's still here," Jeremy said, joining his father as John looped a rope around the horse's neck. "That's good, because a troop of soldiers rode through the reservation yesterday. I thought they might have taken her."

"They don't always have time to stop and catch horses," John answered, although he could feel his heart jump a bit at Jeremy's words. He did not want to lose this horse at the last moment, right before he really owned her. "Very soon she will be ours— Isabel's."

Jeremy said nothing. *He is quiet around the horse, but he is usually so talkative,* John thought. He did not know why this could be. Surely Jeremy did not think the horse liked quiet. His son had been around enough horses and mules to know that they were calmer with talk and even enjoyed it, just as people did. *Jeremy knows his sister well—perhaps he is silent because he has decided the horse is a bad idea for Isabel,* he worried.

Shaking that thought out of his head, John saddled and bridled the palomino. Sun That Rises stood quietly, half closing her eyes. She always liked attention and being touched, even if it was with a saddle and bridle and meant she would have to work. "Today you ride," John announced. He pointed first to Jeremy, then to the left stirrup of the saddle.

"I don't want to," Jeremy protested, putting up his hands and backing away.

"But you have to." John frowned. "You have some experience riding, and if you can ride this horse, Isabel will not have trouble. Besides, I want Sun That Rises to know at least one other rider. She always expects that I will ride."

The palomino stretched her neck toward Jeremy. "See? She thinks when you are around only that it is time to eat," John said. "But I want her to understand that all her friends ride her."

Jeremy shoved his hands into his pockets and shook his head. "Look, Father—I don't really want to," he said. "I don't even like to ride."

"You have to do this. For Isabel." John beckoned vigorously to Jeremy.

"No, I don't. Isabel will do fine with her." Jeremy kicked a clump of pine needles.

"How do you know that?" John demanded. "Isabel has never even ridden a horse."

Jeremy had a complicated expression on his face that John could not understand. "I just . . ." He ran his hand through his hair. "Fine, I'll get on the horse." Before John could reply, Jeremy swung easily into the saddle.

The mare twisted her neck to sniff Jeremy's foot and pricked her ears. John almost laughed at the horse's expression. She might as well have said, "Just what do you think *you're* doing?"

"Are the stirrups the right length?" John asked, checking the girth to make sure it was tight.

"A little short, but they're okay," Jeremy replied.

John stepped back. He did not want to take the time to adjust the stirrups and have Jeremy grow impatient and get off the horse. "Take Sun That Rises along our deer path to the meadow, then stop," he said. "We'll see how she is doing."

The palomino mare set off at her usual energetic walk before John had finished speaking, probably also before Jeremy could cue her to go. Sun That Rises, John knew, could understand quite a few words, even if Jeremy would not believe this. John walked behind the horse and rider to the meadow.

Jeremy stopped the horse. "Now what?" he asked.

John was grateful that his son sounded patient and not unhappy. "Take her around the edge of the meadow at a slow gallop," he said. "But hold on tight to her," he could not help adding. "Both with the reins and your legs."

Jeremy nodded, then looked straight forward. John did not see his son give Sun That Rises any visible cue, but perhaps he nodded to her as well. The little mare sprang straight into a gallop, as she always did. She liked moving fast best of all. Getting her to walk or trot was the more difficult part of her training.

Shielding his eyes, John watched the two. The pale yellow afternoon sun was climbing higher and higher to the deepest blue part of the clear sky, and a breeze lightly touched last year's long stalks of dry grass, shaking them to life. The dark green of the piñons, junipers, and ponderosa pines was deepening under the warmth of the sun as even those trees, alive all winter, woke into further life. John felt his shoulders relax, and he smiled.

Jeremy may not want to ride, but he is very good at it, he thought. John squinted to see his son better. Jeremy had reached the far side of the meadow with Sun That Rises. So far, she was arching her neck and looking and behaving just the way he wanted her to. His son sat straight and still in the saddle but moved easily with the horse's strides.

Why doesn't Jeremy like to ride? John wondered. *Perhaps because he is good at so many other things: his work, making friends. But still, he should understand the importance of horses.*

John began to pace. He could feel his mind wandering off, as it often did when he did not want to think about a difficult subject. *Stand still*, he ordered himself, stopping. *Think.*

But thinking was impossible while he stayed still. That had been one purpose of sitting on the fence after Maria's death. He could not remember one thought he'd had there as he sat gripped with misery day after day.

As a compromise, John began to walk again but forced himself to keep thinking. *The importance of horses has much to do with the old Apache ways*, he reasoned. *I have learned that trying to live in the past is not good—I cannot do it. But not all of the old is bad. Old friendships are good, and so was the bold freedom of Apache warriors, when we rode fearlessly to fight battles and raid. We can no longer fight or raid, but riding is a way to remember those times.*

John frowned. Still, riding and horses did not seem like only a way to remember the joys of the past. He enjoyed horses, and he thought others should too. But why?

Looking out over the meadow, John saw that Jeremy had begun a second circle of the meadow with Sun That Rises. The riding work and growing a bit older—her teeth showed that she was only about three years old—had given the palomino strong shoulder muscles. They bunched powerfully under her golden coat as she leaned into the circle.

If I thought Jeremy could handle her, I would have him take Sun That Rises out to the wide-open land beyond the mountains and run with her, the way I did with Moon That Flies so long ago, John thought wistfully. *But with a little more practice, he could do that in these times as well, and that is a kind of freedom we can keep. I should not forget that now I have the new freedom of ownership—I do not have to worry that what I have will be taken from me. That is because Robert understands the new world, as does Jeremy. Should I listen more to them? But does that mean I give up horses?*

Jeremy had slowed Sun That Rises to a trot. He made several circles with her, showing his father that he could control her, which was exactly what John wanted.

Are horses important anymore? John wondered. *Jeremy would much rather have one of those new machines—an automobile.* Ever since he and Jeremy had seen the automobile in El Paso when they took Isabel to the train, Jeremy had talked about them constantly. He planned to own one someday. Cars went as fast as horses, and Jeremy was sure one day they would go even faster.

So why am I training a horse for Isabel? John asked himself. He was sure he knew, but he wanted to put his reasons into words so that he was not acting like a sad old man again, longing for the past. *We can ride together, as a family,* he thought. *But we could also ride in an automobile. What am I giving Isabel with this horse? I know I am trying to show her the fine part of the old days without the hunger, fear, and sickness. But I am sure that is not all I am trying to do. Riding a horse is good by itself.*

John smiled as he imagined Isabel riding her new horse. His daughter had always spent her days sitting in buildings, first at the reservation and now at school, reading her books and sewing. She had said she ice-skated on a pond at Carlisle, but the pond did not sound very big. *I will give her the open sky and a beautiful and loving animal as a partner,* he thought. *And we will ride together often.*

Jeremy rode over to him and pulled Sun That Rises to a stop. The mare stepped forward again almost immediately, bobbing her head, eyes bright. "She's still ready to go." Jeremy laughed and slid out of the saddle.

John took hold of the reins and rubbed the palomino's forehead. Sun That Rises jerked up her head, as if she had not quite given up on more galloping, then sighed and leaned into the caress.

"She's like another little sister." Jeremy patted the mare's sweaty shoulder, and Sun That Rises closed her eyes completely in bliss.

With a loud crack, a chunk of melting snow broke a branch on a juniper and fell to the ground. Sun That Rises opened her eyes, but she didn't jump. She looked at first Jeremy, then John, and finally dropped her head onto John's shoulder.

Spring is truly here. John reached up to stroke the palomino's soft gray nose. *Soon Isabel will be home, and her horse will greet her.*

16

"I promised Gail Whitman that I'd check on her today," Mrs. Schmidt fretted. Wringing her hands, she stepped to the kitchen window and peered out at the darkening evening sky. "If she's not all right, I said I'd fetch Dr. Hutchinson."

"But you just checked on her yesterday," Jennifer reminded.

"Gail is very close to her time—although the baby would be early if it came now. Still, mothers often know when the baby is coming, and Gail thought it would be anytime now." Mrs. Schmidt turned to Jennifer. "That storm has already dumped an inch of rain," she said. "Your father has the horse and buggy in town, and I doubt he can get back in this weather, but how on earth can I reach the Whitmans'?"

"Dell's with her mother." Jennifer joined her mother at the window. Rain had fallen steadily all day yesterday, and now the wind had risen—another storm might be moving in. "Why are you worried?" she asked. "Mrs. Whitman has eight children. She shouldn't have a problem having another one."

"She hasn't been feeling so well." Mrs. Schmidt frowned.

"Mr. Whitman is with your father, finalizing the purchase of that land, and there's no telling when they'll be back. Paul Whitman went now because the baby *isn't* due, but you never know with babies. If the baby does come, Dell will have to stay with her mother, and there won't be anyone to go get the doctor if he's needed."

I know where this conversation is heading, Jennifer thought. *But I don't want to saddle up one of the horses and ride all the way through a storm to the Whitmans'. I just don't see why it's necessary.*

"I'll ride over." Isabel had walked quietly into the room, carrying a pile of folded laundry.

Jennifer frowned. By this time, after three weeks of living with Isabel, the grimace was practically a reflex, and she didn't try to cover it with a pleasant smile. Isabel hadn't even given Jennifer a chance to tell her mother how much she didn't want to go out in the mud, rain, and wind—but that she'd do it anyway. "It's not so simple," she began. "Father has Tulip with the buggy, and Dandy is barely trained. You'd have to take Celebrity."

"I think I can handle him," Isabel said calmly. "I've been riding him for a while, and he hasn't been any trouble."

Yes, I guess you can handle him, Jennifer thought crossly. *Probably better than me. Even Celebrity is a traitor.*

"Thank you for your offer, Isabel," Mrs. Schmidt said gratefully. "I would just feel so much better if I knew Gail was all right. Jennifer, please get Isabel warm clothes and a raincoat. I'll put away the laundry, dear."

Jennifer felt even worse because her mother didn't seem to be mad at her. She just seemed glad Isabel was such a nice person, even if her own daughter wasn't.

Isabel followed Jennifer into their bedroom, and Jennifer silently handed her a thick sweater from her dresser drawer. Digging into her closet, she brought out waterproof boots and a rain slicker that would come most of the way down Isabel's legs. "All of these are kind of big—men's size small from Sears again," she said.

"That's all right," Isabel said, taking the pile of clothes. "Thank you."

She doesn't seem mad at me either, Jennifer thought, sitting on her bed and picking at her fingernails while Isabel put on the sweater and boots. *I guess everybody is a saint around here except me.* Jennifer gave a big sigh of defeat. "I'll help you tack up Celebrity," she said. She supposed that was the least she could do.

"You don't have to—there's no need for both of us to get wet." Isabel pulled the slicker over her head.

"All right." Jennifer shrugged, and Isabel darted out of the room.

Jennifer picked up her new book, *White Fang,* by Jack London, and flopped back on her bed, stuffing a pillow under her head. *Not much else to do but read,* she thought.

A crack of thunder startled her. Jennifer jumped up and ran to the window. "Uh-oh," she muttered. "I'd better tell Isabel that Celebrity's scared of thunder and lightning." Jennifer tapped her foot, deliberating. "But she can probably handle him. I mean, my riding isn't anything special compared to hers, right? And I can get him through a storm."

Jennifer leaned against the windowsill, trying to decide what to do. Strangely, no more thunderclaps came. She wasn't even sure if it was raining. *Isabel will be all right,* she thought.

"Whoa, boy. Calm down," Isabel soothed Celebrity. The big dark brown horse stood tied to his stall in the barn, watching her approach down the aisle with his saddle. But something was wrong—Celebrity was pawing the floor aggressively with a front hoof and rolling his eyes.

"What's the matter?" Isabel asked, adjusting the saddle blanket and saddle on Celebrity's back. Celebrity skittered forward as far as the lead rope would let him, and Isabel lost her grip on the tack. She grabbed the saddle before it could fall off and quickly pulled the girth tight before Celebrity could move again.

"Maybe you're acting up because you know that I'm worried about Mrs. Whitman."

Celebrity snorted and shook his head hard. "I hope you settle down," Isabel said, grabbing his nose and quickly pulling the bridle over his head with her other hand. "We've got a long ride ahead of us."

Isabel got quickly into the saddle, then rode the reluctant horse across the yard toward the lane through the woods. It was so dark she could barely see the break in the trees where the lane was. "I've noticed that horses can see well in the dark," she said. "I hope that's all horses, including you, Celebrity, and not just the ones I happened to ride."

Celebrity snorted again, and Isabel tightened her legs on his sides. She could feel the tension in his muscles, and it didn't seem to be easing when she talked to him or he moved. *I'm just going to have to watch you and be ready for any problems*, she realized.

The sky grumbled once or twice, then seemed to settle down. Gradually Celebrity relaxed and assumed a steady pace along the lane. To Isabel's relief, he did seem to be able to see easily in the black woods and didn't hesitate. Isabel couldn't even see her hands on the horse's neck.

Mr. Schmidt said no wolves or bears live around the farm anymore, she reminded herself. *I have no reason to be frightened of the dark*. Celebrity huffed out breaths, his gait steady and reassuring. "We'll get there, won't we?" she said softly. "Thank you, Celebrity." Isabel touched the horse's warm, solid neck with her hand.

In less than an hour, she saw the glow of lights through the windows of the Whitman farmhouse. She had scarcely dismounted and wrapped the reins around the hitching rail in front of the house when Dell flung open the front door.

"Isabel! I'm so glad to see you." Dell rushed over, grabbed her hand, and pulled her toward the house. "Mother is in labor, and she's not doing well at all. Can you ride to get the doctor?"

"Of course." Isabel was already turning back to go. She glimpsed Mrs. Whitman lying on her back in the front bedroom, her eyes closed, her face white and drawn. Dell's little brothers and sisters were crowded in a corner of the living room, clutching each other's hands and arms. For once, they were all quiet.

"Do you know where Dr. Hutchinson lives?" Dell asked, her voice still frantic.

Most of the way to town, Isabel thought rapidly. *At least by this time in the evening, he will be at home and not at his office all the way in Carlisle.* "Yes," she said. "I will go as quickly as possible."

"Thank you so much." Dell pressed Isabel's hand gratefully. Before tonight, Dell had been polite but cool when Isabel rode over with Jennifer. That had all changed now.

"I'll be back soon with the doctor," Isabel promised. "I think in about an hour."

"Just hurry," Dell whispered.

Isabel ran across the yard to Celebrity and put her foot in the stirrup. "I must stay calm—otherwise you may become nervous again," she said to the horse. "This wouldn't be the time for it."

Celebrity's dark eyes were huge in the dim light from the farmhouse, but otherwise he seemed himself. With a quick pat to his neck, Isabel swung his head around and headed back to the lane. The turnoff to the doctor's house was only a short way.

"We mustn't go too fast," Isabel instructed. "I have never ridden down this part of the lane, and I don't want to get knocked off by low-hanging branches. I hope I'm not out of luck."

Celebrity whuffed, and Isabel stroked his neck again. "You're very good company," she said. "I'm glad I'm not alone out here."

The big horse effortlessly paced down the lane, and in no time Isabel was knocking on the doctor's door, holding Celebrity's reins in her hand. Dr. Hutchinson opened the door. Isabel had seen him once or twice at Carlisle. He was a middle-aged man with a short, pointed goatee and sharp gray eyes. "You're the Schmidts' girl from the Carlisle school, aren't you?" he said. "What is wrong?"

"Please come to the Whitmans' right away," Isabel said, trying not to gasp from the long ride and the strain. "Mrs. Whitman is having her baby and is very ill."

The doctor reached for his coat on the hook behind him, pulling it on as he stepped through the doorway. "I'll harness my horse and go right over there."

"Thank you so much." Isabel almost sank to the ground in relief. *Thank goodness in Pennsylvania, doctors can help women have babies if they need it and the women aren't left to do the best they can, as they are at the reservation,* she thought. *I've done my job for tonight, and now all I have to do is ride back to the Whitmans'.*

Dr. Hutchinson quickly led his horse from the barn to his buggy, which was in front of the house. Isabel tried to help him attach the complicated traces of the horse's harness. She had only done it once before, under Mr. Schmidt's supervision, but she and the doctor quickly got the harness together. "I'll see you at the Whitmans'," the doctor said, climbing in the buggy. "Get up," he called to the horse, slapping the reins.

Isabel ran back to Celebrity. She was shaking all over from nerves, relief, and cold, but she managed to get in the saddle again. *Just one more ride tonight,* she promised herself as she guided Celebrity away from the doctor's house into the inky darkness looming over the lane. *We'll be fine now.*

But the black air in the woods seemed even heavier than before and clung to Isabel's face like an unpleasant skin. Isabel swiped her damp hair out of her eyes and concentrated on keeping Celebrity to what she thought was the middle of the lane, where the dirt was slightly softer. Celebrity's strides jarred less there. *I didn't hit any branches on the way over, and if I can just stick to the same path, I should be able to avoid them again,* Isabel thought. *If only I could sense low branches in the dark.*

Abruptly, thunder clapped in the dark sky. It smacked sharply over the woods, rattling the trees and shaking the ground. Before Isabel had time to react, Celebrity exploded. He reared, clawing the suddenly bright sky with his hooves. Celebrity's terrified, frantic whinny shook his entire body.

Isabel grabbed his mane with one hand, desperately trying to keep her seat as Celebrity went up in the air so far he was almost vertical. *Lucky for me you have a thick mane,* she had time to think, then Celebrity came crashing down hard on his front legs. Isabel instantly shifted in the saddle to recover her balance.

Before she could gather the reins, Celebrity bolted. The Standardbred had forgotten his training to go only at the pace gait, but he still remembered how to race. He shot after Dr. Hutchinson's horse and buggy at a full gallop, his hooves thudding on the wet ground. Isabel managed to take up the slippery reins and pulled back hard. "Stop, Celebrity!" she cried, but her voice was drowned out by another clap of thunder louder than the first. Celebrity ran even faster, knocking Isabel back in the saddle, and she struggled to sit upright again. In the brilliance from the next lightning strike, Isabel could see the doctor's buggy a quarter mile ahead.

Surely Celebrity will stop when he reaches the other horse, she thought. But suddenly Celebrity veered left. *Oh, no—he thinks he's on the racetrack again!* she realized, grabbing his mane again. She had lost her right stirrup, and the crazy gallop was tipping her off to that side.

I'm going to fall off! Isabel realized. *And the ground is so wet and muddy!* But at that moment Celebrity careened into the Whitmans' yard and slammed to a stop next to Dr. Hutchinson's horse and buggy. Isabel almost went off over Celebrity's head. Still clutching his mane, she hastily worked her way back down off his neck into the saddle.

The doctor was already inside the house. Isabel's shoulders slumped with relief as, looking through the window, she saw Dr. Hutchinson bend over his black bag and take out an instrument. He would be sure to help Mrs. Whitman.

Isabel got off Celebrity slowly. She knew she should hurry, in case he acted up again or the thunder did, but she was just incapable of it. Celebrity stood shivering, his head down low. He was a wreck too.

"Okay, boy, let's go to the barn and I'll rub you down," Isabel said, trying to make her cold mouth work. "You're going to tie up or worse if I don't."

Suddenly rain began pouring down, so hard Isabel imagined a huge bucket had just been dumped on her head out of the sky. She trotted Celebrity to the barn, the horse following her gladly.

The dry, warm barn smelled comfortingly of hay, grain, and horses. The Whitmans' two plow horses, Barton and Danny, whinnied a greeting, and Celebrity gratefully whinnied back. Isabel found a dry towel hanging on the wall and wiped him down thoroughly, then walked him up and down the barn aisle until he stopped breathing hard. Finally she put him into an empty stall with a bit of hay in the net. "I'll give you more later," she told him. "If you eat too much now, you might colic. I can't have that after we made it this far."

Celebrity stepped to the hay net and plunged his nose blissfully into the food. "I'll be right back," Isabel said. "I have to take care of the doctor's horse now."

The big horse glanced up. His calm eyes and sleek, dry coat gave no sign of their mad ride. "I made some kind of mistake in the way I handled you tonight," she told him. "But here we are, so I guess I shouldn't complain."

Isabel ran out into the rain and undid the part of the harness that held the buggy to the doctor's horse. Then she brought the horse into the barn and with difficulty got off the rest of the harness. She dried off the black mare and set her up with her own hay net. "There," she said with satisfaction, wringing water out of the ends of her hair. "Now all the horses are comfortable."

Isabel let herself through the Whitmans' front door and sat in a chair in the living room. She pulled off her boots, which seemed to have at least an inch of water in them, trying not to dump it on the floor.

"Here you go." Susan stood next to her, holding out a towel.

"Thank you." Isabel dried off her face and rubbed the towel over her head. Susan's little brothers and sisters stood behind her, peering at Isabel.

Isabel didn't have much experience with younger children, but she could see they were frightened. The door to Mrs. Whitman's bedroom was closed, but every now and then a pained groan came from the room. "Let's stand around the fire while we wait for your brother or sister to be born," Isabel said. "Which do you think it will be?"

That turned out to be a lucky question because all of the children were very interested in the subject. "It's going to be a boy," Charles, who was four, said confidently. "I know, because we don't have enough boys—there's more girls in the family. Too many girls."

"That's not how it works," Susan said scornfully.

"How many girls do you have?" Isabel asked.

Charles examined his fingers. "One, two, three, four," he began. "Is Mother a girl?"

While the children argued happily, Isabel stretched her hands out to the fire. *I'm sure of one thing*, she thought, pushing still damp strands of hair out of her face. *That had to be the most difficult ride of my life.*

Jennifer jerked awake very early the next morning, before sunrise. For a second, she knew something was wrong but couldn't remember what. She sat up quickly, her feet hitting the cold wood floor. *Where's Isabel?* she thought, tiptoeing over to the other bed.

The bedroom was still dark, but Jennifer could just make out her roommate curled up under the covers. "Thank God," Jennifer said softly, her shoulders slumping with relief. "What an awful night." She collapsed back on her bed.

Once the thunderstorm had started, Jennifer had fretted about Isabel and been unable to sleep. *What was I thinking when*

I didn't warn Isabel about Celebrity's fear of thunderstorms? she had wondered. *Isabel may be the best rider God ever put on this green earth, but even she may not be able to handle Celebrity in thunder.* All Jennifer could hope was that when the storm hit, Isabel had already reached the Whitmans', but she really didn't think Isabel had time.

I am the meanest girl alive, Jennifer thought.

Isabel sat up in bed. Apparently not noticing that Jennifer was awake, she took a book from under her pillow and carried it to the window. She wrote something, then stood for several minutes, gazing outside.

Jennifer walked over and joined her. "Is Mrs. Whitman all right?" she asked.

Isabel nodded without looking at her. "She's resting."

Jennifer let out a huge sigh of relief. "Thank God," she said.

"Yes," Isabel replied, closing her book but keeping the place with her finger. "The situation was scary for a while."

Jennifer gripped the windowsill with both hands. *I would have never forgiven myself if Mrs. Whitman or Isabel had come to harm,* she thought. "Boy or girl?" she asked.

"Another girl," Isabel replied. "With just a tuft of blond hair."

"She's blond like Dell." Jennifer smiled. "I'll have to go see them today."

Isabel had opened the book again and bent her head over the page.

"What are you reading?" Jennifer asked.

"A poem by Alfred, Lord Tennyson," Isabel replied. "It's called 'Armageddon.'"

> *Spirit of Prophecy whose mighty grasp*
> *Enfoldeth all things, whose capacious soul*
> *Can people the illimitable abyss*
> *Of vast and fathomless futurity*
> *With all the Giant Figures that shall pace*
> *The dimness of its stage,—whose subtle ken*
> *Can throng the doubly-darkened firmament*

Of Time to come with all its burning stars
At awful intervals, I thank thy power,
Whose wondrous emanation hath poured
Bright light on what was darkest, and removed
The cloud that from my mortal faculties
Barred out the knowledge of the Latter Times.

"It might sound strange, but last night I just felt all alone out there in the storm—as if I had to fight a tremendous battle, but then I was saved," Isabel said. "The poem seems to be about that, so I copied part of it into my journal when I got back."

"I prefer to read novels myself." *I guess that means I'm superficial, but I might as well be honest,* Jennifer thought, and read the next entry in Isabel's journal.

Clouds bunch into dark masses, then crack into thunder and lightning, frightening me and terrifying my horse, bringing even more unwelcome light into the black air. Even on a sunny summer's day, the clouds wait, ready to crowd into blackness and envelop the sun.

"I keep a cloud log," Isabel explained. "Almost every day, I write down what the clouds are doing."

"Why?" Jennifer asked. *How odd is that?* she thought. "You don't seem to like clouds very much," she added. "Why do you watch them?"

Isabel looked at her strangely, as if she hadn't considered that before. "They fascinate me," she said finally. "Last night they threatened me, I suppose. But sometimes they're beautiful."

"Oh." *Is this a peculiar hobby of Isabel's or should I have been noticing the clouds all along?* Jennifer wondered. *Do they influence her behavior, like a lucky charm?* "I keep a journal too," she said at last. "But I don't think it's nearly as interesting as yours—I mostly write about what's bothering me."

Isabel started to speak, then hesitated, as if she'd surmised some of the entries were about her. *Time to change the subject,* Jennifer thought. "Tell me what happened at the Whitmans'," she said. "Details, please."

Isabel stepped over to her bed and set her journal on her pillow. "It's time to milk the cows. Why don't I tell you as we work?"

"Sure," Jennifer agreed. "We need to get started."

The girls quickly dressed, then put on overcoats in the hall. Outside, the storm had moved off, leaving a pile of gleaming wet leaves on the threshold outside the door and fresh, clean air. *Oh, happy day—the Whitmans and Isabel are all right*, Jennifer thought as she and Isabel walked to the horse barn. Isabel stretched her hands to the midnight blue sky, streaked with feathers of reddish cloud.

"What are you doing?" Jennifer asked. *Maybe it's some sort of sacred Indian ritual*, she thought.

"Letting my feelings of fear and discomfort from that cold, hard night rise into the air and vanish," Isabel replied.

"Is that something Indians do?" Jennifer asked, opening the barn door.

"I think just this Indian," Isabel answered, and Jennifer could hear a smile in her voice.

Jennifer haltered Molly, the nearest cow, and guided her into a milking chute. "So, last night," she said. "Start from the beginning and don't leave anything out."

"Well . . ." Isabel sat down on a stool next to Sadie, one of the younger cows, and drew a pail close. "I'm quite sure that Celebrity doesn't like thunderstorms. But that's the middle of the story."

Jennifer listened in stunned silence, her hands barely moving to milk, as Isabel told of her dramatic ride through the dark to the Whitmans', the crisis there with the baby and getting the doctor, and her battle with Celebrity and the storm.

"My goodness—your ordeal was even worse than I thought," Jennifer said when Isabel finished. "I'd better check on Celebrity."

"I hope he's all right." Isabel sounded worried. "He looked exhausted at first, but then he seemed better, so I rode back here. I knew that your mother would be concerned."

Jennifer felt a guilty flush start to her cheeks. "I was worried too," she said.

"I'm fine." Isabel stood and backed Sadie out of the chute. "Really, Mrs. Whitman is the worst off. She lived after having this child, but I hope she doesn't have any more. This one seemed to take a lot out of her."

"So Dell has another sister," Jennifer murmured. "Did she ask why I wasn't there?"

Isabel shook her head and haltered another cow, Sassy. "She really didn't have time to ask," she said. "We were all so busy. By the time I left, everyone else was asleep, even the doctor in an armchair."

"Oh." Jennifer sighed. "Well . . . I'm sorry I wasn't there," she said softly.

"Only one of us could go—it might as well have been me." Isabel busied herself milking Sassy.

"That's not exactly true. I shouldn't have let you go out on Celebrity alone, especially when it looked like rain." Jennifer bit her lip.

Isabel stood up and looked over the partition. "So you knew about the way he acts in thunderstorms."

"Yes," Jennifer said, but quickly added, "I can control him in storms, and so I thought you could too, since you're such a good rider. But I should have warned you."

"He's not my horse," Isabel said, her voice flat. "Of course I can't handle him as well as you. Besides, I'm not a better rider. I haven't ridden as much as you have or nearly as many horses."

Isabel sat back down on her stool, and both girls were silent as they finished the milking. *I wonder if she can ever forgive me*, Jennifer thought. *I'm not sure if I would.*

As they walked back to the house, Isabel said, "Why don't we go for a ride after breakfast?"

Jennifer stopped walking and stared at her. "You really want to ride after yesterday? Working Celebrity would probably be the best thing for him to stretch out his muscles, but aren't you sick of horses?"

"I'm never sick of horses," Isabel said passionately.

I need to get to the bottom of this story about Isabel and horses, Jennifer thought. *She's hiding something big.* Jennifer opened her mouth to ask, but Isabel was already almost to the house. *We can talk more while we ride,* Jennifer promised herself.

"There's my Isabel," Mrs. Schmidt greeted her. "Come have breakfast. Good morning, Jen."

"Good morning, Mother." Jennifer seated herself at the table and poured coffee for Isabel and herself.

"Did you hear about Isabel's gallant ride?" Mrs. Schmidt asked, handing Isabel the platter of bacon.

"I did." Curiously, Jennifer found that she had no resentment of Isabel this morning. *Isabel deserves all the attention she gets,* she thought.

Mrs. Schmidt fussed over Isabel, handing her dish after dish. "Are you sure you won't have another slice of bacon?" she asked for the third time.

Isabel adjusted her napkin in her lap and smiled. "Of course," she said, sliding the slice onto her plate with her fork. "Thank you very much. I do so like bacon."

I'd better get Isabel away from the table before Mother kills her with kindness, Jennifer thought. *She must be stuffed!* "Ready to ride, Isabel?" she asked, getting up.

"Are you sure you feel like it?" Mrs. Schmidt asked, hurrying around the table to Isabel and gently resting her hand on Isabel's shoulder. "After that adventure you had last night?"

"I'm fine, thank you," Isabel replied. "I'm glad I could be of help."

Thank heaven Isabel didn't tell Mother I put her on a horse that goes crazy in storms, Jennifer thought. *That was nice of her.*

"Be very careful." Mrs. Schmidt kissed Jennifer on the cheek, then Isabel too.

Isabel looked positively blissful. *She must miss getting kissed by her mother,* Jennifer realized. *That would be hard to do without.*

Celebrity and Dandy whinnied eagerly when the girls entered the barn. "You're such a donkey, Dandy," Isabel said with a laugh. "But you, Celebrity, have a beautiful voice." Isabel walked over to Celebrity's stall and rubbed his forehead. The tall brown horse dropped his nose to her shoulder, then rested his chin on it. "I guess we're still friends," she said.

"Are you and I?" Jennifer asked. *I wonder if deep down, Isabel is very angry with me,* she thought.

"I'm not mad at you." Isabel shrugged with the shoulder Celebrity wasn't leaning on. "Celebrity was the only horse I could take to the Whitmans', and I did make it there and back with the doctor."

"I haven't been very friendly to you sometimes, but I never meant for you to get hurt," Jennifer said hesitantly.

Isabel's tone was flat again. "I know—I don't think you're a bad person. But I also know you don't like me, and I am a little mad about that. I've tried to help you all I could."

She actually cares whether I like her or not? Jennifer sat down on a bale of hay. "I know it seems that I don't like you, but really, I do."

Isabel joined her on the bale. "So what's wrong?" she asked, looking at Jennifer intently.

Jennifer dropped her head. "This is going to sound peculiar," she said to her hands, "but I think my mother and father prefer you to me."

She expected Isabel to laugh or deny it, but instead Isabel said promptly, "They feel sorry for me. I don't really live here, and I have to go back to the reservation. They know I won't have a clean bedroom there with books on the shelves or a mother to talk to. I won't have beautiful horses to ride along pretty trails whenever I want. I'll have to work very hard, and it will be just to have enough to eat. And all the horses I ride will just go to somebody else—even if I train them, I'll never have one of my own."

"So you *have* trained horses before," Jennifer said. "Are you finally going to tell me about it?"

"Yes." Isabel stood. "Let's get Celebrity and Dandy ready."

"All right, but then I want to hear all about your horse training." *I wonder what she'll say,* Jennifer thought. *Did she use horses to hunt buffalo or something?*

To Jennifer's surprise, Isabel got Dandy out of his stall. "Do you want to ride him?" Jennifer asked. "I know Celebrity was awful last night, but really he's much better trained than Dandy. Especially today"—she pointed out the barn door at the robin's egg blue sky. "No thunderstorms. Not even a dangerous cloud."

Isabel laughed. "I wouldn't dare get on Celebrity again if I saw even one cloud in the sky," she said. "But that's not why I want to ride Dandy. Celebrity is your horse, and so you should ride him. I think I can handle Dandy's ordinary training problems."

"Now I really want to know how you learned to train," Jennifer said as she led Celebrity out of his stall and began to brush him.

Isabel said nothing until the girls had saddled up the horses and walked them out to the lane. Jennifer smiled at the alert, confident set of Celebrity's neck and ears. *This is going to be an excellent ride on a pretty day,* she thought.

The spring had brought out tiny spearmint green leaves on all the trees, and new shoots of grass pushed aside the brown dead blades from last year. Cheerful, busy birds called to each other from branches. Leaning back in the saddle, Jennifer sighed contentedly. Then she noticed that Isabel looked tense.

"So how did you come to train horses on the reservation?" Jennifer asked. "I really can't imagine."

"I doubt if you could guess," Isabel said, shortening her reins a bit. "Training horses was actually my job, much like yours here. I got all the horses that the soldiers and agent's people couldn't handle."

"Heavens." Jennifer sat back up straight and stared at Isabel.

"No wonder you're such an accomplished rider—some of those horses must have been brutalized when you got them. Not all of the ex-racehorses I've worked were; some of them just are very determined to race very fast in a circle and do nothing else. But was training ever enjoyable at the reservation?"

"Sometimes," Isabel replied. "You're right that all the horses I trained had not been treated well, and they all had stubborn vices. But the horses could be quite forgiving—I was always amazed by that. The training caused a problem with my father, though. After my mother died, he didn't want me in harm's way—he couldn't stand it. If he had known I was riding difficult horses— and they were all difficult or I would not have been given them to ride—he would have forbidden it. But training horses was the best-paying job I could get. Besides, it was the one I liked best." Isabel hesitated. "So actually, I should not be riding horses here at the farm either. I've been afraid all this time that my sponsoring teacher at school would hear about it from your family and report it to my father."

"I don't think my family has said anything so far—I mean, riding horses isn't special news here," Jennifer said. "But I know my mother is going to want to spread around the tale of your heroism with Celebrity. Can't you just say the horses at the farm are well behaved and safe, and now you like riding so much, you want a horse of your own?"

Isabel sighed, then shook her head. "I'm not trying to sound impatient with you," she said. "It's just the situation. If Indians try to own anything, someone always takes it away—our land, our houses, horses. My father is actually quite rich in silver that he got in the old days. But it doesn't do him much good, because if anyone knew he had it, they would take it. And if he tried to buy something, that would be taken, and the silver too, because then that person would know he had the silver."

Jennifer looked at Isabel in bewilderment. "Where did he get the silver?" she asked. "What does he do with it—walk around wearing a silver necklace?"

"In the old days, he found the silver in a wagon and hid it somewhere." Isabel pulled Dandy's head back from the tasty fresh leaves on a bush. "Even I don't know where it is. Stop nibbling, Dandy. I'll have to clean green goo off your bridle if you don't."

"Dandy's so relaxed," Jennifer commented. "I think he's going to work out as a pleasure horse, don't you?"

"He seems to have the right temperament for it," Isabel agreed.

"He's going well for you." Jennifer was silent for a moment. She wanted to make sure she meant what she said next. "Are you really going back to the reservation?" she asked. "My parents would probably let you stay here. You and I could make a lot of money training horses. Plus if you go back to the reservation, your father will find out that you're riding eventually. Then he might not let you do it anymore."

Isabel glanced over at Jennifer. "Yes, I think he'll find out soon if I train again at the reservation. I only got away with it before because he was so sad after my mother died, he didn't pay attention to what I was doing. But he's feeling better now, and he will certainly notice more how I spend my time. Thank you for your invitation," she went on. "Your mother told me last week that I could stay longer at the farm if I want and even to think about making my home here. But the problem is, this isn't my home or my family, though sometimes I've wished it was."

"You could go back to the reservation for the summer, then visit in the fall when you're back at school," Jennifer said.

Isabel frowned and shook her head slightly.

"What?" Jennifer asked. "You're going back to Carlisle next fall, right? Don't you like it?"

"Yes, I do." Isabel sighed deeply. "Or I did. Now I'm not so sure."

"Did something go wrong at school?" Jennifer asked. *Now I'm getting to the real Isabel,* she thought. *Past that mask of perfect politeness.*

"One of my best friends died." Isabel looked over at Jennifer, her expression bleak. "Suddenly, and it was a terrible shock. I think Frances was the most promising of us all. Although I like the school very much, I was glad to get away after that. But . . . I can't always leave a place because of the sadness there. I think . . ." Isabel narrowed her eyes. "I left the reservation because my father urged me to, but part of my going was to escape the place where my mother died. I think I have a bad habit."

"I can't imagine how I'd feel if my mother died," Jennifer said softly.

"As many deaths as I have seen, I still can't accept it." Isabel's voice quivered. "It's hard not to feel that happiness is just impossible."

I feel like such an innocent farm girl, Jennifer thought. "We both have different experiences and family histories," she said finally. "But my life isn't really so wonderful here. The farm can be so dull—I think I would have a much better time living in Philadelphia with my aunt."

"I'd stay at my home if I were you." Isabel's voice sounded strained.

Dandy and Celebrity were walking so close together, Jennifer could reach over and pat Isabel's arm. "The horses are old friends," she said. "Look at that—neither of them is even laying back an ear. How odd—ex-racehorses are usually such prima donnas."

Isabel smiled. "I don't think you should give all this up," she said. "But even if you go to the city, you can always come back here. And life would be much the same—good. I don't know what I'll find at the reservation when I get back. Things change fast there, and hardly ever for the better."

Jennifer studied Isabel for a moment. Her long black hair, tied back with a red ribbon, gleamed in the sun, and her hands were soft and low on Dandy's reins. Isabel's face had an intent expression—even though they were talking, she was keeping a careful watch on Dandy. "Then stay at the farm," Jennifer said. "In a lot of ways, you seem to belong here."

"I like living on the farm very much," Isabel replied. "And my father wants me to make a better life for myself than he had, which I could certainly do here. Thank you for your invitation."

Jennifer smiled. *I'm glad we got all that cleared up*, she thought. *Now we can just enjoy our ride.* "Let's canter," she said. "These Standardbreds need a good workout."

Isabel smiled back. "You first. I'll see if I can hold Dandy in."

"Oh, I know you can." Jennifer asked Celebrity for a canter with a quick nudge of her legs, and he immediately broke into the faster pace. *Celebrity's canter has gotten so smooth*, Jennifer noticed. *Dare I think he's trained?* She looked back over her shoulder to see if Dandy was also behaving.

Dandy slowed his walk at first, seeming stunned at being left alone, then he leapt out at a canter. Isabel let him go quickly for a few moments, since he had gone into the gait she wanted, but then she steadily pulled back on the reins until Dandy was rocking along in a slow, collected canter.

Just right, Jennifer thought approvingly. *Another few seconds at that fast canter and Dandy would have gotten all fired up and bolted.*

Isabel gradually let Dandy catch up to Celebrity, and the two horses cantered side by side. Jennifer grinned broadly as the horses flew through the forest, tails and manes streaming. "I think a bit of racing should stay part of their training!" she called.

Isabel turned to her, her eyes joyous even as they teared from the cool wind. "I think you're right!"

Jennifer tossed her head to flip her hair out of her eyes. The trees ahead leaned over the path, as if they were welcoming the girls on. She couldn't stop smiling. *This ride couldn't be better*, she thought. *I not only have a beautiful horse to ride, I have a friend to ride with who feels about horses just the way I do.*

At last the girls pulled Celebrity and Dandy to a halt by a grove of young maples. "How is Celebrity doing?" Isabel asked. "He's not off from last night?"

"Not at all." Jennifer patted Celebrity's neck. The big brown horse pawed lightly with one hoof, clearly anxious to be off again. His neck was barely sweating. "Do you want to go over to Dell's and see her new sister?"

"I'd like to," Isabel replied. "The baby is very cute, although she has a scrunchy face."

Jennifer laughed, then grew serious. "So who will I talk to if you go back to the reservation?" she asked. "Benjamin was right—it's great having a sister."

"We both have brothers. I know what you mean." Isabel smiled. "They don't like to talk about important things. I'd miss you and the horses and farm very much if I didn't see you every day."

"So what will you do—stay here or go back to the reservation?" Jennifer asked.

"I have thought for a long time about this," Isabel said, "and I've made up my mind."

17

"Here comes the train," John said. He and Jeremy stood by the tracks at the station in El Paso, watching as the black funnel of smoke from the train drew nearer.

"I hope Isabel is on it," Jeremy answered.

Isabel had written several weeks before that she was helping to finish the spring chores on the farm and might extend her stay again. She had promised to write if that was the case, but John had not gotten such a letter. "She'll be on the train," John said, although he could feel his heart ready to rip in two if she wasn't.

The train chuffed into the station and stopped with a last immense puff of smoke. An official in uniform got off, then the passengers began to climb down the steps from the different cars. John searched the few faces, increasingly worried. Isabel was not among them. He saw two missionary women dressed in white, four businessmen wearing derby hats, string ties, and suits, and a young female relative of the agent, her face mostly hidden under a bonnet, but not Isabel.

"There she is!" Jeremy pointed and jogged toward the end of the train. Isabel had just stepped off. She wore a long gray skirt and a ruffled, high-necked white shirt. *She looks so grown up and beautiful,* John thought, stunned. *How could I think a little palomino mare would be a splendid enough gift for such a daughter?* He hurried after Jeremy, who had already reached Isabel and picked up her trunk.

"Father!" The lovely smile that glowed on Isabel's face was so much like her mother's, John thought, smiling broadly back.

He held out his arms and hugged her, careful not to squeeze too hard and wrinkle her fine clothes. "Are you hungry?" he asked. "The restaurant here has very fine waffles."

"No, thank you. I had lunch in the dining car in the train," Isabel replied. "Do you know, the dining car was just remodeled. The seats were a very plush burgundy velvet."

John shifted awkwardly. With those few words, Isabel had reminded him of how different their lives had become.

"How was your train trip?" Jeremy asked, starting for their horse and wagon. "Did you meet any interesting strangers?"

Isabel began to describe the people on the long train ride, including a little girl who kept wanting to pat the soft fabric of her skirt all the way to Chicago. *I am glad that Jeremy can talk to anyone at any time, even his fine sister,* John thought. *I don't know quite what to say.*

Jeremy helped Isabel up into the back seat of the wagon, then got in himself. John climbed up next to him. "How was school?" John asked, slapping the old horse with the reins. The agent had been willing to lend him the horse and wagon to get Isabel, but he had given him the oldest of both. John hoped they could reach the reservation without either the horse or wagon falling apart, but another part of him hoped they would take a long time to get there. He could not wait to show off Isabel to the people at the reservation, but he knew they must now seem shabby to her.

"I enjoyed school very much," Isabel replied. "I learned a lot—
I wrote you about that. But there were some hard parts too."

John looked back at Isabel, but her head was turned as she
watched the countryside and he could not see her expression.
What were these hard parts for Isabel at the school? he wondered. But
Isabel said nothing more about it, and he didn't want to press her.

Soon they had jolted in the wagon to the edge of El Paso,
and the flat, silent desert stretched before them. No rain had
fallen in a very long time, and John could see the faint tracks of
their wagon wheels from the trip out here still in the crusty sand.
The desert looked bleak and desolate.

"I have a surprise for you, Isabel," he said.

"What is that?" Isabel asked, sitting stiffly on the wagon seat.
She was hanging on tight to the board with both hands.

"You will see." John slapped the horse with the reins again.
He tried to look mysterious, but he had never felt so nervous.

He glanced back at his daughter's pretty, solemn face. He
had much to tell Isabel, but now did not seem like the time, with
the wagon swaying and bouncing and the loud creaking of the
boards and wheels. John had finally gone to Maria's grave, and
he wanted to tell Isabel that she should go too. She was now old
enough to face the difficult subject of death, even of her beloved
mother. To John's surprise, his visit to the grave had not made
him unhappy again. He had forced himself to be honest and go
without Jeremy—he knew sometimes he needed his son more
than Jeremy needed him—and he had faced the difficult facts of
his wife's death and burial alone. At the grave, he had begun to
talk to Maria in his old fashion, but he had stopped after a few
words. Maria was there, under that bare patch of earth, but she
herself was quiet and at peace. And, he had realized, so was he.
*Another surprise I have for Isabel is the nice house Jeremy and I fixed
up for the family*, he thought.

The old horse plodded patiently and steadily the entire day,
mercifully not breaking down. By nightfall, when John and his

children set up camp, they were close to the Mescalero reservation. *If I did not think this horse would break a leg in a prairie dog hole, I would keep traveling and try to bring Isabel to the reservation in the dark,* John thought as he piled up sticks for a fire. *I fear she will see it, turn around, and get back on the train to Carlisle.*

Isabel awoke very early the next morning. The air was calm and chilly, and the dark sky was speckled with glowing stars. On the eastern horizon, the light blue of day had begun to push back the night. *If I were in Pennsylvania, it would be time to milk the cows,* she thought. Isabel unrolled herself from her blanket and sat up. She opened her valise and took out her journal and pen.

> *Here, back in the New Mexico Territory, I see few clouds—they are crowded only around the horizon. The clouds are small squares, like the pieces of a quilt, glowing orange as they wait for the sun to rise. Are these the same clouds I would see at Carlisle?*

Isabel got up, still holding her journal. A sharp breeze fluttered its pages, and she gripped the edges to hold them steady. "In here is my whole life," she said softly. In her journal was the story of Lily drawing horses and antelopes and of Albert's lips touching hers in their first kiss, of Miss Hayes serving tea and explaining Tennyson at the Susans' meetings, and of Frances with her cheerful outlook and quirky ways. *They are all with me wherever I go,* Isabel thought. The journal was still half empty, ready to be filled her observations of summer clouds and experiences with her family at home. *I won't leave those pages blank until I return to school in the fall,* she told herself.

Her father was quietly poking up the fire and setting the coffeepot on a hot stone. He smiled. "I was just thinking about your surprise," he said. "As soon as we get home, I will show it to you."

"Thank you—I can't wait." Isabel smiled back. *What on earth can it be?* she wondered. *Father seems very pleased about this surprise, but what kind of good one is possible on the reservation?*

After a breakfast of rolls and coffee, Jeremy helped John hitch up the horse and they set out on the trail again. By mid-morning, Isabel could see the low buildings of the reservation town. She shifted on the uncomfortable wagon seat.

"Let's not go into town just yet," her father said, pulling the horse to a stop.

At the side of the road Isabel saw two horses tied. They were ordinary enough looking—a sorrel chestnut and a gray—but their legs and backs were straighter than the wagon horse's. They were saddled. "Are those horses for us?" she asked.

"One is for you and Jeremy, the other for me," John replied, tying the wagon horse to a pine tree in the shade. "We will come back for this one."

Isabel barely stopped herself from saying, *I can ride—I don't have to go with Jeremy!* Her brother had a strange expression on his face, but he said nothing.

John untied one of the saddled horses and got on. "Follow me," he said.

Jeremy helped Isabel get on the other horse behind the saddle, then swung into the saddle himself. "What is going on with Father?" Isabel asked. "I never saw him ride before," she added.

"I don't dare spoil his surprise." Jeremy lightly kicked the horse forward, and Isabel wrapped her arms around his waist. "You'll see when we get there."

"Where?" Isabel asked. "Whose horses are these?"

"Father borrowed them from somebody," Jeremy said. "And I don't really know where we're going."

"Father is all right, isn't he?" Isabel asked cautiously.

Jeremy shrugged. "Yes—I think. And I also think that what he has planned will please you, although he doesn't know it so well as I do."

Jeremy sounds as strange as Father, Isabel thought. *I can't imagine what is going on with either one of them.*

Isabel glanced around, smiling a little. She had ridden here several times before on the reservation horses, although she didn't say so now. *But I will*, she vowed. Isabel had talked it over with Jennifer before she left the farm, and Jennifer had strongly advised Isabel to tell her father about her riding skills or she might not get to ride all summer. Isabel hoped that because her father was feeling better, he wouldn't be so nervous about her getting on a horse. All the same, she planned to break her riding history to him in stages.

John whistled, a long, clear note. To Isabel's amazement, a palomino mare stepped out of the forest and walked toward him with a determined gait.

Isabel slid easily off her horse and watched as her father haltered the palomino, then pulled a saddle and blanket from behind a tree. He led the horse to Isabel and handed her the lead rope.

"Hi, pretty girl," Isabel said, holding her hand up to the horse's muzzle. The little palomino took a long sniff, then dropped her head to be petted. *This is a very beautiful horse, whoever she belongs to*, Isabel thought, looking her over carefully. She patted the palomino's golden face. The small mare watched her with bright, intelligent eyes.

"Do you like her?" John asked. He had gotten a bucket with brushes from behind the tree and was currying the horse. "Her name is Sun That Rises."

"Yes, very much," Isabel replied politely. *What is going on?* she wondered. *Now we have three horses here . . . Did Jeremy tell Father I would like to ride? I doubt it. But perhaps this is my opportunity to tell Father myself.* "Can we go for a ride?" she asked, praying her father wouldn't say no and give her a lecture about safety.

"That is what I hoped," John said. He threw the saddle over the mare's back, and she stood quietly, nosing the saddle blanket.

Isabel tried not to let her jaw drop. *How very strange this all is*, she thought. *But the mare seems gentle, and if I ride her well, perhaps Father will arrange another ride. At some point, I might even be able to bring up the subject of training.*

Isabel got on the mare, flipping her leg easily over the saddle and arranging her skirt. The little horse seemed very short after the big Standardbreds at the Schmidt farm. Jeremy still sat on his horse, waiting. John led the way onto a forest trail, and Isabel followed with Sun That Rises. Jeremy was last.

John turned to check on Isabel. *Should I pretend to be slightly awkward?* she wondered. *That way I can tell Father I really haven't ridden so much.* John faced forward again with a satisfied look, and Isabel relaxed into the palomino's easy, rocking gait. The sharp, pungent scent of sun-warmed ponderosa and piñon pine was familiar and pleasant. John took a turn on the main deer trail onto a branch that Isabel had never explored.

The little mare looked eagerly around at the woods, pricking her ears at the sound of birds fluttering in the trees and other small animals scurrying about. Then she rolled an eye back to see her rider. *Sun That Rises is a companion horse,* Isabel thought. *She's very interested in people and what is around her.* Isabel looked forward between the horse's small golden, black-tipped ears and settled deep into the saddle with a sigh of happiness. *If only such a horse were mine.*

The trail ended at the edge of the woods, leading to a low, flat mesa. John stopped his horse on the mesa and looked back.

Isabel pulled Sun That Rises to a stop next to her father. A lone cloud in the shape of a question mark stretched almost overhead, rapidly fleeing the sun. *Perhaps that cloud will blow to Carlisle next,* she thought. *Hello, Jen!*

John turned in the saddle. "So, do you like your horse?" he asked.

"I do, very much," Isabel replied. "Will we be able to ride these horses again?"

"Anytime you want." Her father smiled broadly. "Sun That Rises is yours."

"Mine?" Isabel gasped. She looked down at the horse, then back at her father. "How is that possible? Won't someone take her?"

"No, she is really ours," John said proudly. "I have a paper that says we own her, and Uncle Robert told me that is good enough. We can keep her."

Isabel leaned down and flung her arms around the horse's neck. "My very own horse!" she cried. "I still can't believe it. Thank you so much, Father!"

"You're wel—" John began.

A tree branch crashed onto the trail behind them, startling all three horses. Sun That Rises jerked up her head, almost hitting Isabel in the face, wheeled, then bolted back through the trees at a dead run.

Isabel immediately squeezed hard with her legs and sat back, regaining her balance. *She isn't bucking*, she thought rapidly. *So this isn't a temper tantrum; she's just running as fast as she can.* Isabel grabbed the dangling reins and adjusted them to get contact with the horse's mouth, but she didn't want to interfere too much with her while she was turning and twisting at this speed or she risked the horse falling on her.

Sun That Rises darted around a protruding rock, shot between two mesquite bushes, then leapt over a tiny brook. Isabel sat back after the jump and prepared to slow her with the reins, but Sun That Rises wasn't finished with her fun yet. She burst out of the woods onto a meadow and sped up even more. Her hooves were hitting the ground so quickly that Isabel could barely hear the individual beats.

Oh, well—let's gallop across this meadow! Isabel thought, her body moving easily with the fleeing horse. *I guess we might hit a gopher hole, but Sun That Rises seems very smart—she'll jump over them. I think!* Isabel almost laughed at the palomino's expression of glee as she pounded across the grass.

"Isabel!" she heard her father shout. Glancing back, Isabel saw her father racing his horse after her. But Sun That Rises was definitely the faster of the two horses, and John was losing ground. Jeremy was galloping after them, but not very fast.

I'd better stop, Isabel realized as she saw the fear on her father's face. At the same time, she noticed how smoothly he moved with his own horse's short-strided, choppy gallop. *Father is an excellent rider*, she thought. *He always said that, but now I'm really seeing it.*

Isabel gradually pulled Sun That Rises up. The small horse obediently stopped in a clump of cone flowers and stood quietly. While Isabel waited for the other horses, she bent over to pick one of the reddish flowers, outlined in yellow. Sun That Rises stretched her neck toward a clump of grass and grabbed a mouthful. She was barely winded from her galloping spree. "Did you have a good time?" Isabel asked. "I did."

Sun That Rises took a step and reached for more grass, but Isabel kept a tight hold on her. "No more grass," she said. "We have to talk to Father."

The palomino glanced back at her, then huffed out a big sigh. Isabel laughed. Sun That Rises might as well have said, "All right. If you insist."

"Do you talk too?" Isabel asked.

John brought his horse alongside them. "You are all right?" he asked anxiously.

"Yes, we're fine. I'm sorry we scared you." Isabel patted the mare's slightly damp neck.

"She hasn't run away like that in a long time, and I thought she had stopped doing it." John sounded vexed. "I don't know why she does that."

Isabel looked at her contented little horse, who was chewing her mouthful of grass, then at her puzzled father. "I know why she ran. She was picking up on my feelings—I wanted her to go fast. We were both feeling so . . . joyful."

John cocked his head and frowned. "That is a strange way to explain it," he said.

"We both just felt so free and alive when we were galloping. Sun That Rises agrees," Isabel answered confidently.

John looked at Isabel, his expression a mix of pride and bewilderment. "Where did you learn to ride so well?" he asked. "Surely not at the reservation or at the school."

"You are also a very good rider, Father," Isabel said. "Maybe I get it from you."

"I rode my horse over there, with Victorio." John pointed southwest and straightened his shoulders. "Before that, I trained horses for the agent here at the reservation."

Jeremy rode up on his horse. He grinned at Isabel. "Nice riding. Pretty good for a beginner."

Isabel made a face at her brother, then smiled.

Sun That Rises had finished her grass and was looking from one person to the next. Isabel almost laughed at the palomino's alert, understanding expression. Then Sun That Rises tossed her head at the meadow, pulling the reins through Isabel's hands.

"I understand perfectly," she said to the horse. *I do*, she thought. *This is my very own horse, and we will always understand each other. And I know that we have to ride again now.*

Suddenly Isabel remembered the words of Tennyson, as clearly as if they were on a printed page in front of her:

> *I wondered with deep wonder at myself:*
> *My mind seem'd wing'd with knowledge and the strength*
> *Of holy musings and immense Ideas,*
> *Even to Infinitude. All sense of Time*
> *And Being and Place was swallowed up and lost*
> *Within a victory of boundless thought.*
> *I was a part of the Unchangeable,*
> *A scintillation of Eternal Mind,*
> *Remix'd and burning with its parent fire.*
> *Yea! in that hour I could have fallen down*
> *Before my own strong soul and worshipp'd it.*

Tennyson is a dark cloud of historical joy, Isabel thought, smiling. She could almost hear Jennifer saying, "What on earth are you talking about, Isabel?"

Dear Jennifer. I will see her next fall, Isabel thought. *Wait till I tell her about my horse!*

Isabel dropped back down over the palomino's neck and buried her face in her thick, soft gold mane. "I just love you," she said, tears choking her voice.

When she looked up, her father and brother were sitting quietly on their horses, waiting. John's expression was of pure delight, and Jeremy looked satisfied. Isabel stroked the small mare's sleek neck. "I'll call you Sunny," she said. "Unless you don't like that very un-Apache name, Father?"

"She is your horse," John replied, pride in his voice. "You may call her what you wish. And I happen to think that Sunny is a fine name—very like her."

"Let's ride," Isabel said. She leaned forward and let out the reins, giving Sun That Rises her head. Without a bit more encouragement, the palomino mare flew across the broad meadow, her hooves skimming the tops of the sun-drenched grass, leading the way.

TIMELINE OF THE INDIAN INDUSTRIAL SCHOOL

1867: Shortly after the end of the American Civil War, Captain Richard H. Pratt is assigned to command the Tenth Regiment Cavalry, or "Buffalo Soldiers," a unit of recently freed black slaves and Indian scouts who had served in the Civil War. Pratt commented, "Talking with the Indians, I learned that most had received English education in home schools conducted by their tribal government. Their intelligence, civilization and common sense was a revelation, because I had concluded that as an Army officer I was there to deal with atrocious aborigines."

1875: In April, seventy-two "hostile" Indians, considered to have fought against the soldiers in their struggle to subdue the Indians in the American West, are chained, shackled, and eventually sent by train to Fort Marion in St. Augustine, Florida. The imprisoned Indians did not receive a trial, and some of them had helped the soldiers. Captain Pratt is assigned to accompany the group to Florida. Within a month, Pratt writes the War Department:

"The duty of the Government to these Indians seems to me to be the teaching of them something that will be permanently useful to them . . . They have besought me repeatedly to try to get Washington to give them an opportunity to work."

1878: The prisoners at Fort Marion are released to the Indian Bureau. Some stay in the East; others return home. Some of the Indians who stay enroll at the Hampton Normal Agricultural Institute in Virginia, a school for black people. The War Department assigns Captain Pratt to Hampton.

1879: Captain Pratt receives permission from the Department of the Interior and the War Department to start an Indian school in the abandoned cavalry barracks at Carlisle, Pennsylvania. He travels to the Dakota Territory to recruit Indian children for the school, starting with the Sioux tribes. Spotted Tail, a Sioux chief, tells Pratt, "The white people are all thieves and liars, and we refuse to send our children, because we do not want them to learn such things. The government deceived us in the Black Hills treaty. The government knew that gold was there and it took the land from us without giving us its value, and so the white people get rich and the Indians are cheated and become poor." Pratt points out that if Spotted Tail had been able to read the treaty, he would have known about the gold and kept the land for his people. At the end of the meeting, Spotted Tail agrees to send five of his sons to the Carlisle school. On October 6, 1879, eighty-two Sioux boys and girls from the Rosebud and Pine Ridge reservations arrive by train at Carlisle.

1879: When the first students arrive, the Indian Bureau has not sent the promised food, clothing, and other supplies for the school. The students spend the first night sleeping on the cold floor. The Indian Bureau then sends poor-quality clothing and not enough food. At last books and desks arrive. Each Indian child picks out a white person's first name for him- or herself from a list on the blackboard. Plenty Kill Standing Bear, a Sioux boy, picks the name Luther and becomes Luther Standing Bear. The boys' long hair is cut, and they wear military uniforms. The children work half the day at a trade, go to class for half the day, and spend evenings and weekends doing extracurricular activities.

1880: Pratt establishes the outing program in the summer: Carlisle students are paid to work in local homes and businesses and learn trades meant to lead to employment.

1892: At the Nineteenth Annual Conference of Charities and Correction in Denver, Colorado, Captain Pratt says in a speech: "A great general has said that the only good Indian is a dead one, and that high sanction of his destruction has been an enormous factor in promoting Indian massacres. In a sense, I agree with the sentiment, but only in this: that all the Indian there is in the race should be dead. Kill the Indian in him, and save the man."

1893: W. G. Thompson, on staff at the school, teaches the boys football and organizes games against other schools.

1899: Glenn S. "Pop" Warner becomes football coach at Carlisle. He leads the football team to national fame and greatly advances other sports at the school.

1904: Government support for schools on the Indian reservations has grown since Pratt started the Carlisle school. At a conference in New York, Pratt attacks officials at the Indian Bureau for opposing his philosophy at Carlisle of assimilation, or blending, of Indians into white society. On July 1, 1904, Pratt is replaced as superintendent at Carlisle by Major William A. Mercer. During Pratt's twenty-four years at the school, 4,903 Indian boys and girls from seventy-seven tribes were educated at Carlisle. For the rest of his life, Pratt continues to champion his views from his home in New York.

1904–1908: Under Superintendent Mercer, athletics, especially football, is emphasized at the school. The industrial and academic programs deteriorate. In 1908, Moses Friedman replaces Mercer. He is the first Carlisle superintendent who is an educator, not an army officer. In 1904, athlete Jim Thorpe starts school at Carlisle. Francis E. Leupp, Commissioner of Indian Affairs, hires an Indian artist, Angel De Cora, to teach the first native art course at the school in February 1906. "It seems to me that one of the errors good people fall into in dealing with the Indian is taking it for granted that their first duty is to make a white man out of him. If nature has set a different physical stamp upon different races of men, it is fair to assume that the variation of types extends below the surface and is manifested in mental and moral traits as well," Leupp comments in the May 1905 *Arrow*, the Carlisle school newspaper. Until De Cora was hired, the students were taught classical art. De Cora remarks, "I experienced the discouraging sensation that I was addressing members of an alien race." But by March 1906, the *Arrow* reports, "The students are making excellent progress in native art under the instruction of Miss Angel De Cora."

1908–1914: Friedman increases support for the athletics program. The school emphasizes courses that will help the students earn a living, not prepare them for college. Other boarding schools for Indians that are off the reservation, modeled after Carlisle, increasingly compete with Carlisle. In 1912, Jim Thorpe wins Olympic gold medals in the pentathlon and decathlon. He goes on to a career in professional baseball and football. Congress investigates the school's finances in 1913 and finds no wrong-doing by Friedman, but he is dismissed as superintendent. Student numbers decrease.

1914–1917: Oscar Lipps, once an Indian agent, becomes superintendent at Carlisle in 1914. More off-reservation schools now exist in the West, and fewer students attend Carlisle.

1917–1918: John Francis Junior takes over as superintendent at Carlisle. He tries to revive the educational programs at the school. But World War I decreases student numbers even more. In 1918, the War Department closes Carlisle and takes over the school for army use again. The remaining students are sent home or to other off-reservation schools.

1923: Pratt, now eighty-two, dictates the last chapter of his memoirs to his daughter. He dies the next year. The memoirs, called *Battlefield and Classroom: Four Decades with the American Indian*, are not published until 1964.

21st century: The Army War College, a school teaching military strategy to high-level army officers, civilians who work for the federal government, and military officers from other countries, is now at the site of the former Carlisle school. Some of the original structures remain, including the superintendent's quarters, the gym, and the bandstand. The children's cemetery was moved from its original site on the school grounds to the edge of the Army War College. Not all the names of the children buried in the cemetery were known, and so some of the grave markers simply say *Apache* or another tribe and give the date of death.

ACKNOWLEDGMENTS

Many thanks to Linda Witmer, executive director of the Cumberland County Historical Society, for her advice about this book; Barbara Landis, Library Assistant and Indian Industrial School Biographer, for her help in the Cumberland County Historical Society library and a generous and informative tour of the former Indian Industrial School, now the Army War College; and once again Lillian Chavez, Tribal Librarian, Mescalero Community Library, for her vision and guidance.